SOULLESS

Also by Rozlan Mohd Noor

21 Immortals: Inspector Mislan and the Yee Sang Murders
DUKE: Inspector Mislan and the Expressway Murders
UTube: Inspector Mislan and the Emancipatist Conspiracy

SOULLESS

INSPECTOR MISLAN
AND THE
FACELESS GIRL

ROZLAN MOHD NOOR

ARCADE
CrimeWise

An Arcade CrimeWise Book

First North American Edition 2022

This is a work of fiction. Names, places, characters, and incidents are either the products of the author's imagination or are used fictitiously.

Arcade Publishing books may be purchased in bulk at special discounts for sales promotion, corporate gifts, fund-raising, or educational purposes. Special editions can also be created to specifications. For details, contact the Special Sales Department, Arcade Publishing, 307 West 36th Street, 11th Floor, New York, NY 10018 or arcade@skyhorsepublishing.com.

Arcade Publishing® and CrimeWise® are registered trademarks of Skyhorse Publishing, Inc.®, a Delaware corporation.

Visit our website at www.arcadepub.com.

10 9 8 7 6 5 4 3 2 1

Library of Congress Cataloging-in-Publication Data is available on file.
Library of Congress Control Number: 2022931523

Cover design by Erin Seaward-Hiatt
Cover photographs: Man sleeping © Marc Gutierrez/Getty Images; Alleyway © DenisTangney Jr./Getty Images; Haze © Jonathan Knowles/Getty Images

ISBN: 978-1-950691-43-2
Ebook ISBN: 978-1-950994-65-6

Printed in the United States of America

From beasts we scorn as soulless, in forest, field and den,
The cry goes up to witness the soullessness of men
William Inge

SOULLESS

1

IT IS FOUR IN the morning, and Jalan Alor, one of the city's red-light and tourist hotspots, is slowly winding down. Known to foreigners and locals alike, Jalan Alor is a narrow street running parallel to the main artery, Jalan Bukit Bintang. Bukit Bintang, located south of the city's golden triangle, is an upmarket shopping and tourist area with mega malls and five-star international hotels. Behind its trendy, dazzling boutiques and specialty restaurants, Jalan Alor offers without pretension food, drink, street culture, and, for those who dare to venture, an unforgettable experience of sinful pleasures.

Jalan Alor and, for that matter, Bukit Bintang, are predominantly Chinese. Like most commercial areas in Malaysia's cities, they're controlled by triads, or secret societies as they're known locally, and are lucrative sources of revenue from protection schemes and racketeering. The whole area is a prime piece of real estate whose pubs, music venues, and girlie bars have seen numerous gang fights. Jalan Alor, which is roughly a mile long, is famous for its seafood restaurant with alfresco dining. The street is noisy with street musicians and the loud calls of restaurant operators waving laminated pictorial menus as they vie for customers. The smell of deep- or chili-fried seafood and pork fills the air. Concealed behind the seafood restaurants are peddlers of fake merchandise and contraband like cigarettes and liquor, along with the sleazy pubs, girlie bars, and hotels that rent out rooms by the hour. These are attractions much sought after by those looking for a memorable visit to the city.

Overworked and underpaid illegal immigrants are busy clearing and cleaning tables and chairs that occupy half of the narrow road—in blatant breach of municipality bylaws, which the city council chooses not to act upon for whatever reason. Beaming restaurant operators are counting the spoils from overpriced dishes and beer sold to the foreigners and locals. The area is thinning out of visitors. The only ones still about are either drunks sobering up or half-drunk tourists getting drunker, along with the pimps and hookers hoping for a last catch.

In one of Jalan Alor's numerous filthy, malodorous back alleys, Aden Kho, a druggie and outcast from society, is rudely awakened by a flash of torrential rain. Petulantly, he curses the giver of life in incoherent Cantonese as he grabs his pieces of cardboard and crawls deeper under the external staircase on all fours. Covering his skeletal body with the cardboard, he curls up into a shivering ball. He is just about resettled when the dark alley suddenly lights up. "Now what?" he grunts. As the moving light sweeps under the staircase, he pokes his head above the cardboard out of curiosity. His first thought: drug roundup. One of those standard police operations for drug addicts: perform urine tests and throw those who've tested positive into lockup to be charged in court the next day. For Aden, there is no place to go from there but prison, as his family disowned him years ago. He'll be kept in prison at the taxpayers' expense and be released after a period only to resume his drug habit. There are no winners in this game except for the prison food suppliers.

Desperate to remain a free man, Aden scrambles feebly to his feet, intending to make a dash for it, but the light is too close, and his feet are unwilling. Resigned, he slumps down on the hard, cold concrete, consoling himself with the thought, *It's not such a bad thing in this fucking monsoon season. At least I'll sleep on a dry bed, with three meals a day.* Waiting for the inevitable, he leans against the staircase, closes his eyes, and hugs himself tightly to shake off the chill. He readies himself for the "junkie" or "corpse" insults the raiding policemen will vent on him along with the demeaning flashlight-in-the-face routine.

The seconds tick away. Nothing. No name-calling, no flashlight in the face. Aden opens his eyes just as the beam of light passes the staircase on its way out of the alley.

"Bloody hell, I can't even get arrested when I want it," he complains, laughing nervously.

Pulling over a piece of cardboard, he covers himself again. As he rests his head on his skinny arms as a pillow, he hears the thud of something heavy hitting the ground from the direction of the dumpster. He pays no heed, thinking it's about that time of dawn when the foreign laborers take out the garbage from nearby restaurants. He curls on his side to ward off the cold, and his few untoasted brain cells start ticking: *It's raining, the foreigners are a lazy lot, no way in hell they'll go out in the rain to throw out the garbage.* Strenuously elbowing himself up, he peeks at the dumpster located about forty feet away. The area is dimly lit by fluorescent lamps mounted to the rear of shops for security. He sees no one by the dumpster or walking away from it. For most druggies, their greatest virtue is *curiosity.* Indeed, curiosity is the most common excuse given to anyone who cares to ask why or how they became addicts.

Pushing the cardboard aside, Aden gets on all fours. Like a cagey stray dog searching for food behind the restaurant kitchens, he makes his way along the pavement toward the dumpster. It's hard work, but his curiosity drives him on. As he gets closer, he rubs his red, watery eyes to get them to focus. Aided by the faint glow of the fluorescent lights, he sees the shape lying next to the dumpster, but he's still too far away to make out what it is. Crawling closer, he becomes increasingly positive it's a bag of some sort. Closer still, he is pretty certain it's not one of those black plastic trash bags used by restaurants. It's a real bag, a duffel.

Aden Kho sits by the pavement catching his breath, his teeth or what is left of them chattering from the chill of dawn rain. All druggies know that water, be it from rain or shower, is detrimental to their health and to be avoided at all costs. He looks up to the dark sky, stretching out a bony hand to feel for raindrops. "It's stopped," he says with a sly grin. His thoughts return to the bag by the dumpster. *Could be full of stash dumped by bank robbers escaping the police . . . a gift from the big guy above*, he fantasizes, wiping saliva from the corner of his mouth with the back of his hand. A smile comes to his ravaged face. The cold wind is totally forgotten. Consumed with excitement, his toasted brain has overlooked the absence of such crucial details as the blaring sirens or screeching tires synonymous with police car chases.

On bony hands and knees, Aden battles the elements and crawls toward the bag with heightened anticipation. Trembling from the cold, he unzips the bag of his imagined fortune.

A hair-raising scream resonates from the alley, piercing the early-morning quiet. Remnants of the city's night creatures patronizing a nearby stall turn their heads just in time to catch sight of a druggie apparently powered by methamphetamine, known to the locals as horse pill, dashing out at a speed that would have commanded Usain St. Leo Bolt's respect. The seen-it-all stall operator and his customers watch the scene with indifference.

"Junkie running from the grim reaper," the Kelantanese stall operator mutters under his breath to no one in particular. Since he started operating his all-nighter stall a decade back, he has seen muggings, drug overdoses, gang fights, everything the city has to offer.

Exiting the alley, Aden crashes into a parked car and is knocked flat on his back. The car alarm wails. The owner, a pimp having supper at a nearby stall with several of his unbooked butterflies, stares menacingly at the interloper lying on the pavement before pushing back the red plastic stool he's sitting on and walking ominously over to his blaring car. Cutting off the alarm, he first inspects his prized possession. Satisfied nothing is damaged, he steps over to Aden on the ground. Stall operators and other human moths silently wish for something exciting to follow.

Aden staggers to his feet, reaching toward the car for support. The pimp shoves him, cursing, "Asshole, touch my car again and I break your arms."

Too stoned and dazed to comprehend, Aden gawks at the barking pimp and plants his palms on the car's trunk to steady his stance. As soon as his hands touch the car, a kick lands on his rib cage and sends him tumbling into the roadside drain. Jaded onlookers yearning for more action start to hoot, egging them on.

A single sharp siren yelp turns all heads to an approaching Mobile Patrol Vehicle, an MPV. The furious pimp takes a quick glance at the patrol car and snarls at the druggie in the drain. Beer-laden spit flies from his lips and lands on the druggie's head. *"Lei ho choy, keng chat hai li tor,"* he snarls. It's Cantonese for *You're lucky the police are here.*

The MPV's passenger window lowers a few inches. Corporal Hafidz Baharom inquires what's going on from within the comfort of the well-worn patrol car. Ignoring the light drizzle, the pimp walks over to the police officer and puts on a chameleon act, claiming to be an innocent victim trying to stop a drug addict from breaking into his car. Corporal Hafidz, a seasoned city patrolman with fourteen years' experience, has seen and heard it all. Reluctantly, he steps out of the vehicle. Stepping out means he will have to own the situation. Unbeknownst to his partner, Hafidz put in a request through a friend in the personnel department several months back to be transferred to Gurun, his hometown. Since then, he has hated everything about the city—the congestion, air pollution, crime, and people, especially the politicians and religious NGOs, the cost of living, everything.

Hafidz hears groaning and turns to look at Aden. The druggie is sitting in the stinking, saturated drain that's half-filled with water from the downpour that just ended. Stepping away from the pimp, Hafidz walks over to the drain. Aden, who is massaging the pain in his right ribs, lifts his head to look up at the patrolman, his expression begging for sympathy.

Instinctively, Hafidz extends a hand and asks what happened. Aden refuses the proffered hand, denying anything to do with the corpse next to his alfresco bedroom.

"What corpse?" Hafidz asks, perplexed by Aden's blabbering.

"The body with no face," Aden rants, pausing momentarily to wipe a drip of mucus with the back of his hand. With the same hand he points to the alley, saying, "There, back there inside a bag." To sound more convincing, Aden tries to stand up, but his methamphetamine-worn body fails him. Giving up, he sits back down in the drain. "I swear I was sleeping when the body fell near me. The damn thing almost hit me," he exaggerates, catching his breath. "I swear on my mother's grave, boss."

"Fall? Fall from where? The shops?" asks Hafidz

"Car. I think they robbed a bank," Aden says, his addled mind taking over.

Corporal Hafidz gives him a questioning glare.

"*Hai'yaa*, I'm telling you the truth, *loh*," Aden asserts, contorting his facial muscles to show his seriousness but succeeding only in looking frightening.

Hafidz calls out to his partner.

"He said there's a body in there. I'm going to check it out."

He grabs the druggie's arm, pulling him out of the drain, and is instantly splashed with stinking drain water when Aden shakes his bony body like a dog drying itself.

"Show me where," Hafidz orders, while stepping away from the druggie, who smells like the sewer.

Aden grudgingly leads the patrolman into the dim alley, tailed by several curious onlookers. Halfway in, he abruptly stops and points to a bag by the dumpster.

"There," he says, refusing to take one step further.

Hafidz shines his flashlight on the unzipped bag and approaches tentatively. As he stands over it, he exclaims, "*Astaghfirullallah!*"

2

THE CRIME SCENE FORENSICS vehicle pulls alongside the MPV. Stepping out of the air-conditioning, Supervisor Chew Beng Song and his team are engulfed by the post-rain humidity spiked with wafts of soaking wet uncollected garbage. Corporal Hafidz instructs his partner to stop the crowd from following them as he leads the forensics team into the alley. About twenty feet from the cadaver, they halt as if there was a silent command from a drillmaster.

One of the men exclaims, "Holy cow, look at the size of those rats!"

On impulse, the photographer fires a salvo of flashes from his camera at the cadaver to shoo the rodents away.

"Shit, they're not even afraid," he cries out.

"These are city rats, probably have their own cameras," one of his teammates says.

"Look, they're eating the corpse. Shit, did you see that one!" the photographer shrieks, shining his flashlight on a rat running away from the cadaver. "Look, look, it has a piece of flesh in its mouth."

"Chase them away before they devour all the evidence," Chew urgently instructs his team.

Basic human instinct in shooing animals, in this case rodents, is to make loud noises. The men stomp their feet and clap their hands, shouting loudly to scare the rats away. The rats give them a look and continue enjoying their fresh supper.

"Come on guys, grab something and chase them away!" Chew barks sternly.

One of them takes a few steps, pretending to charge the rats. In retaliation, several rats jump down from the corpse to form a defensive line, curling their lips upward to display threateningly sharp fangs.

"Ohhh, shit shit shit." The technician falters, stopping cold in his tracks. "Did you see that?" he squeaks, backing off.

The rest of his mates laugh.

"Yeah, laugh. One bite and it's rabies with a fucking capital R."

With the garbage dumpster off-limits, they search around for something to use against their adversaries. One of them points to the cardboard under the staircase. Without hesitation they go for it, folding the cardboard into improvised bats.

Aden Khoo watches as his bedding is dismantled. He starts to protest, but an admonishing stare from Corporal Hafidz Baharom shuts him up.

Shining their high-powered flashlights and pumped up with raucous war cries, the crime scene forensics team builds up enough artificial courage to mount an assault on their fanged adversaries. The city rats are no match for the city's dedicated forensics team armed with rolled-up cardboard. As the rodents retreat, the men celebrate their victory with handshakes and high fives. Nevertheless, most of them hold on tightly to their cardboard weapons.

Triumphant, Chew steps forward and kneels over the cadaver, gawking at it.

"Call D9," he barks to one of the technicians.

———

Inspector Mislan Latif and Detective Sergeant Johan Kamaruddin of Special Investigations (D9), who are on twenty-four-hour duty, respond to the call. Arriving at the scene, they are met by Corporal Hafidz. Johan hangs back to gather information from the crowd, and Hafidz leads the inspector into the alley.

Approaching the dumpster, Mislan sees Chew crouching over the cadaver, engrossed. Normally, crime scene investigations are handled by

Contingent's Crime Forensics Unit (D10) and not federal unless it is a case of public interest or on top brass's instruction.

"Why are the federal guys here? What's special about this?" Mislan asks, walking toward him.

Chew simpers on hearing Mislan's voice. He has worked with Mislan on several cases, and although the inspector can be difficult to please, Chew admires his adamant attitude and dedication in pursuing a closure.

"Contingent team is engaged at another scene and they called for assistance," Chew replies. "Over here," Chew says, without looking away from whatever he is examining.

Stepping up next to the forensics supervisor, Mislan exclaims, "Holy shit, what happened here?"

Hearing his boss, Johan briskly makes his way to join them. The faceless cadaver catches his attention, and he lets loose a low whistle.

"Where's the face?"

Still kneeling, Chew holds up a reddish cotton swab to them.

"Take a sniff," he says, extending the cotton swab to Mislan.

Mislan laughs, turning his face away. "No thanks."

Johan extends his hand, taking the cotton swab from Chew and sniffing it.

"Yeeak, that stings," he says rubbing his nose. "What is it?"

"Hydrochloric acid."

"You mean it was acid rain just now?" Johan asks.

"No, Sergeant, no known acid rain can cause this," Chew answers, shaking his head.

"OK, guys, let's hold the forensics lesson for later. Who's the IO?" Mislan asks, looking around.

"Inspector Acap Borhan, but he's at another crime scene. Sergeant Gina Yap is interviewing the guy who reported the find," Johan replies.

"Which is Gina Yap, the one always with a cap?"

"Yup, that's the one. Gina Yap Lai Yoong," Johan replies, nodding.

"Then why were we called?" Mislan asks.

"I'm afraid I'm the culprit," Chew confesses. "I asked my men to insist on D9."

Mislan raises his eyebrows at Chew. "It's not like you to make such a call."

"Yes, I know, but in this case I did."

Mislan keeps his eyes on him, waiting for an explanation.

"I don't think this is one of your garden-variety murders. The killer went to great lengths with his handiwork," the forensics supervisor continues, pointing to the cadaver's face. "And this, look at the hands," he says, lifting one of them.

"The flesh is scraped off the fingers," Johan remarks.

"No, not scraped off."

Chew swabs another cotton bud on the fingers' bone or what is left of the flesh, handing it to Mislan.

"Jo is the smell-fool-do-meter, not me," Mislan declines, chuckling.

"Why do you keep doing that?" Johan asks.

"To prove a point. The flesh was not scraped off as you thought. It was burned with acid."

The three men stare at the macabre seminude female deceased in rapt silence. Her face is covered with pinkish and red melted or mangled flesh with milky colored strips of jelly-like substance. The eyelids were corroded or peeled off, exposing one bulging eyeball and a gaping socket missing its eyeball. A red lump sits where the nose once was. Below it, there's a gaping mouth without lips, displaying red gums and a super-white set of teeth. The hair on both sides of the face was burned and melted to form netlike meshes. A jagged bone sticks out of her left arm from a compound fracture. The chest and lower neck are full of strange tiny markings.

A light breeze blows through the alley, and the men instinctively cup their mouths and noses as whiffs of pungent corrosive odor rise from the corpse.

"What are those marks?" Mislan asks, breaking their silence, pointing to the chest area.

Chew takes a closer look. "Lacerations, like it was pinched or twisted with something."

"Pliers?"

"Possible. These groove markings here could've been made by a pair of pliers' grooves. We'll know for certain when we get back to the lab and compare data."

"She was tortured," Mislan mumbles under his breath to no one in particular.

"You mean they tortured her and gouged one of her eyes out," Johan says, shining his flashlight on the hollow eye socket.

"I don't think so, I mean the eye. It was probably eaten by the rats," Chew offers. "There were rats all over the cadaver when we arrived."

Mislan and Johan look at him inquisitively.

"Sewer rats are carnivorous scavengers," Chew explains. "See those tiny puncture marks? Rat bites."

"You said the body's full of acid: wouldn't that keep the rats away?"

"Flies maybe, but these are city sewage rats, mutated. They're immune to toxic poisoning."

"Aren't you going to look for it?" Johan asks, troubled by the fact.

"It's long gone by now." Chew is resigned to the obvious.

"Any ID on her?" Mislan asks.

Chew shakes his head. "Nothing. Not even fake jewelry or accessories. What do you think happened?"

"I don't know, but we can certainly rule out robbery," Mislan answers offhandedly. "Too elaborate. Time of death?"

"From the liver temperature, can't be more than eight hours."

"I'm always puzzled by how you people can tell the time of death by the corpse's body temperature," Johan says. "I watched on TV the forensic pathologist inserting something into the corpse then establishing the TOD. The thing is they never explain, just assume viewers know."

Chew smiles. "The liver's the best test for a dead body's temperature. The body when alive will regulate the temperature at 98.6 degrees Fahrenheit. When a person is dead, the body can no longer regulate the body temperature and it drops between one to two degrees per hour until it stabilizes to the surrounding temperature," he explains.

"What if the deceased was having a high fever?" Johan probes.

"There're other signs that we look for apart from the temperature, like discoloration, the degree of rigor mortis, decomposition, and so on. Anyway, this is only a prelim TOD. The pathologist or entomologist will give you a better indication of TOD."

"What's an entomo?" Johan asks.

"A scientist studying insects."

"Don't you start with the forensics trivia, Jo, or he'll keep us here the whole morning or what's left of it," Mislan kids. "COD?"

Chew and Johan grin.

"The obvious cause of death would be severe acid burn. However, that may have been done postmortem. It's better for the forensic pathologist to give the cause of death," Chew says.

"What's that?" Mislan asks, grabbing Johan's hand holding the flashlight and directing it to the side of the deceased's shoulder.

Chew turns the cadaver slightly, "Tattoo." Turning it onto the other side he says, "And another one here just above the panty line, a blue butterfly with red wings."

"The first one, what does it say?"

"I don't know," Chew answers, turning the cadaver back onto its right.

"It's Chinese, isn't it?"

Chew crouches, taking a second closer look. "No, it is not."

"What is it then?"

"I don't know, looks more like Tamil or something similar to it," he says, standing up. "Why do you think she was tortured?"

Mislan shrugs with a slight shake of his head.

"She could've really pissed off someone, messed with a jealous wife or lover." He lights a cigarette. "Jo, get the detectives to canvass the area. See if anyone saw or heard anything. Persuade Gina to send the deceased to HUKM." Stepping away, he asks, "Who found the deceased?"

"A druggie, Gina is talking to him over there," Johan answers, pointing to the main road.

"Get one of the MPVs to send him to the office. Ask the standby detective to sober him up for the interview," Mislan instructs, walking toward the main road.

"Inspector, are you taking this case?" Chew calls, his voice pleading more than asking.

Mislan stops and turns to face him.

"What do you think . . . should I?" he answers with a question.

"Yes. Yes, I do. No one deserved to die like this." Chew turns to look at the corpse, then back to the inspector. His expression mirrors his feelings.

"Then, Mr. Chew Beng Song, I'll be honored to be the lead investigator," Mislan replies with a gentleman's bow. "That's if my boss has no objection and you, sir, are the lead forensic."

Chew and Johan laugh.

"Much obliged to you, Inspector, sir," Chew reciprocates.

———

Assistant Investigation Officer (AIO) Sergeant Gina Yap Lai Yoong is patiently listening to the accusations and counteraccusations between Aden the druggie and Ah Fook the pimp, both insisting on their version of the incident and talking at the same time. The pimp is accusing the druggie of attempting to break into his car, while the druggie is accusing the pimp of deadly assault. The druggie animatedly shows the cuts and bruises he sustained from the kick and the fall into the drain.

"He was trying to break into my car. I've every right to protect my property," the pimp argues.

"Like hell I was, your car banged into me."

The spectators laugh at Aden's claim. One of them shouts, "The car was parked. You banged into it!"

The realization makes the now-sobering Aden giggle.

"OK, I banged into it and fell. Then when I got up he kicked me into the drain. Here look, look at my ribs," he insists, lifting his smelly, discolored T-shirt.

"Do you want to make a police report against him?" Mislan interrupts, approaching them.

"Damn right I do," Aden sneers angrily at the pimp.

"Yeah, I want to make a report, too," the pimp says.

"OK, you," the inspector points to Aden, "can do it at contingent HQ. Gina, take the car owner to the station if he wants to make a report for the attempted theft, otherwise take down his particulars for later. Let's clear the area before the morning rush hour starts."

Walking to his car, he reminds Johan to instruct the detectives to canvass the area.

"See if anyone noticed a vehicle leaving the alley in a hurry."

3

AFTER ENDING THE BRIEFING that has the moniker "morning prayer," Superintendent Samsiah Hassan, head of Special Investigations, puts down the twenty-four hour report on the last case Mislan attended and looks at him squarely.

"Explain our interest in this case?" she asks.

"The body was found or rather the body found the complainant, a drug addict bunking under the back staircase of 22 Jalan Alor, Bukit Bintang around 4:15 a.m.—"

"I can read your report," Samsiah cuts him short. "My question, what's our interest in the case?" she states firmly, taking her glasses off and placing them deliberately on the report. "Are you running out of cases? If that's the reason, I can get the other IOs to pass some of theirs to you."

Mislan grins. "Thanks, but no thanks."

"Convince me or the case goes back to the district," she says sternly.

"As for now, we still don't know the vic's identity."

"That's nothing new," she rebuts drily.

"No it's not, except in this case the killer went to great lengths to erase the vic's identity. Her face was totally gone; only bits and pieces of flesh were left where there once could've been a beautiful face," Mislan says, injecting a little melodrama for impact.

Samsiah stifles a giggle at her officer's feeble attempt to convince her.

"Wiped out with acid, at least that's what Chew said. The same goes for all her fingers, just mangled flesh and bones. A compound fracture on her left arm and pinched markings all over her chest. That's intriguing and puzzling. Well, at least to me."

"Tortured?"

Mislan puckers his lips, nodding.

"And that pissed you off."

"Aren't you?"

"A lot of things piss me off. What else?"

"That, and the fact the killer tried to rid her of her identity. I mean, if the killer wanted her or in this case her corpse to disappear, he, she, or they could've just dumped it in the river or sea or buried her in a construction site." Smiling, he adds, "Or fed her to a python."

"Python, that's imaginative."

Samsiah knows something is bothering him, and she also knows he is not one who will easily let go. Unless she puts this to sleep, he will be on her back like a roadside musical monkey.

"Your theory?"

"They wanted her found."

"But they do not want her identity known," Samsiah completes his thoughts. "Reason?"

"I don't know yet, and that's what I'd like to find out."

"Because?"

"No one deserved to die the way she did—that's quoting Chew."

"No one deserves to die by another person's hand," Samsiah replies, more to herself than Mislan. "What was she tortured for?"

The officers around the table are all ears.

"No idea, but more baffling, who is the vic and what did she do that the killer or killers felt the need to erase her identity?" Mislan poses.

"A public figure, perhaps a celeb," Inspector Reeziana offers.

"I doubt it," Mislan disagrees.

All eyes focus on him to elaborate.

"If she was, we would've gotten a missing person report or at the very least the tittle-tattle spreading by now."

"Maybe it's too early," Reeziana argues.

"Gossip in our society? You must be kidding," Mislan mocks. "The vic has a tattoo on the back of her left shoulder that Chew said looked like Tamil characters or something similar."

Samsiah tightens her lips, staring at him questioningly.

Mislan grins impishly. "I'll ask the pathologist to photograph it and find out what it is."

The room falls silent.

"So, ma'am, can we keep the case?" Mislan asks, beaming like a five-year-old bringing home a stray.

"Go with it until we can establish the victim's identity. We'll form an opinion from there," Samsiah decides, putting the issue to rest for the moment.

———

Having achieved what he wanted, Mislan and Johan drive off to the Crime Forensics Department in Cheras. Parking the car, they head straight for Chew's office on level one, finding him slumped at his desk, catching up on lost sleep. Mislan puts a finger to his lips, signaling for Johan to be quiet. He sneaks into the office, picks up a stack of files from the cabinet top and drops them onto the desk, jolting Chew awake.

"Is this what the taxpayers pay you for? Sleep on the job?" Mislan jests.

"Inspector," Chew squeaks, mortified. "Don't you guys ever sleep?"

"We sleep all the time, during meetings, briefings, and in court while being cross-examined," Johan quips, laughing.

"Have you done the victim's clothing or what little she had on?" Mislan asks.

"No, we haven't," Chew replies, standing up and rubbing his eyes. "But now that you so tenderly woke me up, let's go and see what we have."

Chew tells one of his technicians to prepare the victim's brassiere and panties for examination. Turning to the two officers, he asks if they had breakfast. The officers shake their heads.

"We can go down to the cafeteria for a quick bite, if you want," Chew suggests.

"Can I smoke there?" Mislan asks.

"I'm not sure, but I did see some smokers outside on the pavement."

"The way you people are treating us smokers, very soon we'll become extinct like the dodo," Mislan snarls. "No smoking here, no smoking there. Making dumb statements like 'secondhand smoke is more dangerous than firsthand smoke.' You know what's dangerous? Secondhand theories."

Johan and Chew raise their eyebrows at each other.

Returning from breakfast, they find a female technician examining the victim's undergarments at the workbench. Her face is devoid of excitement or expression, which Mislan interprets as her having had no success in finding anything interesting.

Disappointed, he asks Chew, "You can get prints off fabrics, right." It comes off as more of a statement than a question, causing the technician to glance at him.

"Yes and no," Chew replies. "Yes, we can if we have the equipment. No, we can't, because the lab doesn't have VMD equipment." Noticing the blank expression on Mislan's face, he adds, "Vacuum Metal Deposit, for lifting prints from soft fabrics using metal dust like gold or zinc."

"Gold!" Johan exclaims, "that must be costly."

"Forensics is an expensive business," Chew says with swagger. "No *lah*, the quantity used is microscopic."

Lah has no particular meaning, and is commonly used to change a verb into a command or to soften its tone. It is a Manglish style of speaking.

"What about superglue?" Mislan asks.

"That's used for smooth hard surfaces."

"If we freeze the cadaver to harden it, we can perform the procedure?" Mislan pushes on.

"Ingenious," Chew admits, chuckling, "We can, but we don't have a clear chamber large enough for a full cadaver. Anyway, latent prints from skin are not reliable. They're usually distorted by movement during transfer, shedding of old cells and growing skin tissues. In the case of the victim, it was subjected to handling, mutilation, bodily fluids, weather, and decomposition."

"What about from the bag?"

Chew again shakes his head. "Rough canvas material like in duffels used in World War II by the US Army? No, no print."

Mislan grunts at the stream of *nos* he's receiving.

Seeing his boss's dejection, Johan remarks rather curtly, "Then how come those TV guys. . . on *CSI, NCIS*, can get prints from any damn thing or surface?"

"TV science. They can get prints from water for all they care. We're dealing with real science and real evidence," Chew replies, feeling offended by Johan's remark.

"The undies look expensive. Can you show me the brand?" Mislan asks, turning his attention to the female technician.

"*Guia La Bruna*, Italian," she reads aloud.

Johan steps closer to have a look. "If it's ori, it'll thin your wallet quite a bit."

"Spoken like the expert that you are," Mislan jibes. Addressing Chew, he asks, "Can we find out if it's original?"

"For that, my dear inspector, you have to check with the supplier or manufacturer," Chew answers.

"Can you do that for me?"

"No promises, but I'll get my technician to check with them."

"Chew, can you also get your guys to check for foreign material from the undies? It may provide us with the lead to the primary scene's location," Mislan requests. "The victim was without her shoes. It'll also be good if you can get the pathologist to collect samples from her body, especially her soles, and send to Trace for analysis."

Chew nods and instructs the technicians.

The technician cuts a short strip of clear adhesive tape, pasting it on the bra to collect foreign materials that may be trapped within the fabric. Johan watches as the technician meticulously repeats the process to cover the entire bra and panties.

"Such tedious work," Johan remarks.

"Forensics work is not as glamorous and exciting as you see on TV," Chew says. "For one, we don't get to go out chasing after criminals with guns. Most of the time we're stuck here in the lab or some horrible crime scenes doing repetitive work, not to mention dirty and stinky. On top of all that, we get blamed if we don't come up with the evidence." He faces Johan squarely and furrows his forehead, which ages him several years in a few seconds. "We don't manufacture evidence. We analyze and explain their relevance or irrelevance to the case scientifically."

"Where is all this resentment coming from?" Mislan asks, perplexed by the usually soft-spoken Chew's outpouring.

"Sorry, it's my fatigue talking," Chew apologizes with a smile.

Mislan notices the frustration and beckons for Johan to leave, saying, "I know our work is ninety-nine percent frustration and one percent exultation. Let's all go get some rest before we start going at each other's throats."

Chew grins, acknowledging Mislan's suggestion.

4

LEAVING THE CRIME FORENSICS Department, Mislan drives over to another part of Cheras to what was formerly called Hospital Universiti Kebangsaan Malaysia (HUKM) or Malaysia National University Hospital. It has now been renamed Pusat Perubatan Universiti Kebangsaan Malaysia (PPUKM) or Malaysia National University Medical Center. The renaming stems from one of the many bureaucratic malaises Mislan cannot understand and that he attributes to Malay superstition. Government workers and politicians being mainly Malay, they believe when a newborn is always sick or crying, it means the name given to the baby wasn't suitable. Change the newborn's name, and the sickness and crying will cease. In the case of poorly performing government agencies, it's thought giving them new names will improve their performance.

He drives around to the back of the complex, where the morgue and Medical Forensics are located. After parking, the officers head straight for Dr. Nursafia Roslan's office. The receptionist informs them she is with the chief pathologist and invites them to take a seat.

"Is she doing the autopsy?" Johan asks his lead investigator.

"I don't know, but I'm hoping so," Mislan answers. "Why don't you check with her?" he says, gesturing to the tudung-clad receptionist.

Just as Johan makes a move toward the receptionist, Dr. Safia appears through a side door.

"Hi," she greets them. "Sorry, do we have an appointment?"

"Doctor," Johan returns her greeting, then turns to his boss for confirmation. Mislan responds with a smile, giving her a slight shake of the head.

"Good, I thought I forgot about our appointment," Dr. Safia says, smiling. "Have you been waiting long?"

"We just arrived," Johan replies.

"Problems?" Mislan asks, cocking his head to the office behind her. Dr. Safia answers with a tiny shake of her ponytailed head.

"Why're you here, you have a case?"

Mislan takes her shake of the head at face value.

"The faceless victim, are you doing the autopsy?" he asks.

Dr. Safia narrows her eyes at him, not making the connection momentarily.

Mislan gives her a hard stare. *Something must be bothering her. It's not like her to let her work schedule slip her mind. Probably just got a serious shelling from the boss*, he figures.

"The victim with acid-burned face," Mislan says refreshing her memory. "They brought her in this morning."

"Sorry, yes, I saw the scheduling this morning. I believe she's scheduled for eleven," she says, glancing at the wall clock behind the clerk. "You're sitting in?"

The officers nod.

"Anything I should know about this case?" she asks warily.

"Have you seen the deceased?"

She shakes her head.

"Then I won't be the spoiler. You'll know when you see it," Johan hints.

"OK, let me put this in my office," she says, waving a letter she's holding. "And we can go straight to the morgue."

———

The deceased is already prepped on the autopsy table, covered from chin to toe with white cloth, when the three of them walk in. *There is something about a morgue that gives you an unnerving feeling*, Mislan reflects. *On second thought, unnerving is not the right description, it is more of uncanny. The room's chilled temperature, the strong sensitizing agent odor, the stainless steel fixtures, and mainly the blank or zombielike expressions on the faces of the attendants complement each other to give you that feeling.*

No matter how many times he has been to the morgue, the feeling overwhelms him upon stepping in, and it lingers for a moment like drops of water on a hot wok before evaporating.

Though the two officers have seen the victim, they still cringe on seeing the mangled flesh with milky streaks in place of a face. Dr. Safia throws Mislan an inquisitive grimace.

"What happened to her?" she asks, snatching the clipboard lying on top of the deceased and giving it a quick read.

"I'm hoping for you to tell me," Mislan answers matter-of-factly.

She flips though the report. "It says she was found by a drug addict who claimed she fell from a car." She lifts the deceased's broken hand and gives it a cursory examination. "This is not consistent with a fall from a moving vehicle."

"It was the other way around," Mislan says.

Dr. Safia looks at him, puzzled.

"She found him," Johan says. "She was dumped where the druggie was sleeping."

"OK," Safia says, turning to the deceased. "Let's see what she can tell us."

She signals her assistant that she is ready to begin. The two officers step back and watch as the pathologist carefully examines the corpse. It never fail to amazes Mislan that she explains in whispers to the unhearing corpse every move she is about to make.

Is she expecting the corpse to protest or refuse to be subjected to the examination? Mislan muses. *Maybe she can talk to the dead, or the dead can speak to her. After all, she did say, "Let's see what she can tell us." It's like Mr. Nakata of* Kafka on the Shore *who can speak to cats, and she can speak to the dead. That's why she's good at what she does.*

Inquisitively, she takes closer looks here and there, gestures to her assistant to snap some shots, then delicately scrubs a spot, examining it and making notes. She seems to have stepped into another world. Respectfully, she removes the white cloth covering the deceased's modesty, handing it to her assistant. She pulls the flexible lamp arm closer, examining the body from head to toe, using the light to examine the deceased's ears and earlobes, puzzling over them.

Mislan watches her curiously.

"Find something?" he asks.

"It's what I didn't find that's puzzling," she says, without turning to him.

The two officers step away from the counter they were leaning against, moving closer to the operating table.

"There's no laceration on her ears, specifically the lobes," she says, as she continues examining the ear.

"Why's that puzzling?"

"A woman rarely goes out without earrings and—"

"What makes you think she was going out?" Mislan asks, cutting her off.

"I can see traces of cosmetics and smell the faint scent of perfume over the acid odor. Do you know of any woman staying home or going to 7-Eleven who puts on perfume? In any case, she looks like she was roughed up or slapped around. Usually, there'll be a tear or laceration made by the earrings on impact. In this case, there's none."

"The crime scene guys didn't find any earring at the scene," Mislan says, pushing her hypothesis aside. "Fie, can you get several shots of the tattoos?"

"Sure." She turns the body onto its side, instructing her assistant to take several close-ups of the tattoos.

"Thanks. This looks like it's going to take a while. Can I get a print-out of the tattoos and check with you later?"

Dr. Safia nods to her assistant, who uploads the photos into the computer and prints out copies for the officers.

"We better make a move and get some rest. It's been a long day."

"You want me to call you when I'm done?" she asks.

"I'll call. Perhaps we can meet up later after work for coffee."

Dr. Safia flashes them a smile, then immediately ignores their presence and dives back into her realm.

———

Mislan drops Johan off at the office and asks if he wants to join them later for coffee. Johan declines, saying he needs to catch up with an old buddy from Penang.

On his drive home, Mislan makes a call to Dr. Safia.

"Fie, sorry to disturb you, one quick question. Can you determine the deceased's age?"

"Medically, that's still a research in progress."

"I thought you can determine anything medically or through DNA and bone analysis like on *Bones*," Mislan teases.

Dr. Safia laughs heartily. "Nothing close to it, and as a police officer, you should stop watching those shows. They're for entertainment and very misleading."

"OK, how about a ballpark age?"

"Ballpark, based on build and the cartilage ossification, I'd say mid-teens to her early mid-twenties."

"Can't you narrow it down to within five years?" Mislan explores with a hint of disappointment.

"Even the latest blood test developed in Rotterdam can only give you plus-minus nine years or a twenty-year range. However, scientifically, it can give you plus or minus one to two years through the method of racemization of the aspartic acid in the dentin, or tooth enamel, or radiocarbon dating of the tooth enamel," she explains. "Anyway, I don't think we have that field of forensic anthropology here."

"What do you mean?"

"There's no department or agency conducting such studies or analysis here, or at least none that I know of. UM has a Faculty of Anthropology and Sociology. You can try checking with them."

"You mean Universiti Malaya?"

"Yes. Why do you need the deceased's age?"

"I thought of getting the detectives to check the missing persons reports for women of the victim's age," Mislan says.

"Sorry, Lan."

"Are you doing a rape test?"

"That's standard."

"Thanks."

He makes a call to Johan, asking him to instruct the standby detective to check for missing persons reports of women between the ages of fifteen to twenty for the last month.

"KL?"

"Let's cover nationwide to be safe. Jo, get them to cover kidnapping, too."

"You think it was kidnapping gone bad?" Johan asks.

"I doubt it was kidnap for ransom. The torture and the act of getting rid of vic's identity don't fit in."

"Why not?"

"If it was kidnapping for ransom, the hostage is the bargaining merchandise. Damaging the merchandise would only be done to send a message, to apply pressure on the family. That doesn't include killing and defacing the merchandise, at least not until it's a confirmed nonpayment. Even then, defacing isn't part of the game plan."

"Maybe they did apply pressure but the family still refused to pay up?" Johan suggests.

"It would likely be a single bullet to the head or a blade across the neck. Kidnappers want the family to know she is who she is to screw with their guilty conscience. Destroying the vic's identity could only mean they don't want her to be identified for whatever reason. My money is on crime of passion."

"Who knows anymore why people do what they do these days? Too much anger and not enough love in us," Johan opines. "OK, I'll get the detectives to do some digging."

"Jo, there's another thing I need you to do. Can you show the tattoo photos to Buddhist and Hindu temples? Ask the priest if he knows what the tattoo meant."

"Why Buddhist?"

"Chew said it's similar to Tamil writing. I remembered reading once that Buddhism and Hinduism literature were written in Pali or Sanskrit."

"What's Pali?"

"Old language. My money's on the vic being Buddhist."

"Why?"

"Buddhists are more likely to have religious tattoos for luck or to repel evil spirits."

"OK, on it."

5

THEY DECIDE TO MEET for an early dinner. Dr. Safia suggests they go for satay, pleading it has been a while since she had some. A disturbing thought flashes through Mislan's mind: *Is she pregnant and craving satay? She hasn't said anything or displayed any signs.* They were always careful when making love, and he never once came inside her, never, although he loves to and finds it more satisfying. She did suggest he wear a condom, but he's not a latex person. He deems it superficial, skin against latex. Pushing the thought aside, he suggests she take the Light Rail Transport to Ampang Park, and he'll pick her up there.

"Why don't you pick me up at home then go to Kajang?" she asks.

Kajang is a district in the state of Selangor, bordering Kuala Lumpur. It was once known as a satay hub, thus the nickname Satay Kajang. Satay or Sate is bite-size marinated meat skewered on a thin bamboo stick and grilled over open fire. It is eaten by dipping it into peanut sauce accompanied by sliced cucumber, onions, and rice cakes called ketupat.

"No, we're not going to Kajang, they're overrated. I'll take you where they serve the best satay in town."

"You and your best in town," she says, chuckling. "OK, I'll call you when I'm leaving."

"Money-back guarantee," he says with a swagger.

On his way to Ampang Park to pick Dr. Safia up, he again makes a call to Johan, inviting him to join them for dinner. The detective sergeant declines, saying he is meeting an old buddy.

"Just in case you change your mind and decide to join us, do you know where O'Mulia Satay is?"

"It's at Jalan Tun Razak, Jalan Semarak," Johan says.

"Yes. Jo, I'm on my way to pick up Fie then head straight for O'Mulia. If you're coming, bring your friend along if he wants to join us."

"I know where it is. I'll ask if she wants to."

"She? I thought you said it was an old buddy from Penang," Mislan jokes, calling him out.

"Did I? I must have gotten my two appointments confused," Johan replies, chortling.

———

Mislan drives past the Petronas Twin Towers, pride of the nation, which has grown into the city's unofficial symbol. He makes a U-turn at the traffic light and heads back in the direction he came from on Jalan Ampang. As he slowly approaches the Ampang LRT station, he spots Dr. Safia standing by the roadside. Flashing the headlights to attract her attention, he squeezes in between the rows of waiting taxis.

"Hi," she greets, climbing into the passenger's seat. "Where's this place that serves the best satay? Is it far? I'm starving."

He looks at her, contemplating whether he should ask her what he had thought her craving is about, but decides against it. *If she is, she will say.*

"Jalan Tun Razak. I'm not really into satay, but I know the satay there is really good."

"How do you know then?"

"My grandma used to take us there. It was her favorite satay hangout."

"Sorry to ask. Is she still . . . ?" she asks, letting her sentence hang.

"She passed away a long time ago."

"You never did tell me anything about your family," she says with a hint of disappointment.

"What's there to tell? Both my parents have passed away, and I don't like to talk about dead people." He flashes the all-too-familiar let's-not-talk-about-it grin.

"Except if it's your case," she says dejectedly, but she knows not to push it.

Johan is already waiting at the O'Mulia restaurant, alone, when they arrive. Mislan raises his eyebrows and Johan shrugs, grinning. Mislan lets his inquiry slide. They pick a table on the sidewalk, alfresco, and Mislan orders an iced black coffee, lights a cigarette, and offers it to Dr. Safia, who declines. She reviews the menu.

"What would you like to eat?"

"Anything," Mislan answers matter-of-factly.

"Jo?"

"I'd like to try the oxtail soup," Johan says, "and iced lemon tea, please."

"Twenty chicken, ten beef, ten intestine, three ketupat, two iced lemon teas," she says to the waiter. "Is that enough?"

"We can order more if we want later," Mislan suggests. "How did the autopsy go?" he asks when the waiter leaves to place their orders.

"Can we wait until we've eaten?" she replies, narrowing her eyes in annoyance at his impatience. "Autopsy and dinner don't go well together."

Johan senses a hint of anxiety from his superior and decides to initiate casual small talk.

"How do you know this place?" he asks his boss.

"His grandmother used to bring him here. It seems this was her favorite satay hangout," Dr. Safia mischievously answers for him.

"Yes, I remember you saying your grandma stayed somewhere around here, didn't she?" Johan asks.

"Kampung Baru," Mislan answers, pointing in the direction of the junction. "Did you visit the temples?"

"I went to the Buddhist temple in Petaling Jaya."

"Wat," Dr. Safia corrects him.

"What is 'what'?" Johan asks, confused.

"It's a wat, w-a-t," she says, spelling it out. "A Buddhist temple is called a wat."

Johan beams. "I visited the Buddhist wat, and the priest, sorry, monk, confirmed the tattoo is a form of Buddhist prayer, the five sacred lines."

Flipping through his notepad, he continues, "Hah Taew Sak Yant. It's the most popular yant among women. The yant is supposed to bestow blessings, love, kindness, and success in all aspects of life, charm, good luck, and protection against evil. The Hah Taew is part of some prayers. The priest, I mean monk, said a lot more, but I couldn't understand most of it. Something to do with the five outstanding attributes of Lord Buddha."

"So the vic is Buddhist," Mislan mulls.

Johan nods.

"Still doesn't give you her identity," Dr. Safia observes. "Not even her ethnic group."

"Or nationality," Johan adds. "She could be local or Thai, Myanmar, Vietnamese, Cambodian, Laotian, who are mostly Buddhist."

Mislan's forehead wrinkles in thought.

Their order arrives, and the conversation stops momentarily. Dr. Safia and Johan sample the satay in harmony and nod their approval.

"Much tastier and fresher than in Kajang," she mumbles between bites.

Johan agrees, and Mislan beams.

Mislan takes a stick, dips it into the sauce, and nibbles on it. He watches as his dinner companions dig in heartily. In record time, all that's left of the forty sticks of satay and three ketupat are the sticks.

"You want more?" Mislan asks.

"Not for me, I'm up to here," Johan declares, placing his index finger across his throat.

Dr. Safia shakes her head, saying, "It's really good, but no thanks."

"Now can we talk autopsy?" Mislan asks, lighting a cigarette.

The pathologist gives him a sharp glance, taking a slow sip of her iced lemon tea. Mislan hands the cigarette to her and lights another for himself.

"The cause of death was from blunt force trauma to the occipital bone," she says after a deep drag on the cigarette.

Mislan gives her a stare, and she bursts out laughing.

"The back of the head, the lower part of the skull," she explains, indicating to the spot on him.

"I thought the acid burn was the cause of death," Johan interjects.

"The acid burn would've eventually killed her. However, before it did, she received the fatal blow to the back of her head."

"You're saying, the killer poured acid on the vic's face while she was alive?" Mislan asks disbelievingly.

"Antemortem, before death," she says. "There're traces of acid in her throat and lungs, indicating she swallowed and inhaled the acid."

Johan shakes his head disgustedly, saying, "How cruel mankind has become."

"Mankind has always been cruel, it's just gotten worse by the day," Mislan corrects him. "The deceased must have screamed like mad when they poured acid on her face. The killer or killers might have feared someone heard the screaming and smacked her head to silence her," Mislan theorizes. "Perhaps there was no intention of killing her, they'd just wanted to deform her but it went a little too far."

"Could be, but there was no way she could have survived the burn on her face," Dr. Safia comments. "The acid burns on her hands were, however, postmortem."

"Could be an afterthought. To make sure her identity was totally wiped out," Mislan says. "The markings on her chest and arms I suppose were done antemortem."

"Yes. Looks like a viselike or clipping device, perhaps a pair of pliers. I've sent the photos to forensic for matching. Traces of tissue hematoma or contusion were found on her wrists, indicating she was restrained. In my years of practice, this has to be the worst case of death I've seen," Dr. Safia says, followed by a tiny quiver.

The three remain silent as they contemplate the findings.

"There're also numerous puncture markings and tear wounds all over the deceased's body," she continues. "They're not deep enough to cause any serious damage or harm, more superficial. One of her eyes was gouged out. I used the term 'gouged out' because it wasn't done surgically and it was more like the eyeball was ripped off."

"Probably from the rats," Mislan offers.

"Rats? What rats? There was no rat mentioned in the report. I wasted so much time trying to figure out what could've caused the wounds," she reproaches them.

"Chew said he and his team had to fight off sewer rats when they arrived at the scene."

"The rats even got one of her eyes," Johan says, with a shudder. "I hope I don't go out that way, as rat food."

"We all will be worms' food one day," Dr. Safia says, laughing.

"Did you perform a rape test?" Mislan asks.

"Told you, it's part of the standard autopsy requirement on female deceased," she snaps. Then toning down, she says, "No trace of tearing or semen found, but she is not a virgin. She had experienced sexual intercourse. You think this is related to a sexual crime?"

"I doubt it, but you can never tell."

Dr. Safia and Johan give him an inquisitive look, not believing the reasoning given.

Seeing the looks on their faces, Mislan grins. "Long shot, I was hoping the victim had sexual intercourse prior to being killed. If we can get DNA of the male donor, match it, we could learn a little more about her."

Their expressions change to that of consensus.

"One other thing before I forget: the crime lab said you made a request for the scraping of the deceased's soles to be sent to Trace. What are you looking for?"

"Where they found the vic was not the primary scene. I was hoping Trace might find something to probably lead us to the primary scene."

Dr. Safia's face lights up like a woman about to announce she is engaged or pregnant. Mislan feels a cold shiver running down his spine.

"I remember you saying it wasn't the primary scene, so I decided to take samples from the deceased's stomach in case you want to send it to Toxi for analysis. Who knows, you might get lucky, she may have eaten something unique as her last meal, which might lead you to a restaurant or a specialty shop selling such food or using such ingredients. And if you're luckier, the restaurant operator or shopkeeper might know your victim."

Mislan gives her the do-I-look-lucky-to-you gaze, which she ignores.

Holding up her hands to stop from being interrupted, she continues, "And guess what I found?"

"Her ID card," Mislan jests.

The two officers laugh and watch as she fumbles in her oversized handbag. She mimics a drumroll and holds up a small exhibit bag.

"What is it?" Mislan asks, holding out his hand.

"An earring."

"In her stomach?" Johan asks, puzzled.

The pathologist nods.

"Just one?" Mislan asks.

"Just one, and I almost missed it. If not for the clinking sound it made hitting the receptive bowl, I probably would've missed it."

"Why is it in her stomach?" Johan asks, his curiosity mounting.

"Maybe the killer shoved it down her throat," Mislan answers off-handedly. "But why only one?"

"And when she choked, they decided to knock her off," Johan suggests, completing Mislan's theory.

Mislan examines the round stud earring. It's made of clear crystal, about the size of a green pea, and embedded inside it is a tiny pink heart.

"Admit it, I was right. A woman never leaves home without her earrings," Dr. Safia says by way of nudging him.

"Except in our case she wore it in her stomach," Johan teases.

"Did you find any defensive wounds on the victim?" Mislan asks, changing the subject.

Dr. Safia shakes her head. "Told you, her hands were bound, remember? Any luck with anthropology?"

"Dead end."

"Didn't expect you would. We're very far behind in the field compared to developed countries."

"We're lagging in most fields compared to them," Mislan moans.

6

MORNING PRAYER KICKS OFF at eight thirty daily except weekends. Contrary to the moniker, it has nothing to do with any religious matter, except for unsanctioned utterances of "*Oh my god*" or "*Holy shit*." No one exactly knows how the morning briefing got its name. Mislan figures it was most likely coined by some old-timer investigators. Their legendary conducts were used as examples by instructors during training of what young officers were not to repeat. These old-timers, mainly investigators, would go into the morning briefing with a "bullshit and pray" attitude. Bullshit their way on the investigations and pray they would not get their asses chewed.

The briefing is short and sweet, or sour or bitter depending on the cases and the preliminary actions taken by the investigator. Should there be a need for lengthy consultation, the unit head usually addresses it on a one-to-one basis. Officers who are required to attend court are released.

The session usually starts with the outgoing shift investigator briefing the attendees of incidents for the last twenty-four hours. The morning prayer is a good way to keep other investigators updated. And at the same time, it provides them a chance to contribute input or suggestions based on their own experience.

This morning, it is Inspector Reeziana who starts, as she is the outgoing shift investigator. She updates the team on two homicides. One involved a known drug runner; the case is being handled by the district investigator of narcotics. The other was an argument between two foreign workers that turned into a physical fight; when the restaurant owner tried to intervene, he was stabbed by the cook. This case, too, is being handled by the district.

When she finishes, the unit head opens the table for the investigators to raise any matter related to work. If none, which is usually the case, prayer is adjourned until the following morning.

Before this morning's briefing is adjourned, the head of Special Projects, Assistant Superintendent of Police Ghani Ishak, takes center stage, requesting for the standby detectives to be assigned to his team for one week.

"Where are your detectives?" Superintendent Samsiah asks.

"They're overworked, and I really need additional men," Ghani states.

"Overworked with what? I see them sitting in the office every time I pass by. Sometimes I wonder how they hope to get any lead by warming their bums in the office. How long has it been since your last intel on the VIP housebreaking gang, two months?" she asks, staring intently at Ghani.

Ghani pretends to ponder her question.

"Before you request any additional men, forward all your detectives' journals to me," she demands.

The detective journal is an official diary of activities, the cases the detective is working on, information gathered, arrests made, raids conducted, and so on. At the end of the month the journal is forwarded to the detective's superior for evaluation. Detectives will be cautioned or reprimanded if they're found to be slacking. Unproductive detectives are known to piggyback on other detectives' achievements to avoid being put on notice.

Ghani frowns, shrinking lower in his chair, making himself as small as he possibly can.

"What's the status on your Jane Doe?" she asks, turning to Mislan.

"All we know so far is she may be a Buddhist," Mislan replies. "Jo showed photos of the tattoo found on the vic's back to a Buddhist monk and was told it was an extract from a Buddhist prayer."

"That's a start," Samsiah responds encouragingly.

"Not much of a start," Mislan grunts. "Knowing her to be a Buddhist doesn't even tell us her nationality."

Samsiah nods. "Since that's the only lead you have, work on it," she advises.

"Ma'am, I read about a DNA test that can determine the ethnic group of a person used by the FBI in the Precious Boy case. Can we get our forensic to conduct such a test?"

Samsiah looks at him curiously.

"Since when have you been reading DNA literature? Find out more about it before I speak to Catalina from the crime lab and hear what she has to say."

———

At his office, Mislan heads for the emergency staircase, his private self-authorized smoking area. He lights up and makes a call to Dr. Safia.

"Hey, can you talk?"

"Yes, what's up?"

"Have you read or heard of DNA tests that can determine the ethnic group of a person?"

"You mean a DNA ancestry test?"

"I can't remember what it's called. What can that test determine?"

"It can determine a person's heritage or ancestral makeup based on markers across your twenty-two pairs of autosomes, that's the non-sex chromosomes," she explains. "It takes into account contributions from your full spectrum of ancestors. The standard test gives you information about your direct maternal and paternal lines, which is your parents and siblings."

"I lost you at twenty-two pairs of autobahns," Mislan says, chortling. "A yes or no answer, OK. Can DNA tell a person's race?"

"I don't know," she answers agitatedly, "and don't you use the courtroom yes or no line on me."

"Sorry, didn't mean to."

"The discovery was about five or six years back. Perhaps by now they can," she continues, accepting his apology. "Anyway, if the heritage is of a single ancestral makeup, that already tells you the race, doesn't it?"

"I suppose so. Thanks."

"Are you requesting for such a test?" she asks excitedly.

"I'd like to give it a shot."

"Can you keep me in the loop? I'm keen to know, too."

"Sure, if our crime lab can do it."

———

Stubbing out his cigarette, he flicks the butt down the stairwell, getting rid of any evidence of him smoking on the floor. He is pretty sure one of these days the cleaner is going to file a complaint to building management of occupants smoking in the emergency staircase. Once that happens, management will be sending cleaners to every floor to look for evidence. No way is he going to leave any evidence behind.

Leaving his unsanctioned private smoking landing, Mislan again heads for the boss's office. He enthusiastically passes on to Superintendent Samsiah his newly acquired knowledge and impresses on her the need for a DNA ancestry testing to be done. It may well be the only way for him to have a workable lead.

———

Johan joins Mislan at his desk, handing him the list of missing persons compiled by the standby detectives. He scans the list dispassionately.

"Most of them are Malay girls," Mislan remarks, shaking his head.

"Runaways, the parents claimed kidnapped. You read of them almost weekly in the Malay dailies," Johan points out.

"I don't think our vic is in here."

"Why?"

"Last night I did some research on the tattoo, the Hah Taew Sak Yant. From the literature, I'm guessing the vic isn't a Malaysian Buddhist. Religious tattooing is a practice more attuned to strong Buddhist countries like Thailand, Myanmar, Vietnam, Cambodia, and Laos."

"The vic has a fair complexion, like the Chinese," Johan points out.

"I'm thinking Thai or Vietnamese. They've lighter skin compared to Cambodian, Myanmar, or Laotian."

Mislan makes a call. After a couple of rings he asks teasingly, "Chew, how's your mood today?"

"Hi, Inspector, how may I assist you?" Chew replies, ignoring Mislan's teasing.

"Chew, do you have facial reconstruction software?"

"I don't understand. You mean like at airports?"

"No, that's facial recognition. You know, something like 3D software that can construct a person's face from the skull," Mislan explains. "Or maybe a technician who reconstructs faces using plaster or clay."

"Sorry, heard you wrong," Chew says chuckling. "No, we don't have a facial reconstruction sculptor. I haven't received any such request before, don't know if IT has any software on it. Let me check and get back to you."

"Thanks, Chew."

"Can't we check with immigration?" Johan asks as soon as Mislan terminates the call.

"We can if we have her name or know what she looks like," Mislan replies, letting out a frustrated sigh.

His cell phone rings.

"Mislan."

"Inspector, our IT technician says he can download one of the Facial Compositing softwares and give it a shot," Chew says. "But no guarantee."

"Great, when can we do it?"

"He needs the 3D photo of the skull. Can you arrange for it?"

"I can take him to the morgue. He can snap as many photos as he wants," Mislan eagerly offers.

"He said it has to be a clean skull."

"Oh!" Mislan exclaims, followed by a brief silence. "Chew, let me run it by my boss and get back to you. Keep the tech on standby."

Armed with the new input, Mislan again heads for Superintendent Samsiah's office. Knocking on the door, he interrupts her by asking, "Ma'am, can you spare me a minute?"

Samsiah puts down her reading glasses and indicates the chair.

"I've spoken to Catalina Rembuyan, if that's what you're here to inquire about." She pauses, reading the expression on her officer's face, which instantly lights up with expectation as he holds his breath. Her heart feels for him. "We don't do it here."

Mislan's chest deflates as he empties his lungs of disappointment.

"But," Samsiah continues, and sees her officer's face light up once again. "If there is justifiable need, she'll put in a special request for it to be done in a private lab in Australia."

"Thanks, that's encouraging and I may take you up on it, but not now. It's something else I need your advice on," Mislan says, sliding into a chair. "I did some research on our vic's prayer's tattoo, and I believe she's a foreigner, probably Thai or Vietnamese. There's no way of knowing unless we can somehow do a facial composite. To do that, we need to clean her up." He pauses, tightening his lips at Superintendent Samsiah as if what he is about to say is difficult. "This's where I need your advice."

"Are you talking about forensic anthropology?"

"Yes, that's what I was told," Mislan confirms, smiling. "They do have a name for everything, don't they? Checked with Universiti Malaya: we have an anthropology department but not forensic anthropology."

"What are you getting at?" Samsiah asks.

"I'd like to try facial reconstruction, and to do that, I need to clean up the vic's skull. Which means detaching the head from the rest of the body, clean it of the flesh, then take 3D snapshots."

Samsiah laughs. "You've been reading again. I'm amazed at the effort you're putting into this case."

"No, not reading, inquiring—it's much easier." Mislan chuckles. "Can we do that?"

"If we've exhausted all other means, and, more importantly, if the forensic evidence will assist us in identifying the victim, yes."

"Why the hassle? The head's already a skull anyway."

"She's somebody's daughter, Lan. Just stop for a moment and picture how the parents would feel seeing their daughter's head is a bare skull," she sneers at her officer's insensitivity in chasing for closure.

"It's more merciful than letting them see her the way she is now," Mislan contends.

Samsiah hikes her eyebrows.

"Sorry, there're too many dead and loose ends, and I don't like either," he grunts.

"I know," Samsiah says, acknowledging her officer's frustration. "Speak with the pathologist and make the decision under advice."

7

LEAVING SUPERINTENDENT SAMSIAH, MISLAN makes a brief call to Dr. Safia, asking if she can meet him at the morgue. Anticipating disapproval from her on his plan, he decides not to tell her the purpose of their intended meeting. He is too hyped up to risk being shot down over the phone.

He isn't anticipating her to object, but the fact remains that the hospital's staff are mainly Malay, therefore Muslim. To Muslims, even an autopsy is something they are opposed to. It is looked upon as desecrating the dead, torturing the soul. He personally hasn't experienced such opposition but has heard other investigators grunting about it. The deceased's family could go to great lengths, even to their parliamentary representative, to stop an autopsy. He doesn't know about the Buddhist community, but this is another hassle he can do without.

Arriving at HUKM Medical Forensic Department, the two Special Investigations officers head straight for the morgue, where Dr. Safia said she'll be waiting.

Pushing through the morgue's heavy double-leaf swing door, they see Dr. Safia by the autopsy table. She asks the purpose of this secretive urgent meeting. Mislan enthusiastically explains what he has in mind while she listens prune-faced. When he finishes and catches his breath, she is staring at him unblinkingly. Mislan knows he has somehow managed to capture her attention, total attention, for she is at a loss for words. Something he knows does not happen to her often.

"Fie, you OK?" he inquires.

"Are you serious?" she finally asks.

"No, I was just kidding to see how you'll react," he says, mocking. "Yes, I am, and the IT tech is on his way. I've never seen it done before. You think I can hang around to observe it?"

"I've never performed it before. This's not my field, but disturbed as I am, I must admit I'm as excited as you are," she says. Narrowing her eyes quizzically, she asks, "Are you sure you're authorized to request for such procedures to be performed?"

"As the investigator, I am," Mislan says as confidently as he can manage. "Look, Fie, this is a sudden death case, and the CPC sanctioned the police to determine the cause of death through autopsy. It empowers the medical officer to dissect any part of the deceased, take samples, and so on."

"I know what the Criminal Procedure Code says. That is to determine the cause of death, which I've already established was due to a blunt force trauma," she replies, stopping the inspector in mid-sentence.

"What good is the cause of death if we don't know who the victim is? Who do we inform? Where do we begin?" Mislan snarls, annoyed at her need for any clarification to perform the procedure. "This's the only way for me, I mean the police, to identify the deceased."

"I don't know, Lan, I'll have to consult my chief on this."

"Why don't you do that, and I'll wait for you outside, I need a smoke anyway." Mislan gives in and gestures for Johan, who was quietly observing them, to follow him.

Stepping out to the parking lot, he lights up, inhaling deeply. Spotting a bench, he moves toward it and plonks himself down. Johan slides next to him.

"Are you sure we can do that?" Johan asks, jerking his head toward the morgue.

"I really don't know. The CPC is silent on using medical science to establish the identity of the deceased," Mislan says. "The legislature is not keeping up with modern science, but that shouldn't prevent us from doing our job. I suppose if it is done in good faith, why should we be wrong?" He extinguishes the cigarette. "What good is the cause of death without knowing the identity of the deceased?"

"You got a point there, but are you sure this is the only means of establishing the vic's identity?" Johan asks, concerned.

"The truth is, I don't even know if it'll work," Mislan laments, lighting another cigarette. "All I know is, we have to try."

His cell phone rings.

"Yes, Fie."

"Where are you?"

"Parking lot. What did your chief say?"

"Put your request in writing, and we'll comply," Dr. Safia answers, sounding disturbed.

"OK, we'll be right in." Turning to his assistant, he says: "Jo, can you check with Chew where the hell the IT tech is. He's supposed to be here by now."

Walking back to the morgue, they find the IT technician Saifuddin Rahim waiting at the entrance.

"Inspector, Sergeant, sorry I was caught in the jam."

"Sai, nice to see you again," Johan returns his greeting. "How's the family?"

"Fine, thank you," he replies, following them into the morgue.

The Jane Doe is brought to the autopsy table by the morgue attendant on instruction of the pathologist. Following the officers into the morgue, Saifuddin stops dead in his tracks when he sees the deceased.

"Oh, my God! What happened to her?" he cries.

Mislan turns to look at Saifuddin, whose face is turning pale, his eyes anxiously scanning the room searching for something. Mislan recognizes the nauseous look with ballooning cheeks holding the puke in from his early days in the police force doing weekend pub roundups.

He pats the IT technician on the back and points to the row of sinks. Covering his mouth, Saifuddin makes a dash for the sinks to throw up loudly. The two officers, Dr. Safia, and her assistant watch as Saifuddin empties his stomach. When he is done, he turns around, sees the deceased on the slab, makes a 180-degree turn, bends over the sink, and throws up whatever little is left inside him.

Mislan chuckles. "Wimp."

Dr. Safia gives Mislan an admonishing smack on the arm, glares at them, and goes to Saifuddin's assistance. The men titter, but no one makes a move to assist. After several pats on his back from the pathologist's soft hand and some words of encouragement, the IT technician is ready to give it another go.

Mislan completes the formal request and hands it to Dr. Safia.

"Here, now can we start?" he says, the words coming out rather curtly.

"Can I have a word with you, in private?" she says with a pout, walking briskly toward her office.

Mislan follows her while Johan and the morgue attendant seize the opportunity of their absence to further torment and mock Saifuddin. When Mislan enters the office, Dr. Safia is standing behind her desk, arms folded across her chest.

"Close the door, please." Without waiting for the door to be closed, she goes straight to the point. "Are you sure you want to go ahead with this?"

Mislan leans against the door, staring at her, not answering.

"Do you really want me to perform the procedure?" she repeats firmly.

"What's going on here?" he asks, irritated by the harshness of her tone.

"Nothing's going on. I ask if you—"

"I heard what you asked," Mislan stops her mid-sentence. "What I'd like to know is, what's going on. One minute you're all excited to go, and the next minute this. Was it Sai?"

"Who?"

"The IT geek?"

"What about him?"

"I don't know. Are you angry because we laughed at him?"

Dr. Safia replies with a rebutting laugh.

"It was the meeting with your chief, wasn't it? I saw the look on your face when you came out of his office yesterday."

"It has nothing to do with the meeting with my chief. I'm just concerned about what we're about to do. Severing her head and defleshing it."

Mislan notes her referring to the corpse as her. He knows just too well how she has always treated the dead with respect and dignity.

"Do you know how to do it? I mean, are you trained to perform such procedures?" he asks, his tone soft and sincere.

"Trained—no. Read the procedures—yes. Done it before—no. Excited to perform it—yes. Concerned if something goes wrong—bloody hell yes. Does that answer your questions?"

"Whoa, never had it like that before from you."

The pathologist allows herself a tiny smile. "Well, now you have."

"What could go wrong? First, you detach the head from the body. Then you put the head in a pot and boil it until the flesh softens. Once the flesh softens, you remove it from the head until you get a skull," he says, smiling.

"Since when did you became an expert in medical forensic?" she mocks.

"Since I started watching *Bones* on TV." He grins. "I mean, if an actor can do it, surely a real pathologist can."

"It is not that simple, OK. First, to get rid of the flesh you have to dry it before dermestid beetles are unleashed onto it. The beetles only consume dry, leathery soft tissue and that'll take two to three days. Then the skull is cleaned with hot water and detergent. After that you bleach it."

"Why all the steps? Can't you just go to the defleshing?"

"I can skip the dermestid beetle process and boil the skull to deflesh it. But overboiling may damage the skull."

"Sooo, it's not the procedure that's bothering you, you do know what to do," Mislan says, walking toward her. "What's it then? Did I do something wrong?"

"No," she answers, avoiding eye contact. "Let's get back to the case. OK, I'll proceed, but it'll take some time before the skull is ready for photography. You may want to go back to your office, and I'll call you once it's ready."

Mislan gives her a hard look and thinks he sees a gleam of sadness in her eyes. He opens his mouth to ask something, but she is already walking away from behind her desk toward the door. Without a word, she leaves. He stands there perplexed. *What just happened?* Walking out of the office, he tries to recall if he did something that might have offended her. *A lot*, he reflects. *Perhaps it was when she asked about my family. Was it her way of saying she wanted our relationship to move to the next level? What's the next level, marriage? I don't think I'm ready to give it another go.* Poking his head into the autopsy room, he signals for Johan and Saifuddin to come out.

Stepping outside, Johan asks, "Why, what's happening?"

"Nothing," Mislan replies straight-faced. "The procedure will take some time, and Dr. Safia will let us know when it is ready for photography."

Johan gives his boss a disbelieving look.

"What?"

"Nothing, it's not like you to want to miss witnessing something like this."

"Can we, I mean witness the procedure?" Saifuddin asks eagerly.

"You're kidding, right?" Mislan says, mocking him. "Do you have a puke wish or something?"

"Sai, you can't lose your potbelly by puking, OK," Johan jokes.

8

ON THEIR DRIVE BACK to the office in the Kuala Lumpur Police Contingent building along Jalan Hang Tuah, Johan again asks his boss if something happened while he was with Dr. Safia. Again, Mislan shrugs it off with a brisk nothing-happened gesture. Johan looks at his boss, a superior officer who turned into a friend, a true friend over the years. Together, they have been through thick and thin, stood side by side in the face of death and adversaries. Needless to say, most of the confrontations can be attributed to his boss's unbending character. They shared their most private thoughts, fears, dreams, and fantasies. There is no one they trust more than each other. With Superintendent Samsiah, whom they both trust implicitly, their trust is confined to work-related matters.

Johan senses something is upsetting his boss.

"Is everything OK with Daniel?" he asks, initiaing his around-the-bush probe.

"He's with his mom until school reopens."

"Johor?"

"Hm-hm, Kulai."

Johan knows how tight his boss is with his son. He remembers how close his boss was to throwing in the towel because he wanted to spend more time with Daniel. After his wife left him, Mislan, assisted by his Indonesian maid, Ani, took care of Daniel. He went through a nerve-racking existence trying to balance his two obsessions, Daniel and work. Nothing else mattered to him until Dr. Safia came into his life. Then it was Daniel, work, and Dr. Safia in that precise order.

"The maid is with him?"

Mislan nods.

Johan knows Daniel does not go anywhere overnight alone. It is either with him or the maid, not even with Dr. Safia.

"So Daniel is fine," Johan states, eliminating one possible cause. He asks the next question: "Is there something wrong between you and Fie?"

Mislan gives him a glance. "Not that I'm aware of."

"There're a lot you're not aware of," Johan mumbles under his breath.

"What's that supposed to mean?"

"For one, there're not only dead victims that need you. There're actual living and breathing people who, for whatever screwed-up reasons, do like and care about you."

Mislan lights a cigarette and lowers the window.

"OK, nothing is obviously wrong to you, but I can sense something is developing. You know, after being with someone for some time, you tend to develop these freaky extrasensory vibes, sixth or navel-string sense. I don't know how to describe it, but I'm sure you know what I meant," Johan pushes on.

"There's no such thing. That's just you reading the all-too-familiar or unfamiliar body language of the other person. Like now, I can sense you're nosing into something that is none of your business."

Johan laughs heartily. "That's it, see you developed it, too," he says, tittering.

Mislan glares at him.

"Touched a raw nerve, did I?"

Mislan looks straight ahead, his mind drifting back to Dr. Safia and her sudden mood swing. *It's not like her to allow work to rule her emotions. What was bothering her?*

Mislan jams on the brake as the traffic light turns red at the junction of Jalan Maharajalela and Jalan Hang Tuah, prompting his detective sergeant to throw him a quizzical gaze.

"Are you OK?"

"Sorry."

"You want to talk about what you were thinking?"

"Just thinking about our vic," Mislan says, flicking the cigarette out, raising the window, and looking straight ahead to avoid his assistant's scrutiny.

At the office, Mislan heads straight for his desk, drops his backpack, and slumps heavily into the chair. Walking to his desk, Johan observes his boss through the corner of his eyes. Hearing the chair scream under Mislan's weight, Inspector Reeziana turns to Johan, tilting her head in Mislan's direction inquiringly. Johan shrugs.

Their wordless conversation is interrupted by the front desk clerk announcing fretfully from the doorway that one of the detectives from the Special Projects team got seriously wounded in a shoot-out.

"Who? Where?" Johan asks anxiously, springing to his feet.

"Ganesan, Jong Goldsmith, Jalan Kencana."

Turning apprehensively to his boss, who does not seem to have moved a muscle, Johan asks, "Are we going?"

Reeziana watches amusedly as the two of them lock eyes.

"Where?" Mislan asks.

"Kencana."

"Why? Are they still there?"

Johan turns to the front desk clerk to ask.

"No, ASP Ghani's team is there. The robbers escaped after the shooting," the clerk says.

"Ma'am?" Mislan asks.

"On the way to GH."

"No point in us going now to the scene or GH. Let crime scene and the doctors do their jobs. We'll wait here for ma'am to brief us," Mislan states calmly, lighting a cigarette while heading for the emergency staircase.

As the emergency door closes behind his boss, Johan walks with heavy feet back to his desk.

"Was that our Mislan who just walked out?" Reeziana remarks, gawking at Johan.

Johan throws her a nasty glance, then stares at the fire-rated door behind which the inspector is feeding his nicotine addiction, showing no concern for the shoot-out or the injured personnel.

———

Taking long drags of his cigarette, Mislan racks his brain trying to recollect memories of Detective Ganesan. All he remembers is that Detective Ganesan is a quiet man in his mid- or late-twenties and always wears a smile. Their rapport was limited to formal greeting of each other whenever they crossed paths in the office corridor. His recollection is interrupted by the ringing of his cell phone.

"Yes, ma'am . . . All . . . Yes, will get the standby detectives to assist. . . . How is Ganesan?"

"The doctors did the best they could, but they said . . ." she stammers, unable to finish her sentence.

Mislan can hear her taking deep breaths to steady her nerves.

"One shot went through the heart, he lost too much blood," she continues, barely audible.

Mislan understands the unspoken underlying message.

"Get them all in, including Ghani. I'll be back in twenty."

The line goes dead before Mislan can reply. He stamps out his half-smoked cigarette, kicking it down the stairwell. Stepping into the office, he instructs Johan to get the front desk clerk and standby detectives to round up every available officer and man. He makes the call to ASP Ghani himself.

———

The meeting room buzzes with tense whispers when Superintendent Samsiah enters looking ashen and grave. Her expression silences the room. She calmly sits at the head of the table. Her eyes roam the room, stopping momentarily on each and every face. Somehow, they know they have lost a member. Tears start welling in the eyes of the men and women of the Special Investigations Unit. For most of them, this is the first time they lost a colleague in the line of duty. As police officers, they knew the risk and are constantly reminded of it, but none actually thought it could happen to them. The city's streets are filled with violence, but somehow police officers are never prime targets. Mislan gazes at his unit head and feels the grief she is grappling with.

"Ghani, what've you got?" Samsiah asks, her voice shaky with contained anger.

"I believe it's the same gang I've been monitoring. The MO is similar—"

"If it's a gang you're monitoring, why are they still at large? Why haven't they been picked up? That's the gang you claimed robbed three gold shops, right?" she asks, cutting Ghani short, spikiness evident in her tone. "Where're they?"

"I've identified two houses they use as safe houses, one in Brickfields and the other in Meru, Klang."

"I want round-the-clock surveillance on both houses. I'll get Selangor to give us access. Your team will take the house in Klang and Mislan, organize a team and take Brickfields."

She pauses, deep in thought.

"Tee, you organize another team to act as backup for Mislan."

Again, another deep pause follows. Silence descends on the room. All eyes are fixed on her, and no one says a word or moves. Even their breathing is controlled.

"For the next few days, this is our home," Samsiah finally continues. "We'll all be on standby here. Those who are not in any of the teams have one hour to go home, pack your stuff, and report back."

Another pause follows. Mislan has never seen his boss in such a fragmented state of mind.

"Those who have to attend court shall return here immediately after court. All leaves are temporarily suspended until further notice. Except for the investigator on duty, all pending cases shall be put on hold. I want the bastards who did this to my man."

Samsiah laboriously stands. Mislan notes the shakiness in her legs.

Looking straight at her head of Special Projects, she says, "Ghani, I want them alive."

———

Long after Superintendent Samsiah has left the room, no one moves or makes any comments. Even the gung-ho Ghani Ishak remains quietly in his seat. It is as if they are offering a moment of silence for their lost member.

Mislan leaves the mourning group and heads for his boss's office. He finds her leaning back in her chair, staring out the window into nothing, tiny teardrops trickling down her cheeks. Noticing his presence, Samsiah wipes her cheeks and greets him with a forced smile. Mislan closes the door behind him, taking a seat.

"What happened?" he asks. "Was he on a stakeout?"

Samsiah shakes her head.

"I was told he's off today. He went to the goldsmith to pick his wedding ring," she says, tears welling in her eyes again. "He was talking to the workers when the shop was hit, and he reacted. Ganesan didn't even manage to get his gun out of the holster. Caught two bullets in the chest." Samsiah dabs her eyes. "The doctor found the wedding ring tightly clenched in his hand." Her lips quiver, and she bites them. "Did you know he was getting married next month?"

Mislan shakes his head.

Samsiah discards the wet tissue and pulls out new ones, dabbing her eyes.

"I forgot, you're a bit off on social networking," she mocks, pursing a grin. "I can still see him standing there. The excitement on his face when he came to get my signature on his marriage application," she continues, her eyes shifting to the doorway. Her lips carve a memory-induced smile. "He said, he met her on one of the cases he was working on. Love at first sight was what he told me."

A moment passes as she stares at the spot where the late Detective Ganesan once stood.

"Is there something you wanted to see me about?" Samsiah asks, snapping out of her bereavement.

"No, no, nothing," Mislan says, deciding whatever he wanted to update her on his case can wait.

"Then go and get your team ready," she says, opening a file and putting on her glasses.

Mislan hesitates.

She looks up at him inquiringly.

"Will you be all right?" Mislan stammers.

"Yes, thanks for your concern. Now go and get me those bastards."

9

THE MORGUE ASSISTANT NODS his readiness to Dr. Nursafia Roslan. As this is the first time such a thing is being performed by the hospital, she was instructed to film the entire procedure for future reference. Speaking into the overhead microphones, she signals for the assistant working the video camera to come closer. After identifying herself and the case number and briefly outlining the objective of the procedures, she lets out a long low sigh. She nods several times, more to herself than to the assistant, before proceeding.

With skillful precision, she surgically detaches the head from the body at the atlas vertebra and places it on a stainless steel tray. She gazes reverently at the headless body before pulling the plastic sheet over it and shifting her attention to the disembodied head. She looks at it unblinkingly. Her prolonged motionlessness causes the assistant to peel his focus from the video camera's screen to peek at her. Having assisted Dr. Safia in several hundred autopsies, he has never seen the pathologist in such a hesitant mode. He has always liked assisting her. She is always respectful of the dead and very sure of her procedures. Never cutting more than what was required and never once violating the sanctity of the dead.

Sensing the assistant's baffled stare, Dr. Safia flashes him a tiny smile, inhales deeply, and steps closer to the head. Her lips move like she is saying something to it before she begins. The assistant resumes filming the procedures, and everything is back to normal. She begins with the tedious task of carefully removing the brain and what is left of the eyes, placing them neatly into another tray. *What do I do with them*, she asks herself, looking at the tray. *Damn, I did not think of it before. I probably should put them in a biodegradable container and place it with the body to be buried together.* Next she slowly removes the tangled and caked hairs. After what seems like an eon, she lifts the hairless head from the tray. The head feels strange in her hands. Replacing it on the tray, she takes several still shots of the bald red and white flaky face. Stepping to the apparatus counter, she checks on the boiling water's temperature. Satisfied, she carefully lifts the head, placing it into the boiling water. Dr. Safia steps back, leaning against the counter, desperately needing a smoke. She closes her eyes, blocking out the craving. But closing her eyes means opening the floodgate of thoughts to her personal predicaments.

Hush, Fie, you're making a mistake, a voice in her head tells her.

It's my mistake, and I'll make as many as I choose to make, she snaps back angrily. *And what the hell do you know for you to judge me?*

The boiler timer rings, startling her and chasing away the voice in her head. Pushing herself away from the cabinet, she moves over to the boiler. Putting on thick cotton gloves, she examines the medical equipment tray for a suitable utensil to lift the head from the boiling water. Picking a large surgical tong, she gingerly removes the steaming head, which is not yet a bare skull, from the container, placing it on a tray. Again she gazes at the hairless, eyeless head, asking herself, is it the right thing to do, desecrating a human body even in the name of science?

Yes, Mislan has his reason, a valid reason, but he's not the one doing it. He's not here to see the process and result of his request . . . to see this.

She forgets she was the one who asked him to leave, with the excuse the procedure would take a long time. The truth is, she did not want him to be around for personal reasons.

Pushing the thought aside, she picks a pair of surgical forceps and delicately tugs at the tissue to test its adhesiveness. The tissue comes off easily. She begins to carefully remove the soft flaky tissue, shred by shred.

Minute after minute, the container begins to fill with red and white flaky tissue, and a light dull yellow skull emerges from the hairless, eyeless, and now tissue-less head. She turns on the boiler and places the skull back into it, this time adding some bleach. The procedure is painstakingly tedious. She indicates to her assistant to stop the video as she needs a short break. Taking off her surgical gloves, she convinces herself she's not performing an autopsy and therefore taking a short break won't compromise the procedure.

She heads for the parking lot and lights a cigarette under the car shed. Leaning against a pole, she again grapples with her decision. It is not a forensic decision she is beleaguered with, it is a quandary begging a conclusion. She has deliberated over it a hundred times over the last few months. The countless nights of lying awake in her cold bed debating with herself till the crack of dawn. It was not an easy decision, not a winning decision, but it was a decision nevertheless. She is fully aware of its harshness and finality. Once acted upon, there shall be no turning back. But what choice does she have? It is one of those decisions made using the heart and not the brain. Pushing the thought aside, she tells herself there is no point in thinking about it anymore, *what is done is done.* Crushing the cigarette, she walks back to the autopsy room.

10

THE HOUSE WHERE THE suspects are believed to be hiding out is located in a low- to medium-cost development in the police district of Brickfields. It is about half a mile off the main road, Jalan Tun Sambanthan, known as Little India because this stretch of road is lined with shops selling Indian traditional and religious merchandise, colorful garments, sweets, and delicacies.

Mislan drives into the development. Johan points out the target as they survey the surrounding area. The target is an intermediate unit in a row of single-story townhouses. No vehicles, car, or motorbike, no shoes or flip-flops at the front door, which is rare for a Malaysian's house. No clothes on the clothesline. Nothing to indicate the house is occupied. To his disappointment, there is nothing close by they can use as a stakeout point. Unlike in Western movies, where policemen sit in their car when on stakeout, it is nearly impossible to do so locally when the outside temperature is a scorching 93 to 96 degrees. They would suffer heatstroke or dehydrate in a car without the engine and air-conditioning running. But if they were to sit in the car with the engine and air-conditioning running, they would be made by the residents within minutes. If he is going to have eyes on the target, he needs to come up with a solution.

As they're driving out, Mislan surveys the row of single-story houses opposite their target house. Pulling up to the curb outside the development, he asks his assistant to call detectives Jeff and Syed over.

"Jo, I noticed two houses opposite the target I believe to be Malay houses."

"How do you know?"

"The one just across the target has a *baju kurung* hanging on the clothesline. But that is too close to the target. If they're watching the street, they may notice us visiting the house." *Baju kurung* is the national Malay dress for women.

"OK."

"There's another house about five units down the same row. I think I saw a framed Quranic calligraphy on top of its front door. I don't want to give it another pass-by to avoid suspicion. Get Jeff and Syed to give it another look to be sure."

When detectives Jeff and Syed arrived on a motorbike, Johan gives them the instructions.

"You think the owner will cooperate?" Johan asks the inspector.

"That's the only location where we can stake out the target without being spotted."

Among Malaysia's three main ethnic groups, Malay, Chinese, and Indian, the Malays are more likely to assist the police, especially if the policemen are Malay.

Detectives Jeff and Syed return and confirm Mislan's observation.

"I want the two of you to pretend like you're visiting the house and quietly introduce yourselves. Tell them you're on a stakeout, but tell the occupants nothing else. Say it's in regard to a spate of housebreaking in the area. Ask if you could be allowed in to observe a suspected house."

"What if the owner refuses?"

"Use your powers of persuasion. Tell the owner there may be a commendation letter should the stakeout be successful. That'll surely make the owner cooperate and, if you are lucky, serve you guys food and drinks."

The detectives laugh and get back on their motorbike.

"Where will you be?"

"Around," Johan replies. "Keep us updated every half hour."

"Don't make any moves without my instruction," Mislan adds.

Mislan drives out to the main road and parks by the curb. It is less conspicuous sitting in the car by the busy main road than on the narrow roads in the development. Johan leaves to buy cold bottled drinks from a sundry shop close by. It's almost five hours since Jeff and Syed staked out the house, with no movement observed. Mislan is starting to doubt the accuracy of ASP Ghani's intelligence. The windless late afternoon is getting really hot and humid. He steps out of the car to stretch his legs and butt. The time on his cell phone shows 3:11 p.m. when he receives a call from Detective Jeff.

"A man is coming out of the house," Jeff says in a whisper. "He is pushing out a motorbike from inside the house."

"Just one?" Mislan asks. "What do you mean he is pushing a bike from inside the house?"

"Yes, one. The motorbike is parked inside the house. Wait, it looks like he's talking to someone inside the house."

"Can you see how many are inside the house?"

"No. He is leaving on a bike. You want us to tail him?" Jeff asks anxiously.

Mislan signals for Johan to take the wheel.

"You stay there and watch the house, get Syed to tail him. What's the bike make and number?"

"Honda Cub Ex-5, gray, registration W-A-D 3-0-2. He's heading to the exit road."

In the background, Mislan hears the sound of a motorbike coming to life and figures it has to be Syed.

"Is Syed on him?"

"Leaving now. Boss, the man isn't wearing a helmet," Jeff adds.

"He must be going somewhere close by. OK, keep us informed if there's anything new." Terminating the call from Jeff, he makes a call to Inspector Tee, who is stationed at Brickfields police district headquarters located about five minutes away.

He tells Johan to drive back to the development. A hundred yards in, Johan spots a motorbike heading their way with Detective Syed tailing behind. Mislan tells his assistant to take a left onto a side road, make a U-turn, and follow them.

The suspect rides past them and heads for the main road, turning left to Jalan Tun Sambanthan. The two officers look at each other questioningly. Wearing helmets is mandatory for motorbike riders and pillions. Could they have been wrong in their deduction that the man was not going far because he isn't wearing a helmet? To their relief, about thirty yards before Jalan Sambanthan, the suspect stops and parks in front of the corner mamak restaurant.

Johan pulls over to the curb and parks, paying no heed to the yellow line. Syed is parked next to the suspect's motorbike in front of the restaurant. He sits on his motorbike and makes a call on his cell phone as if he's waiting for someone. It is way past lunch hour. Mislan and Johan follow the suspect into the deserted restaurant, taking a seat at one of the tables. The suspect is standing at the serving counter, reviewing the dishes on display and pointing out his order to go. Mislan sends his location to Inspector Tee.

"We'll take him outside as he gets on his bike," Mislan tells Johan. "Make it quiet and snappy. . . . We don't know who is who here."

One of the restaurant's Bangladeshi workers comes over to their table asking for their order and Mislan tells him they are waiting for another friend before ordering. As the worker leaves, Johan casually stands and walks out to the pavement in front of the restaurant.

The suspect pays for his order and walks out with it to his motorbike, with Mislan following close behind. As the man sits on his motorbike, Syed grabs his arm and prevents him from inserting the ignition key, saying in a commanding tone: "Police."

The suspect twirls to break loose but Syed's grip holds fast. Johan instantly moves in and cuffs the suspect's other arm.

"*Ajo*, what's this? What wrong I do?" the suspect protests.

Mislan glares at him, hissing *shssss* to shut him up.

"What's this?" the suspect continues. "I've not done anything wrong."

Johan gives him a tap on the head, saying menacingly, "My boss said be quiet."

The suspect turns to Johan to object, but another tap to his head from the detective sergeant changes his mind. They bundle the suspect into the car. Johan is patting him down when Inspector Tee and his team arrive. Mislan signals for Tee to follow them, then pulls out of the parking lot and heads out to Jalan Sultan Abdul Samad. Johan pats the man down again, pulling out his wallet.

Syed asks for one of Tee's men to assist in riding the suspect's motorbike.

Johan reads out the suspect's particulars listed on his identity card. "Letchmanan son of Kuppusamy, from Pandamaran, Klang,"

"Letchmanan, what do people call you?"

"Letch."

"OK, Letch, what gang?"

"Where got gang one?" he protests, before claiming he is no gang member. "*Ajo* boss, I swear no gang one."

"How many of you in the house?" Mislan asks, pulling into one of the side roads with Tee and the two detectives on the motorbike close behind.

"Only I alone."

"You're alone, but you bought four packs of rice?"

"Hungry, *lah* boss, last night I no eat."

"OK, let's see you eat all the four packs."

Mislan figures the suspect and the rest of his gang must have just woken up from a night of romping. They're hungry, and the suspect was buying them late lunch. He asks Johan to uncuff one of the suspect's hands.

"If you don't finish them all, I'll shove every grain of rice down your throat," Mislan says, looking at the suspect through the rearview mirror.

The suspect blinks rapidly at Mislan, unsure if he meant what he just said. Johan yanks the suspect's hands, unlocks one of the cuffs, and places the four packs of rice on his lap.

"Now eat," Johan commands.

"*Ajo*, cannot *lah* boss."

Mislan swings around in the driver's seat, grabbing Letchmanan by the back of his neck and pulling his face a couple of inches away from his.

"Start eating, or I'll start shoving them down your throat," he says ominously.

The suspect closes his eyes, turning his face sideways.

"Sorry boss, sorry."

Still holding onto the back of the suspect's neck, Mislan asks, "How many of you in the house?"

"Four."

"Names?"

"Kuna, Morgan, Rao, and me."

"They have guns?"

"Sorry boss, I only take care of house. I don't know about gun."

Criminals face capital punishment for illegal possession of firearms. They know the simple rule of having an unlicensed gun for criminal purpose equals death, either at the hand of the police or the court of law. To voluntarily admit to possession or be associated with those in possession is a big No-No.

Johan gives him a warning tap on the back of the head.

"If they're armed, I'll shoot you first," Johan declares.

The suspect throws him a disbelieving glare.

"You don't believe me?" Johan asks. "I'll shoot you then throw your body inside the house like you died from a shoot-out."

"Who among them have guns?" Mislan barks at the suspect.

"*Ajo*, boss, I'm only their *machai*. They never tell me anything one." *Machai* is the local slang for "lowly follower."

"Who's the leader?"

"Rao, he always gives orders one."

"Is the front door locked?"

Letchmanan looks at the inspector, not understanding the question.

"After you left the house, was the front door locked?"

The suspect nods.

"Do you have the key?"

"No key. Have to call to open door."

"Who normally opens the door?"

"Not sure one . . . sometimes Kuna . . . sometimes Morgan."

"Rao?"

"Rao boss, where open door one."

Johan recuffs him, and they step out of the car and walk over to Tee's team. He updates Tee and the team.

"You want my team to go in?" Tee asks.

"No, stick to the plan. You do the cutoff."

"You want me to call for backup?"

"Yes, but we don't have time to wait for them. If the machai doesn't come back with the food soon, they'll get suspicious."

———

Mislan outlines his plan. Johan will ride pillion with the suspect using his motorbike, but it will be Johan who does the steering from behind. Just in case someone in the house is watching, it will look like the suspect is driving.

"The suspect is pillion but sitting in front," Tee reconfirms.

"Yes. Your team'll take up position at the rear. Johan will use him as a human shield walking up to the front door. He'll call for those inside to open the door. Once the door is open, Johan will push him from the line of fire. Syed, Jeff, and I will rush in."

"You said there are three of them and there are only four of you. Are you sure you don't want two of my men to join you?" Tee offers.

"OK, give me two men as backup. They can guard the suspect."

"Lan, don't take any chances, OK. I know the suspect said there is no gun, but you know there're too many guns floating out there. Treat them as armed and dangerous," Tee cautions.

Mislan nods his acknowledgment.

———

Mislan gives Tee and his team a two-minute head start to get into position behind the house as the cutoff. As the raiding team moves, he calls Jeff and tells him to join them in front of the target. Parking the car about ten yards away from the target, he sees Jeff casually walking toward them. He gives the target and its surrounding area a final eyeball to check for any new activities. There is nothing out of the ordinary compared to other houses in the area. Except for the grille door and windows, no other reinforcement is visible. Still no vehicle parked in the driveway, which indicates no additional arrival. Several cars are parked along the road, but the neighborhood is deserted and quiet. No children playing or stray dogs loitering around. Probably, at this time of day, too hot to be outside. With what is about to go down, Mislan feels it is better so.

He hears a motorbike coming toward them and sees the suspect with Johan riding from the pillion seat. Johan somehow manages to maneuver the motorbike to the front of the target house without any untoward incident. Getting off the motorbike, Johan makes himself as small as he possibly can, hiding behind his human shield as they walk up to the front door. Mislan and his raiding team move in to take up their positions, and he nods to his assistant.

Standing behind the suspect, Johan knocks on the door. He whispers to the suspect to call to those inside to open the door. With the muzzle of a 9mm semiautomatic pressed to his spine, the suspect complies without argument.

A nervous moment ensues when nothing happens. Johan quickly glances at his boss, who is taking cover behind the wall across, as if asking what next. Mislan signals for Johan to focus on the door and wait a little longer. Johan hears the door knob turn from inside and gives the signal with a tilt of his head to his teammate.

The instant the door cracks open, Letchmanan is violently shoved to the side. Tee's men grab him and push him to the ground. Mislan springs into action and grabs the individual who opens the door, spinning him around into a grip lock from behind. His steel-cold Beretta 9mm muzzle presses hard against the back of the man's spine. Johan, Jeff, and Syed rush past the inspector shouting *police* repeatedly. Their announcement is curtly greeted by two gunshots. Syed drops to the floor, holding the side of his stomach and groaning. Johan reflexively lets loose several blind shots into the house as covering fire for Jeff to attend to Syed.

Mislan lets loose two shots and spins the man he is holding, shoving him into the arms of Tee's men outside the door. He and Johan drop to the floor and scurry for cover. He gestures for Jeff to pull Syed away from the line of fire. Once they are safely out of the line of sight and fire, he instructs Jeff to call for the paramedic and turns to Johan.

Johan indicates to the end of the hallway toward the kitchen, puts a finger to his ear and holds up two fingers. Mislan nods his agreement, it sounded like the two shots came from two different firearms.

The house is deafeningly quiet, except for the low groaning from Detective Syed, who is safely tucked behind the wall in the living room. Their ears still buzzing from the blast of gunshots in a confined space. Mislan turns toward Jeff, using signs to inquire on his injured detective's condition. Jeff indicates his partner is OK, that it is only a flesh-wound. Nodding his relief, Mislan turns his attention to the standoff.

He surveys the house, doing a quick ground appreciation of the situation. A narrow hallway of about four feet wide and twenty feet long stands between them and the shooters. There is nothing along the hallway that can be used for cover from gunfire. There are two doors on one side of the hallway and one door on the other. He knows these are bedroom doors.

What're the chances the shooters or more men are hiding in any of the rooms? he considers. *Don't think so, no escape route.* He concludes it is suicidal to rush the shooters to take them down. His thought is interrupted by Tee's voice over the walkie-talkie.

"Lan, is everything all right in there?"

"Officer down, I repeat officer down. Call the paramedic, I repeat, call paramedic."

"Roger that. The shots sounded like they came from two weapons."

"Roger that."

"I'm told Delta 8 is rolling, Echo Tango Alpha any time now."

Delta 8 mentioned by Tee is the Special Operations Unit.

"Roger. Watch the back door, they may make a run your way."

"Lan, wait for Delta 8 OK."

The radio goes silent.

"Lan, wait for Special Ops. Ma'am wants them alive," Tee anxiously reminds him.

"No promises."

Mislan signals for the backup detectives to bring in Letchmanan.

"Who's back there?" he forebodingly asks.

"R-rao and K-kuna," Letchmanan sttammers, his unblinking eyes fixed on the hallway.

Mislan instructs the detectives to take Letchmanan back out to safety, wait for the paramedics to arrive, and guide them in.

Once they're out of the house, Mislan turns his attention back to the standoff. *It is too quiet. What the hell are they doing back there?* He glances toward his assistant. Johan reads what is on his boss's mind.

"Waiting for us to make our move," he says softly. "They know they have high ground."

"But they also know we'll be calling in reinforcement," Mislan counters. "Where the hell is D8?"

"They'll be here any moment now," Johan says, calming his boss to avert any reckless decision by him.

A loud bang from the rear of the house stops the two officers' exchange. By the sound, they know it is an outside-in blast. It tells them the Special Operations must have blasted the back door open. Instantly, Mislan barks: "Down, flat down on the floor! Assume submissive position." He knows there will be several deafening blinding explosions. "Close your eyes," he instructs. The three of them fall flat on their stomach with both hands over their heads.

The big bang is immediately followed by two loud blinding blasts from flash grenades and boots pounding the concrete kitchen floor. Hectic shouts of *Police* and *Down* fill the house. Something heavy drops to the floor with a dull thud, instantly followed by two shots from a small firearm from somewhere up on the roof. The two shots are answered with eight to ten rapid shots from MP5 semiautomatics from ground level.

Screams of agony fill the house.

As instantaneously as the commotion begin, it ends.

For a few seconds everything is silent, as though time stands still. Mislan glances to his assistant. Suddenly, there is a thundering crash in the ceiling, a loud thud, and raucous clanking of cooking utensils hitting the floor.

Another momentary silence follows.

Someone barks, "*Go, go, go,*" and the stampede of boots on concrete floor accompanied by shouts of *Police* reverberates from the kitchen area. The heavy *tum-tum-tum* and frenzied shouts pass them all the way to the front door. The sound of pounding boots stops and the sweet pronouncement of *clear* greets the D9 officers and men lying facedown on the floor.

Mislan and Johan get to their feet, holster their weapons, and walk to the kitchen. The hallway and kitchen are thick with the pungent smell of gunpowder. A shirtless Indian man lying on his stomach in the middle of the small and crowded kitchen is the center of attention. Three MP5 barrels point at him ready to blast him to the next world should he even think of making a move.

A bloodied body of another Indian man with gaping wounds in his chest and abdomen lies sprawled faceup on the kitchen sink. His head and upper body are squarely plastered in the double-basin sink, hands spread wide across both sides, with his legs dangling over the kitchen cabinet. Fresh warm blood drips from his barefoot legs to the floor, which is littered with cooking utensils, broken pieces of porcelain, and glass.

"What went down?" Mislan asks ASP Sim Poh Len, the Special Operations team leader.

"When we came in, they were trying to escape through the trap-door. I suspect they were going to punch through the roof and out to the other side," Sim says, looking up at the ceiling. "That one," he indicates with the barrel of his MP5 to the man lying on the floor, "was hanging up there, and we managed to pull him down. Him," he turns toward the man in the sink, "fired two wild shots, caught a few in return, and came crashing through the ceiling."

"Lucky you guys got here just in time or they would've escaped," Tee remarks.

"Who is he?" Mislan asks Tee, motioning to the sink.

"He says," indicating to the suspect on the floor, "Rao."

"OK, our work is done here, we're clearing out," ASP Sim informs them. "Who's in charge?"

"Tee," Mislan volunteers.

"OK Tee, they're all yours. I'll get my sergeant to forward you the report when we get back."

"Thanks."

"Anytime. Always glad to be of assistance. Keep my boys in shape."

11

Superintendent Samsiah was informed earlier that the funeral is to be held this morning at Buntong Crematorium, Perak. She remembered reading something about the crematorium being a center of controversy a few years back when the chief minister announced the state government was to build a non-Muslim crematorium on the site. It was strongly opposed by the Indian community, which objected that the land was gazetted as a Hindu cemetery.

She asked a personal favor that the attending public relations officers be dressed in ceremonial uniforms, a dress code used only for honoring VIP funerals and other high-profile official ceremonies.

Although she could have requested an official vehicle, she decided to go in her personal car. Driving up to Ipoh, she realizes she has never been to a Hindu funeral before.

"Has any of you been to a Hindu funeral?" she asks the two PR officers.

"Not funeral, but visited the family at their houses," Inspector Rumaizah Abu Bakar answers. "I went with the CPO to hand over the insurance check."

"Is he going to be buried or cremated?"

The two PR officers look at each other, unsure.

"You didn't find out?"

"Sorry."

Samsiah sighs.

"Why, is there a difference in the ritual?" Rumaizah inquires.

"I don't know, never been to one before. Just thought it would be comforting to know," Samsiah says, more to herself. *Knowing the culture of others is respecting them, yet how little we know of others' religions and rituals. Yet we demand they know and respect ours*, she thinks disgustedly.

They arrive at Buntong Crematory in full ceremonial uniform complete with decorative service ribbons. A uniformed policeman stationed at the open parking space salutes her and points to the crematorium. She thanks him and leads her entourage.

At the crematorium entrance, Superintendent Samsiah and her party are greeted by other uniformed police personnel. They tell her they are from the district police headquarters and the contingent welfare unit. She thanks them for coming to represent Perak police to pay their respects. The welfare officer tells her she missed the officer in charge of the police station by ten minutes, then leads her entourage in and introduces them to the late Detective R. Ganesan's parents and family. Samsiah and her officers offer their condolences and are introduced by the parents to the would-have-been Mrs. R. Ganesan.

Samsiah braves a smile only to be betrayed by her sad eyes that mirror her heart. She cannot bring herself to console the never-to-be Mrs. R. Ganesan, for she herself is inconsolable. The passing of Detective Ganesan is not the first subordinate lost in her career, but he is the first officer lost under her command. Although his passing was not in the line of active duty, Detective Ganesan did succumb to shots fired by criminals. It was a senseless death, brought about by those with no regard to human life in feeding their greed. This was a death worth avenging.

Samsiah extracts herself from the grieving family, making her way to the open casket. The PR officers follow suit. The late detective R. Ganesan is dressed in white *jippa* and *veshti* garlanded with fresh bright flowers. His forehead is painted with white, yellow, and red *tilaka*. A priest is seated next to the casket, chanting prayers. The room is filled with the smell of burning incense.

Standing erect beside the casket, Samsiah gives a smart last salute to her fallen detective, holding it a little longer than required, fighting back tears. Images of the joyful late detective standing in her office, seeking her signature on his marriage request, flash vividly in her mind. She whispers, "Have a good rest," drops her hand smartly to her side, and steps away, resisting a second look.

The PR officers gape at Samsiah's breach of protocol, saluting a member of the rank and file. Inspector Rumaizah steps up and hesitates for a moment, unsure if she should follow suit. Superintendent Samsiah only asked them of the favor of dressing in full ceremonial. Nothing was said about giving a detective a last salute. A few awkward seconds tick by before her right arm rises into a smart salute.

Seeing the PR officers giving their last salute, Superintendent Samsiah allows herself a tiny smile of satisfaction. She glumly reflects on the absence of ceremony in sending off a dead police personnel. A retiring or transferred senior officer is given grander farewells than a member of the rank and file killed on duty. Unlike in the United States, there is no gun-salute nor the symbolic recognition of folded national flags for our fallen heroes. Samsiah lets out a silent sigh, thinking, *There is no glory in death after all, at least not for a policeman.*

The officers stay just long enough not to be seen as disrespectful, before taking leave. On hitting the North-South Expressway, Samsiah pulls into the first rest area she comes upon. Parking the car, she asks if the two officers would like to change into something more comfortable and less obvious. They inform her they didn't think of bringing a change of clothing. She nods her understanding, tells them to hang on, pops the trunk of the car, steps out of the car, takes out a bag, and heads for the washroom. A few minutes later, she emerges in civilian clothing with the ceremonial uniform on a hanger.

Getting into the car she remarks, "I never could stand being wrapped in those costumes. Why can't they design something more suited for our climate?"

"Style, ma'am."

"That's our biggest mistake, a lot of form and no substance."

The PR officers narrow their eyes disapprovingly at her statement.

Back at the office, Samsiah heads straight to the investigator's office. The general area is crowded with officers and detectives, with Inspector Tee holding center stage. She quietly stands behind the rows of detectives who are raptly listening to Tee recount the Goldsmith Gang's takedown. She lets her officers bathe in the rare moment of glory for which they strive daily, risking their lives. The detective standing directly in front of her becomes aware of her presence. He makes a move to allow room for her to pass, but Samsiah instantly puts her hand on his shoulder, stopping him. Placing a finger to her lips, she indicates with a smile and a shake of her head not to announce her presence.

After several minutes, Tee finishes his narration to thunderous applause and cheers. It is all the reward her officers need after a victory in a life-and-death encounter.

Samsiah breaks through the rows of people, smiling and applauding. "Well done, all of you," she says. "Well done. I'm sure Ganesan will now rest in peace."

The officers and detectives slowly melt away, leaving her and Tee.

"Where are they?" she asks, referring to the suspects.

"Bukit Aman took them."

Bukit Aman is the location of the Federal Police Headquarters.

Samsiah nods, hiding her disappointment. It is one case she knows will not cross her desk. There were arrests made, therefore there is glory to be reaped. The top brass will be clamoring for it. She will only be left with the memory of her slain detective. Cases like this will only remain on her desk if there is no arrest, therefore no glory at the end of the tunnel.

12

Dressed in her favorite black silk negligee with her jet black shoulder-length hair bundled under a towel turban, Dr. Nursafia Roslan makes her way to the kitchen. She brews a mug of Earl Grey tea and walks out to the balcony, looking out into the hazy city skyline. *The haze is back and this time worse than before. Malaysians blamed the Indonesian farmers, but in reality the felons are the big corporations—Malaysian companies—but no action is taken against them.* Stepping back inside, she closes the sliding glass door, switches on the ceiling fan, slides a CD into the player and leans back on the sofa. The voice of John Charles Waite, lead vocalist of Bad English, fills the living hall. Closing her eyes, the lyrics of "When I See You Smile" resonate within her.

It has been a long and tiring day at work. As intriguing and challenging as the procedures were, it still bothered her that she was the one who separated a head from the rest of its body. The body will be laid to rest incomplete.

How does one go into the next world headless? How would she see where she's going? Would her dead relatives or friends recognize her without her head? She sips her tea and chides herself for asking stupid questions. *She is a soul . . . a spirit . . . She doesn't need her body—souls or spirits don't need forms . . . silly.*

Her chest constricts, and her breathing is labored as her thoughts drift to the impending change in her life. She has not until this moment decided whether the change is temporary or permanent. It is drastic, an uprooting change, and her subconscious mind knows it would be permanent. *No one reverts after taking a huge leap, or do they?*

Tears roll down her cheeks, down her neck and disappear into her cleavage. She keeps telling herself, *This is not a rash decision. You've thought long and hard for months.*

For months she patiently waited for a sign. Any sign to indicate she is making a mistake. She even looked for it in her dreams like a desperate fool, then woke up in the morning angry with herself. Looking at her puffy eyes in the mirror, she admonishes herself. *You're a forensic scientist. You don't expect clues in dreams. You look for clues using your brain, not your heart, not through divine intervention. If the evidence is not there, it's not there.*

She glances over to the coffee table where an open monogrammed envelope of Luton & Dunstable University Hospital lies. Under any other circumstances or if she received it four years ago, she would have been the happiest forensic pathologist in the country. But it is now, and she is overwhelmed with mixed emotions: thrilled, sad, afraid, undecided, lost, hopeful, hopeless, angry, bitter, and relieved. She really does not know what she feels. She knows she has to decide and decide soon, as explicitly expressed in the letter. Dr. Safia stretches her hands to reach for the envelope and accidentally knocks over her favorite tea mug. It crashes to the floor into three pieces. "Damn!" she exclaims, getting up. Letting out a heavy sigh, she declares, "Maybe that's the sign I've been waiting for."

Distraught by the supposed sign, she heads for the bedroom without cleaning up the mess. She turns on the air conditioner, switches off the lights, and dives into bed, hugging the pillow tightly.

———

Daniel and Ani the maid have been away for only four days, and to Mislan it seems like four months. As always whenever his son goes away to be with his mother during school breaks, his three-bedroom apartment turns into a single-bedroom one. He uses the kitchen to make his coffee and his bedroom to work and sleep.

Mislan enters his empty apartment, heading straight for his bed-room. After a quick shower, he goes to the kitchen to make a mug of black coffee, taking it directly to his bedroom. Earlier he was told by Dr. Safia that the victim's skull was bleached and is now settling over-night before it can be worked on. The information gets him all excited. He knows sleep is not something he can look forward to tonight. He has already made a call to Chew of the Crime Forensics Lab to put Saifuddin the IT guy on standby as soon as he comes in tomorrow morning.

Sitting at his work desk, which was the first furniture he moved from the back room to his bedroom when his wife left, Mislan lights a cigarette and switches on the television and his laptop. He has never been a television person, unlike his ex-wife. Nevertheless, he always turns on the TV just to hear voices. Tonight it is Discovery Channel, one of his son's favorites. The channel is airing, what he is sure is for the thousandth time, a program about Komodo dragons on some remote island in Indonesia. He wonders if the Astro cable television owners actually watch Astro and, if they do, whether they realize they're the Master of Reruns. Letting the rerun run, Mislan turns to his laptop, clicks on the case folder, and pulls out the victim's photos. He wishes he owned a touch-screen laptop like the ones he sees some officers using. Swipes the screen left, right, up, down, enlarges by spreading the fingers apart, and all the air-gesture technologies. He knows it's a luxury he cannot afford with his police salary, unless he gets a 2.6 billion ringgit donation like a certain politician.

Mislan enlarges the photo the conventional way by clicking on the zoom icon. He moves the frame from side to side, searching for something he might have missed on his previous scrutiny. The victim is about five feet tall and slim. Her breasts look tiny, like they haven't fully developed. He zooms in, and the pixels break up, making the image ghostly. He zooms out, and in a moment of frustration thinks of calling Saifuddin for advice. Glancing at the time, he decides against it.

Flipping through other photos, he remembers Dr. Safia putting the victim's age at mid-teens to early mid-twenties. *What did she base her estimate on? Probably a woman knows a woman's body better, and she made her judgment based on that.* Based on the mantra tattoo and the skin complexion, he believes his victim is from either Thailand or Vietnam.

Mislan takes a sip of his cold black coffee, clicks on Google Search, and keys in *common Buddhist mantra tattoos*. Strings of sites instantly fill the screen. Clicking on one randomly, he begins reading. After a paragraph he gives up, letting out a throaty groan of disappointment. Everything he reads is Greek to him. Closing the site, he clicks on another. This site talks about Theravada and Mahayana Buddhism and its history. He closes it and clicks on the image prompt on the sidebar and a matrix of Thai Buddhist religious tattoos appear. He searches the images until he finds one that looks similar to that of his victim. He cuts and pastes it on his desktop. Then he keys in *Vietnamese Buddhist religious tattoos* and repeats the process. He opens the two images side by side on the screen.

Not understanding what is written, Mislan applies the only technique he knows how. Compare the characters line by line. Instantly he spots the differences. Both consist of five lines of characters, but several of the characters in the same sequential position are written with different bends, twists, curves or loops.

"Got it," Mislan says, rewarding himself with a cigarette. Now all he has to do is get someone to tell him what the differences mean, and he will pin down the victim's nationality.

Satisfied with the discovery through old-fashioned detective work, Mislan logs off his laptop and takes a sip of his coffee, making sure there is enough left for tomorrow morning's sip to wake the bowel up for toilet call. In the Army, they termed it as the morning gun salute.

Switching off the light, he gets into bed, missing his son, and the excitement of discovery gives way to longing for Daniel. If he had listened to his infamous obstinacy, Daniel would never have known his mother. It was she who left him to chase after what she repeatedly termed her schooldays dream. A dream that he is damn sure does not include having a young son tagging along. *What kind of a woman goes off chasing after her schooldays dream after starting a family? Isn't starting a family a dream? Schooldays dream my ass,* Mislan sighs, recalling his ex-wife's explanation. He always gets upset whenever his memory bank replays the mentally recorded and imprinted conversation he had with her. He remembers how dazed he was at the calmness she displayed during the whole episode. The next few days, she persistently talked about divorce. She even obtained and completed the necessary Syariah court forms, citing "incompatibility" as the reason. What in hell did that mean? All that was required was for him to sign on the dotted line. In the form she implicitly stated she released any custody and claim of their son, their one and only child—Daniel.

Then after a couple of months of disappearance, she wanted to come back. When asked what happened to chasing her schooldays dream, she shrugged, refusing to talk about it. Much as he wanted her back for Daniel's sake, he told her he would only consider taking her back if she truthfully told him what really happened. He remembered vividly saying to her, *If I don't know what went wrong, there's no way in hell I can try and make it right.*

That was his only condition for her return. For reasons only known to her, she did not take up the offer and he chose not to speculate. That was the last of the matter. When his anger finally subsided, he conceded. Daniel should be given the chance to know his mother and likewise the mother to know her son. The only way for him to do so was to allow Daniel to be with his mother during school breaks. Now, lying in bed alone and missing his son, he hates himself for the silly decision.

13

DETECTIVE SERGEANT JOHAN ARRIVES at Hospital Universiti Kebang-saan Malaysia Medical Forensic Department. At the reception, he asks for Dr. Safia and is informed she is waiting in the laboratory. Upon getting the directions, he makes his way to the laboratory, wondering why Dr. Safia called him instead of his boss. Outside the laboratory door, he peeks through the round peep-glass and spots her standing beside a technician at a workbench. Johan knocks and enters.

"Morning, Doctor," he greets her as he approaches them.

He always addresses her formally, even after years of associated friendship.

"Morning, Jo, thanks for coming," she greets him, with the tiniest of smiles.

Johan nods to the technician, then makes eye contact with Dr. Safia, lifting his eyebrows in asking the purpose of his presence.

"Oh, sorry," she says, reading his expression. Tapping a box on the workbench lightly: "Here, the victim's skull for facial composition as requested. If you'll sign for it, the skull will be released into your custody."

"Shouldn't you release it to Inspector Mislan?" Johan inquires, puz-zled. "He's the lead investigator and requesting officer. Releasing it to me will only add another person onto the chain of exhibit handling?"

"You and he are a team, right?" she states rather than asks, her voice masking an underlying tone of resentment.

Johan nods with a smile.

"Then, you can deem this as me releasing the exhibit to the team and not you as an individual," she emphasizes, handing Johan the clipboard with the release paper attached to it.

Johan deduces this is not the time or place to get into a procedural debate with her. He signs the release form and hands the clipboard back. When their eyes meet, he catches a glimpse of desolation in them, which she quickly blinks away. He wonders if it has anything to do with her calling him and bending protocol.

"Doctor, if you can spare a minute, can we talk in private?" he inquires.

Dr. Safia motions for him to follow her as she heads for the door, reminding him, "Don't forget your exhibit."

Johan picks up the box, telling himself, *She really wants me out of here pronto.*

In the quiet cold corridor outside the laboratory, Safia stops without notice and turns around to face him. Her action almost causes him to bump into her.

"We can talk here," she says, apologizing with an amused grin.

"I'm sorry to ask you this, but is something wrong?"

"I don't understand what you mean?"

"I mean, you called asking me to come without telling me why. When I arrived you release this," Johan says, motioning to the box in his arms, "to me. You know Inspector Mislan is the lead and . . ." Johan lets his sentence hang.

Dr. Safia remains silent, averting eye contact.

"I don't mean to pry into your personal affairs, but I'm sure by now you know he's more than just a boss to me. The two of you are like the siblings I never had. If there's something I can do for the both of you, I'd like to be given the trust and opportunity to try."

She flashes him a half smile. He thinks he sees tears welling in her eyes.

"Thanks Jo," she says, her voice cracking. She places a hand on his shoulder. "Everything is fine between us. Say hi to Mislan for me."

Instantly, she turns away and Johan watches as she walks toward the laboratory and disappears behind the door.

————

Walking to the car, Johan makes a call to his boss who is attending the morning prayer, asking what he wants done with the victim's skull. Mislan lifts his phone to Superintendent Samsiah, who is chairing, indicating he needs to answer the call. Samsiah nods and he steps out of the meeting room.

"You got the skull?"

"Yes, Dr. Safia just released it to me."

"Oh."

Johan doesn't like the tone of the "Oh." It is not the usual "Oh" OK tone. It sounded more like "Oh, but why?'

So he tells a fib, not wanting to turn the situation into something more than whatever it already is. "She said she called you, but it went to messaging, so she called me. I told her you're probably in morning prayer."

"Where are you?"

"On the way back from HUKM. You want me to go straight to forensics?"

"No, come back and we'll go together. Call Chew and remind him to put Sai on standby."

Mislan rejoins the morning prayer just as Samsiah ends it. She gives him the come-with-me gesture with her head as she is leaving. Mislan walks besides her, heading for her office.

"What's the call about?" she asks.

"Jo has the vic's skull with him. Just picked it up."

"Have you given any thought about what to do with the rest of her?"

Mislan glances at his superior, baffled.

"What're you going to do with her corpse? You cannot release the body the way it is, not after what you did to it."

"What did I do? I mean, did you see her, the state we found her in?" Mislan responds. "I'm trying to identify her, not mutilate her."

Samsiah stops in front of her office.

"I didn't say you did, but in trying to identify her, you've taken away the most sacred part of her anatomy, her head. You cannot release a headless body to the family when you finally identify her, can you?"

Mislan remains quiet, unsure of how to respond.

Noting Mislan lost for words she says, "I thought so. You said she has a Buddhist mantra tattoo."

Mislan nods.

"Being Asian, chances are she was a Buddhist if there is no evidence of her converting to other faiths. And from what I understand, Buddhists do practice cremation. Perhaps you'd want to look into it."

Mislan nods with a relieved grin. "Thanks."

"Give her a decent ritual. That's the least we can do for her."

"I will. Thanks, ma'am."

———

Johan enters the office carrying a box under his arm, closely watched by the ever-curious officers and detectives. He carefully places the box on Mislan's desk and returns to his own, taking a seat like there is nothing to what he just brought back.

"What's in the box?" Inspector Reeziana asks, coming over to his desk.

"Skull," Johan answers matter-of-factly.

"No shit! You guys really did it? Let me see," she says excitedly.

"Can we?" Johan ask his boss from his desk.

"You didn't verify it when you signed for it?" Mislan asks.

Johan shakes his head. "It's a skull, what's there to verify? I wouldn't know one skull from another."

"Open it," Reeziana urges, making her way to Mislan's desk.

Hearing the conversation, the others gather around. They are all curious to see what it looks like. Although they've seen many dead bodies, none of them, including Mislan, has ever seen a clean decapitated human skull.

Mislan looks up at their faces.

"Nobody takes any photo, OK?" he warns sternly. "I don't want this to be on social media."

Carefully, Mislan cuts the masking tape, opens the lid and takes a hesitant peek inside. Faking an expression of shock, he jumps back exclaiming, "What the fuck!"

The others around his desk spontaneously leap away.

"What, what?!" one of them asks from a safe distance.

Mislan laughs, stepping back to his desk. "Got you, didn't I?"

They let out a hollow laugh and step closer.

"Do that again and I'll shove the skull up your bloody ass," Reeziana pouts.

They watch agape as Mislan delicately extracts the skull from the box. Not a soul dares move or utter a word. The deafening silence of so many normally boisterous people is nothing like Mislan has ever experienced. It's not even close to the silence of grief in the meeting room when the superintendent announced the demise of one of them.

This silence has a touch of numinous eeriness. Like the spirit of the victim is among them, brushing against their bare skin and demanding respect. One by one the people slither away, back to their desks without a word. Even the zappy Reeziana is at a loss for a droll poke.

After a while, Mislan and Johan are the only two left. They cannot take their eyes away from the chalky white skull. Mislan is amazed by its size; he had expected it to be bigger but the skull in his hand is like a husked-out coconut. The eye sockets seem large for a small skull. Disproportionate, like those of aliens in movies. The nose is now a tiny pear-shaped hole but the jaws are still lined with perfect teeth. Mislan warily turns and twists the skull in his hands. He tries hard to visualize a face on the skull, but all he sees are the faces of his previous victims. Terrified lifeless faces permanently etched in his memories.

Johan shifts his attention to his boss, watching the changes of expression on his face.

"What are you thinking?" Johan asks, unable to hold back his curiosity.

Mislan looks at his detective sergeant inquiringly.

"Are you expecting to see something? I mean, like a psychic. You know like when they touch the victim's personal belonging or exhibits from the crime scene, they get flashes of images."

"No, but if I did that would be good."

"Do we have such people here?" Johan asks.

"Sure we do, thousands of them."

"Really?"

"Sure. They're called quacks. The Malay call them *bomoh*, the Chinese *sifu* or whatever. I don't know what Indian quacks are called. Remember the Raja Bomoh at KLIA with coconuts and the flying carpet that doesn't fly looking for the missing airplane?"

Johan laughs. "The missing MH370. That was a real joke, even CNN reported it."

"To us, but to those KLIA, MAS, and government officials who let them perform that crap, those quacks are for real."

"So, do you see her?" Johan asks, motioning to the skull.

"Soon I hope, once Sai performs his magic," Mislan says, grinning and placing the victim's skull carefully back in the box.

14

Saifuddin is on his second cigarette, anxiously waiting at the canteen for the delivery of his probably once-in-a-lifetime experiment. Spotting the two Special Investigations officers approaching the staircase, he puts out his cigarette and trots toward them.

"Inspector, Inspector," Saifuddin calls as the officers turn the corner going up the staircase.

"Hey, Sai," Johan turns to him and says. "Where's the fire?"

"Fire? What fire, there's no fire," Saifuddin replies, not getting it. "I was waiting for you over there and was afraid you would miss me," Saifuddin explains, pointing to the canteen without realizing his overt excitement. "Anyway, I thought the inspector would like to have a smoke before going up." He grins boyishly to Mislan. Motioning to the box in Johan's arms, he asks, "Is that it?"

Johan nods.

"Are you all set?" Mislan asks, climbing the steps.

"Since Chew told me this morning. Can I?" Saifuddin asks, extending his hands to Johan.

Noting Saifuddin's excitement and fearing the worst, Mislan says, "Better wait till we're at the lab."

The three are greeted by Chew as they enter the laboratory. Mislan notices there is a reception committee for their arrival, a whole bunch of white-coat technicians. In all their visits, they never had such a thing. It is the skull. Saifuddin is about to embark on something that will be the talk of the local forensics community. This is possibly the first time they've been offered the opportunity to witness it. The news of what is about to take place would have gone viral among them. Mislan is surprised the head of forensics himself isn't here. Crime Forensics Supervisor Chew points to a bench where an array of cameras has been set up.

"What's all that?" Mislan asks.

"Documentation, the boss wants it."

Mislan nods warily. He knows his request has reached the highest level of the Crime Forensics chain; screwing up is not an option.

"Here, let me have it and set it up," Saifuddin once again offers with extended hands to Johan.

Johan gladly hands the box over. Saifuddin instantly steps away and places the box on the bench. As if that were the signal they've been awaiting, the group of watching technicians moves closer. He carefully removes the skull from the box and places it on the clear pedestal in the middle of several prefixed cameras and lights.

Like a man about to perform brain surgery, Saifuddin focuses on the cameras. Checking and rechecking the exposure settings and angles set earlier, he moves from camera to camera making minor adjustments. He checks the laptop screen, makes a slight adjustment to one camera and the lighting. Upon reexamining the result, he nods his satisfaction. Punching in several commands on his laptop, Saifuddin looks up with pride to the mounted big screens at his masterpiece. Murmurs of awe ooze from the anxious police officers and technicians as the static image of the skull from different angles fills the three mounted big screens. Saifuddin turns to his spectators and is rewarded with approving nods and thumbs-up.

Pleased, he draws a remote from his lab-coat pocket, points it to the pedestal, and presses a button. The dais on which the skull sits slowly rotates clockwise.

"Why so many cameras?" Mislan asks Chew. "I thought you only need one 3D camera."

"I'm not familiar with the process. You'll have to ask Sai that. This is the first time it's being done here."

They watch as Saifuddin works the laptop keyboard. The cameras come to life, tilting rhythmically up and down as various lights automatically switch on and off with the skull rotating on the middle. To Mislan it is like watching a slow robot dance. After almost two minutes, the cameras stop tilting and the dais comes to a rest. The spectators' attention returns to Saifuddin.

"Done," he announces, to their dismay.

"Where is she?" one of them asks, motioning to the static image of the skull on the big screens.

Mislan steps closer as he, too, had expected to see the victim's face.

"She's in there somewhere. She'll only appear after information is fed into the program," Saifuddin says, removing the skull for it to be repacked. "What I just did was capture the skull in 3 and 2D from all possible elevations and angles. The software will compute distance, length, width, and size of all nodule points on the skulls. These computations will be used to compare the skull's dimensions with known databases of indigenous features from every country, but in this case I'll confine it to Southeast Asia. Once the similarity markers are confirmed, we'll try and match it with regions, ethnic groups, and so on. Only then can we come out with a fair composite."

"Shit, I thought we just capture the image and a face will come out of it," Johan grunts. "Why do TV series always make it look so easy?"

Chew and Saifuddin laugh.

Mislan, who shares Johan's sentiment, lets out a long, tired sigh. "When is the earliest we can see her?" he asks.

"Can I let you know the answer after I do a little work on it first?"

Mislan nods dejectedly.

"I'll need every bit of data you have on her."

"Like what?"

"Height, weight, shoe size, everything, panties, bra sizes."

"I'll email them to you, but don't hope for much."

––––––

Mislan taps Chew's arm, signaling for him to follow as he steps away from the crowd.

"Chew, you know of any Buddhist monk?" he asks once they're out of earshot from the rest.

"Buddhist monk, no, not really. Why?"

"Ma'am wants me to cremate the victim, give her a proper ritual. Much easier to keep the ash than the body until we're able to identify her and locate the family."

"Ma'am is right. Never would've thought of it myself," Chew acknowledges. "I can ask my mom, I'm sure she knows."

"Thanks."

"Can you do it? I mean, cremate the victim without family's consent."

Mislan gives him a what-kind-of-a-question-is-that look. Chew crinkles his nose, realizing the silliness of his question.

"Who's paying? I thought the government only allocated a budget for Muslim burials."

"I don't know, never handled an unclaimed body case before, never even thought about it until now." It's Mislan's turn to crack a grin. "But I'm sure we've a law related to it. We're one country that has a law for everything."

"Come to think of it, what do they do with all the unclaimed bodies?" Chew ponders aloud.

"What do you think they do? Bury them, of course. Did you find anything more on the victim's garments?"

"Nothing out of the ordinary or that can provide you with a lead, sorry."

Mislan pouts. He turns around looking for his detective sergeant and calls to him, signaling it is time for them to leave. Johan, who is rapt watching Saifuddin work the computer like a child at a magic show, reluctantly extricates himself.

———

On the drive back to the office, Mislan asks his detective sergeant if he has any experience dealing with unclaimed bodies from the hospital during his MPV years.

"No, why?"

"Our vic, she's going to be one soon unless we can identify her and inform her next of kin."

"Hmmm, have you?"

Mislan shakes his head. "Ma'am asked she be given a proper ritual." he says, lighting a cigarette. "Cremation, do you know of any Buddhist monk who could assist?"

"Won't the government do it?"

"I think JAKIM handles the Muslim burials, but I'm not sure who does it for non-Muslims." JAKIM stands for the Department of Islamic Development Malaysia.

"JAKIM doesn't just handle Muslim burials. I read in the newspaper they've even raided burial ceremonies if they think a Muslim is being buried as a non-Muslim," Johan says. "And weddings," he adds, laughing. "Let me check the Buddhist association at Petaling Street, I'm sure they have some welfare fund for something like this. You know how extremely jealous religious fruitcakes are?"

"Check with the hospital, too. See if they have procedures or allocations for non-Muslim burials. In the meantime, I'll check with ma'am."

"What makes you so sure she is Buddhist?"

"The mantra tattoo and she being Asian."

"I searched the net, and you know what, even Angelina Jolie has the same tattoo. Does it mean she's Buddhist?"

"With the Westerners, who knows what they believe in? During the Beatles era they were into Sai Baba and Hare Krishna just because John Lennon was into it. I think it's just a fad to them." Mislan laughs and flicks his cigarette out the window.

15

SUPERINTENDENT SAMSIAH HASSAN FINISHES rereading her report on the slaying of Detective R. Ganesan. Putting it down, she walks over to the cabinet to brew herself a cup of tea, and her phone rings. Her personal assistant informs she has just been summoned to the Ego Chamber—the office of the Officer in Charge of Criminal Investigations (OCCI), Senior Assistant Commissioner Burhanuddin Mohd Sidek. It is nicknamed the Ego Chamber by officers because of the numerous framed newspaper clippings of himself adorning the office wall. She thinks of making him wait until she has her tea but decides against it. She has no stomach for a confrontation today, not after writing and rewriting that report.

Walking up the staircases instead of taking the elevator, she mulls on why she was summoned. Her thoughts immediately hover over her maverick investigator Inspector Mislan Latif. In the case dubbed UTube, the OCCI had demanded that Mislan be suspended from active duty with clear intent to dismiss. He almost got his wish if not for the intervention of the federal police head of Sexual and Child Abuse. It is no secret to the officers in her department that the OCCI hates Mislan's guts. She, for her part, interpreted the root cause as envy.

Burhanuddin Mohd Sidek came up in the police paramilitary wing. It used to be called Pasukan Polis Hutan or Police Field Force and was generally referred to as PPH or PFF respectively. Now it's called Pasukan Gerakan Am or General Operations Force, but it's the same outfit downsized and rebranded. In Burhanuddin's case, never having the opportunity to be in crime investigation, which is something every young man joining the police force romanticized, is a missing credential in his career. Being the egoistic individual he is, it's an open wound.

Samsiah's theorized that Burhanuddin felt that if, upon joining the force, he was given the chance to be a crime investigator, he would be better than Mislan. But Samsiah also determined that Mislan had achieved what Burhanuddin could never have done as a crime officer.

Nevertheless, by means of cronyism and internal politics, he was handed the most powerful of crime investigation chairs in the country, the Officer in Charge of Criminal Investigations Kuala Lumpur.

———

Reaching the landing of her intended floor, Samsiah asks herself, *What has Mislan done this time to piss him off? With Mislan anything is possible.* Walking down the quiet corridor, she pushes the thought out of her mind.

When she enters the OCCI's general office, the personal assistant greets her warmly, gesturing for her to go right in. Samsiah acknowledges her greeting and knocks lightly on the door, pushing it open and standing at attention. Burhanuddin makes her wait a few seconds longer than necessary before beckoning her in.

A bloody childish show of rank, she says to herself as she steps into the office.

Assistant Superintendent of Police Amir Muhammad from the Integrity, Standards, Compliance Department, once known as the disciplinary department, is seated in one of the visitors' chairs. He stands to greet her. She returns his greeting with a puzzled expression. Shielding his face away from the OCCI, Amir gives Superintendent Samsiah a roll of the eyes, inferring this is another of Burhanuddin's storms in a teacup. She responds with a tiny smile and takes the empty visitor's chair next to him.

"You've certainly overstepped formal protocol this time," Burhanuddin snarls, his face set in the familiar frown of a man struggling with lifelong hypertension. "I've a report here," he continues, palming a file in front of him, "saying you saluted in public, mind you, in public in front of dozens of people, a policeman whom you know for a fact is below your rank, waaay below. A member of the rank and file who did not merit such protocol."

Samsiah looks disbelievingly at Amir, then to her superior.

"This report will go to Datuk' KP, and what do you think will happen?" Datuk' KP refers to the state chief of police.

"I'm honoring my man, a fallen policeman, and whatever will happen to me for doing so, I'll gladly accept it. Is this what I was called in for, or is there something else?"

"He is a *rank* and *file*!" Burhanuddin snaps.

"He was *killed* in the line of duty," Samsiah snaps back. "He deserves my respect, our respect."

"I was told he was off duty, he was—" Burhanuddin say in rebuttal, his face flushed with anger at being snapped at in return.

"Police officers and personnel are on duty 24/7," Samsiah says, cutting him off mid-sentence. "He was a detective, and detectives are never off duty." The last sentence she says softly, more to herself.

Samsiah impels herself to stand. She knows that if she continues debating with this insensitive lout of a boss she will lose control of herself and tears will fall. She cannot and will not allow him the pleasure of seeing her break down.

Taking a deep breath she asks, "Is that all, sir? If it is, may I be excused?"

Before Burhanuddin can respond, she turns on her heel and heads for the door. Once outside the office, she hurries for the emergency staircases. Stepping onto the landing, she closes the door and leans against it. Tears well in her eyes and roll down her cheeks. She wipes them away with the back of her hand, inhaling deeply to check her emotions. After a good two minutes, she feels calm enough to continue down the staircase to her office.

———

In the solitude of her office, she brews herself a cup of tea and sips it by the window, letting the soothing jasmine tea infuse its calming effect.

She hears a light knock on the door and turns around to find ASP Amir Muhammad standing by it.

"Have you got a minute, ma'am?"

"Yes, yes, come in," Samsiah replies with a smile, walking to her seat. "I'm having tea, would you like one?"

"Thanks, but no thanks." Holding the door, Amir asks: "May I?"

Samsiah nods, and Amir closes the door behind him.

"I apologize for what happened up there," Amir says. "The PR officer filed the report, but she didn't intend for you to be hauled up."

Samsiah dismisses Amir's apology, saying, "I'm sure she didn't, think nothing of it."

"I was surprised when he called to ask if there is any action that can be taken for your conduct."

"Is there?" Samsiah is eager to know herself.

ASP Amir Muhammad laughs. "Strictly going by the IGSO, only an officer of the rank of Sub-Inspector and above is eligible for salute. So technically, saluting rank-and-file personnel is a breach of the IGSO."

"Inspector General Standing Orders?"

Amir nods.

"Hmmm, he was right then, it was a misconduct."

"Ma'am, he was from the field force, paramilitary. Regimentation is their way of life, especially where protocol and status are concerned."

Samsiah remains silent, deep in thought.

"There's no glory in dying in the line of duty," she finally says, dismally. "Not even allowed the honor of a last salute."

Amir listens without response.

"In the United States, fallen policemen and women are given the full honor. Why can't we do the same for our fallen men and women?"

The room falls silent again.

"Here all they get is a minute in the news. The family has nothing to show for their loss." Samsiah lets out a heavy sigh. "Do what needs to be done. I'll accept whatever the consequences of my action are. As for the PR officers, they're not to be acted upon, I was the most senior officer there, and they were following my lead."

Amir nods. "The way things are now, there's no glory in being a policeman, fallen or serving. The public damn us no matter what we do, be it right or wrong," he says, standing to leave.

"We only have ourselves to blame for that."

"And our political master," Amir adds.

"Amir, if I'm to be transferred for my misconduct, can you recommend that I be transferred to Kelantan?"

Amir smiles, "Back home, are you thinking of calling it quits?"

"Lately, it did cross my mind," Samsiah says, flashing him a mischievous smile.

16

AT THE OFFICE, MISLAN reviews his investigation notes on the faceless victim, aka Jane Doe. He scans the photos and scribbled notes on the victim before emailing them to Saifuddin. In doing so, he realizes he has nothing much on her except she is a female, about five feet tall, weighing 101 pounds, fair complexion, short black hair, manicured nails, and a full set of well-cared-for teeth. There were two tattoos, one of a Buddhist mantra on the left shoulder blade and another on her back just above the panty line, a blue butterfly with red wings. Facts telling him nothing about who she was, not even her race or nationality. He cannot even precisely determine her age.

The manner in which Jane Doe was killed tells him it could have been an act of vengeance or rage killing, most likely jealousy. Why the trouble taken by the killer or killers to wipe out her identity? And after all the effort of making her unidentifiable, dumping her body in the back alley of a red-light hotbed, next to a city dumpster where she is sure to be found? Could it have been an afterthought, the nagging conscience of the killer or killers or just plain stupidity? Could it be that there was a sick message the killer or killers wanted to send out? Perhaps she was one of the working girls in the area who was the boss's favorite, and she was pushing her weight around. The rest of the working women had done her in to get even and to warn future would-be favorites.

Mislan chuckles. *Boy, you're really desperate aren't you, pushing your theory to the limit?*

Noticing the inspector chuckling to himself, Johan asks what is going on. Mislan replies with a shake of his head. Johan comes over to his boss's desk.

"Come on, share with me, I need something to cheer me up, too."

Mislan looks up at Johan amusedly. "Problem with your gal?"

"The usual thing: it's-been-a-year-now, followed by where-are-we-heading stuff. Every time one of her friends gets married, the same thing creeps up. I've scientifically narrowed the timing to school vacations," Johan says, laughing. "That's the wedding season, when single self-declared career women get all mushy and crappy."

"I thought you said she's the noninstitutional type."

Johan laughs louder. "She was until she hit the three zero mark, and she just did last month."

"What're you now, thirty-three? Why don't you marry her and settle down?"

Johan flashes his boss a grin.

"After all, you did say she's your kind of a woman, the kind you can live with."

"Live with, not be married to," Johan says with a swagger. "That's a big difference there. What about you? You and Fie have been together what, four years now?"

"Don't go changing the subject, we're not discussing me. We're discussing you."

"You and I, we're both in the same boat."

Mislan smirks.

Johan holds up the exhibit bag containing the victim's earring, examining it. "Why do you think they made her swallow this?" he asks. "You think they caught her stealing the earrings and made her swallow it?"

"Could be."

"If that was the case, this could be valuable. You think it's diamond?"

"You don't know anything about precious stones, do you? Diamonds aren't rounded. See the heart symbol inside it. It could just be of sentimental value to whoever it was the vic stole it from. Why don't you take it to a jeweler and get it appraised? Hopefully, it'll give us a lead."

"You think she was tortured and killed because of the earring?" Johan asks, his face lighting up with excitement. "Maybe it's one of those ancient earrings like a national or religious artefact worth millions, and Jane Doe is a mule for a smuggling syndicate."

"Look at it, does it look old or aged to you?" Mislan mocks his assistant.

"No, but it could have been well-preserved."

"What movie have you been watching?"

Johan gives the inspector a grin.

Mislan is intrigued by his detective sergeant's far-fetched imagination. It seems he isn't the only one with a wild, desperate theory. *Desperation must be contagious.*

17

JOHAN BORROWS ONE OF the detectives' scooters and rides across the city. He knows parking at Kuala Lumpur Hospital is murderous, and at this hour going on a scooter is his best option. Riding out of the contingent headquarters, he cuts through the city into Kampung Baru, a Malay reserve area in the heart of the city that has long since been turned into an unofficial Indonesian settlement. He rides on along Jalan Raja Abdullah, entering the hospital complex through the back road.

Parking his scooter in the morgue compound next to a hearse van, he gives a friendly wave to the elderly, half-asleep security guard. Unsure of whom to address his inquiries to, Johan heads for the morgue reception and asks to see the person in charge of administration. The attendant manning the counter directs him to the admin office next door.

Having gotten the information he needed from the morgue administrator, Johan hops back on his scooter and rides toward Petaling Street. Cutting off to Jalan Hang Kasturi, he heads on to Central Market, a tourist art and cultural center.

The building used to be the city's wet market a long time ago, dominated by Chinese traders. It is located across the tiny river to Dayabumi, once the pride of the nation until the Petronas Twin Towers were built. The Dayabumi Complex, built in the early 1980s, was once shrouded with political and financial controversies unknown to the younger generation. Now, no one gives a damn about it.

Central Market is now a Malay-dominated area, with a handful of other ethnic traders allowed or allocated business spaces, the Indian

Muslim at the top of the list. Indian Muslims, locally known as *mamak*, are individuals of Indian origin who somehow became Malay through marriage. Johan remembers his discussion with Mislan, who said that only in Malaysia can people officially change their race from anything to Malay. All they need to do is convert to Islam and marry a Malay. The government will issue you a new identity card with a Malay name. Your father will be named Abdullah, meaning the slave of Allah, and *wal-laa*, you are officially a Malay. From then on you get to enjoy the special privileges of the children of the land.

Parking his scooter illegally along the roadside with many other illegally parked motorbikes, he walks to a promenade by the side of Central Market, an area where tourists loiter for a breather, smoke, discuss where to go next, take photos, or do what curious Westerners do while sitting under the hot tropical sun in the humidity.

Johan's presence is instantly spotted by the numerous unscrupulous con men and human maggots preying on unsuspecting tourists. Their scoops are either peddling fake branded items, drugs, tickets to nonexistent tiger shows, pimping for sex, or pickpocketing. All forms of creative nonviolent crimes are tolerated by the unofficial controller of the area. Violence is frowned upon and acted against. Scamming foreign tourists is less risky, as the victims usually do not make police reports due to their short stays in the country. The trick is not to relieve them of their travel documents, as tourists do not want their travel plans disrupted.

On spotting Johan, the scammers quickly slither away, leaving their potential clients or more likely victims baffled by their indecorous mid-transaction disengagement. Johan smiles inwardly: his Walking Tall reputation earned during his Mobile Patrol Vehicle (MPV) days still commands respect from the lowlifes hanging out at the area.

Nonchalantly, Johan crosses the promenade, which was once a vehicular road, walking toward a row of prewar shop houses. Approaching it, he is invigorated by memories of his uniformed days, days when the dark blue uniform of the Malaysia Police commanded the respect of the public while terrifying the shit out of the lowlifes. Today, it is the total reverse: fear and hatred by the public and comradeship from the lowlifes. Sadly, what remains is only respect or fear for the individual and not the dark blue uniform.

Johan stops in front of a heavily grilled intermediate shop unit. The signboard on top of the door is in the traditional black thick wood carved with Chinese characters painted in gold. The Malay wording in compliance with City Hall's signage requirement reads *Tukang Emas Yeoh*, meaning Yeoh Goldsmith.

After a few long seconds of showing his face, Johan is confident his presence in front of the shop is spotted by whoever is monitoring the CC cameras. Stepping up to the grilled door, he presses the bell. The wooden door behind the heavy grille cracks open and the pale face of a Chinese man peeks through it. The face bobs up and down, inquiringly.

"Chong *ada*?" Johan inquires, asking if his friend Chong is available.

It is obvious to him the pale face peeping through the crack is a new employee who doesn't know him from his MPV days.

"Who're you?" the pale-faced Chinese man asks.

"*Sa'soon* Johan. Tell Chong I need to see him." *Sa'soon* is Chinese for three stripes, a common term for a sergeant.

Pale-face pulls away, the lock on the wooden door clicks, and Johan waits. A moment later the heavy grille door clicks open, followed by the wooden door. Johan knows the drill. During his MPV years, he visited these premises many times on his patrolling route. He's familiar with the Yeoh family. Stepping through the heavy doors, he faces another grille door. The grille and wooden doors behind him close automatically, trapping him within a small cagelike compartment.

Yeoh Chong Seng, the third-generation goldsmith in the Yeoh family, was happily residing in England spending his father's hard-earned money when he was summoned home to take care of the family business. After being back for five years, he still speaks with a British accent, and it becomes more pronounced whenever he's excited. Recognizing Johan, he nods to a man seated closest to the caged grilled door. With another click, the grille door opens and Johan gladly steps out of the cage.

The shop hall as Johan remembers it hasn't changed, dim, gloomy with rows of tiny wooden desks and stools as workstations. Each desk is fitted with a flexi-arm yellow lightbulb. No air-conditioning, just a few ancient ceiling fans. All of the workers are male in their sixties or older. The hall is so quiet, no conversation, no laughter, no movement except for their hands working the tools. If not for the movement of their hands and the occasional cough, one might think that they were props. Johan figures, at their age they need all their energy to work and not waste it on conversation and laughter.

Chong in his shorts and crew-neck T-shirt sits at one of the desks, but his is larger, with a proper chair. He is in his late forties, all skin and bones, with his signature pose of half-smoked rollie between his index and middle finger.

"Jooo, it's been a while. What brings you here?" Chong asks curiously, stepping to the cage to meet his friend and proffer his hand. "I hope it's not one of the street lies about us buying stolen gold."

"Hi Chong, how have you been? What lies, I always thought they were unproven truths," Johan jests.

"You mean like the 2.6 billion donation," Chong says, biting his index finger, tilting his head to one side while feigning a girl caught doing something naughty. "Oh dear, are you here to arrest me then, Sergeant?"

"Detective Sergeant," Johan says, laughing.

"So I heard. Please accept my sincere apologies," Chong says, grinning. "Are you here to investigate all the lies?"

"It all depends."

"In that case, shall I bribe you with, sorry I stand corrected, *donate* you a drink for a start?" Chong says, walking to his table at the deepest end of the floor. "Coffee, right Jo, black?"

"Since you're buying, make it iced coffee with cream, thanks?"

They catch up on old stories as they wait for the iced coffee to arrive. Johan loves the traditional kopitiam-style iced coffee with its full aroma and strong thick flavor. It's unlike those you get from the *mamak* restaurants or roadside stalls, which are watery and look like water scooped up from the Klang River but with a boatload of sugar added. As he takes a swig, it crosses Johan's mind to pack one for his boss. His boss, being a coffee person, would surely love it, too. Putting the glass down, he pushes the thought aside and pulls out the exhibit bag.

"Chong, I need you to take a look at this and tell me what stone it is," Johan says, handing him the bag.

Chong reads the label on the exhibit bag and arches his eyebrows. "Police case," he remarks.

"I hope you're not superstitious."

"Shit, Jo, I don't even believe in God," Chong says, laughing. Taking the earring out the plastic bag, he holds it against the light. "This is crystal."

"Is it valuable?"

"No man, it's glass. OK, with the workmanship, retail value at fifteen ringgit, twenty max."

"You're kidding, right? Hey look, I'm not selling it to you, so you can give me the true value."

"No shit, Jo, I can order them from China wholesales at a ringgit fifty apiece tops. Why, some lowlife suckered a poor old broad into buying it as a precious stone?" Chong asks, throwing out a wild guess.

"Something like that," Johan says, to avoid talking about an ongoing investigation. "Can you take a real look at it?"

Chong looks at him questioningly.

"Put on the one-eyed thing, like your father always did."

Chong laughs, pulls open the drawer and takes out an old-fashioned loupe. "You mean this?"

Johan nods in earnest. "What do you call it?"

"Magnifying glass," Chong says. "I can never hold this damn thing in place," he continues, putting it aside.

Pulling a circular magnifying glass attached to a circular fluorescent lamp on a flexible arm fixed to his desk, Chong switches it on. He adjusts the magnifying glass onto the earring to examine it.

"This's how we do it now."

"Not much of advancement from the old ways is there, except for the size," Johan mocks.

Chong doesn't respond to Johan's jest. His forehead contorts. He pushes his spectacles onto his head, his slit eyes narrowing even more as he readjusts the magnifying glass onto the earring. Frustrated, he barks something in Chinese to the man sitting next to him and is handed a large handheld magnifying glass. Holding it close to his right eye with his left eye shut tight, he studies the earring.

"What is it?" Johan asks anxiously. "What did you see?"

"I don't know what it is but it's some kind of writing on the heart symbol. It looks like Tamil, but I'm not sure. The last word is cursive Latin lettering, Na . . . Nadear."

"Let me see it," Johan demands, coming around the table.

"Why, you know what 'Nadear' is?" Chong is taken aback by Johan's assertiveness.

Shaking his head, Johan takes the earring and magnifying glass from Chong. He raises the earring up toward the ceiling, looking through the magnifying glass.

"And?" Chong asks. "Here, come closer to the light."

"Hmmm, another ancient writing," Johan remarks, frustrated.

"What ancient writing?"

"Buddhist mantra."

"Sanskrit, yes it could well be."

Johan puts down the magnifying glass and returns the earring to the exhibit bag.

"Where was the earring found?"

"You know I can't reveal that information, it's classified. Why do you want to know?"

"The earring has a screw lock. It's rather uncommon for cheap earrings. I'm guessing the earring stud was replaced from its original."

"Why would you want to do that on a cheap earring?"

"Exactly," Chong says, shrugging.

"OK, wrong question. Why would you want a screw lock earring?"

"Why else, so you don't lose it. It doesn't fall off easily, unlike a clip or hook. Usually, earrings with expensive stones are designed with screw locks."

Johan thanks his jeweler friend for his assistance and the iced coffee and asks him not to speak of the earring and his discovery.

"What earring?" Chong answers jokingly.

"Thanks."

18

AT THE POLICE CONTINGENT headquarters, Johan goes up straight to the office and takes a seat at his desk, beaming excitedly. Mislan amusedly watches his detective sergeant without saying a word. Johan looks at his boss bug-eyed, willing him to say or ask something, but Mislan feigns disinterest.

Unable to contain his excitement any longer, he asks, "Aren't you going to ask me anything?"

"Your gal dumped you," Mislan says, "and now you're reborn as a free man."

"Nooo, but that, too, would make me beam."

"Then?"

"The earring. Well, I took it to my friend, and he said it's crystal, glass. It's worthless, possibly about fifteen ringgit retail."

Mislan gives his assistant a told-you smile. "And that excites you."

Taking the earring out, Johan walks over to Mislan's desk and holds it in front of him.

"Inside the heart-shaped symbol," he says, bringing the earring closer to the inspector's face, "there's some ancient writing on it—like the tattoo on the victim's back—and the word 'Nadear.'"

Mislan frowns at the mention of ancient writing. "I'm guessing 'Nadear' is written with the normal alphabet, I mean the Latin alphabet. Is it a place, god or deity?"

Johan shrugs, indicating he doesn't know. "But here's the interesting part. The locking device is a screw lock."

"Translated?"

"According to Chong, the goldsmith, a screw lock is used for precious-stone earrings like those made for diamonds. The reason is for it not to come off easily. Cheap earrings are designed with a hook or clip. What you said earlier about the earring being of sentimental value makes a lot of sense."

"Or religious significance."

"Yeah, that, too, and," Johan adds, grinning childishly, "it could even be magical."

As the two investigators are deliberating over their new discovery, Superintendent Samsiah walks in. Seeing Mislan and Johan are the only two in the office, she heads straight for them.

"Ma'am," Mislan and Johan greet her, standing up.

She returns their greetings with a smile and waves for them to sit.

"What do you have there?" she asks, gesturing to the earring. "Buying earrings for your partner, Jo?"

With the killing of Detective Ganesan and the shoot-out and arrest of the suspects, Superintendent Samsiah has been too tied up to supervise other cases handled by her unit. Now she's now making herself available and getting updated on other ongoing investigations.

Johan blushes at Samsiah's jest.

"Dr. Safia found this in the victim's stomach," Johan answers, holding the earring toward her. "We're trying to figure out why it was in her stomach."

"And have you?" she asks, examining the earring.

"Inspector Mislan's theory is the victim may have stolen the earring and, when she was caught, she was forced to swallow it."

"And your theory?"

Johan grins, shaking his head indicating he has none.

"Always modest, Jo, aren't you?" Samsiah says. "This is crystal, something teenage girls like to wear, not something you kill for." She turns the earring around. "But something isn't right with it. The lock is a screw lock. Makes it difficult to put on and take off. Teenagers prefer the hook."

"Why is that?" Mislan asks.

"They just don't have the patience to put it on and take it off. Furthermore, they change them every day, especially the fashionable ones, almost every day if not by the hour."

"That's what Chong said, too," Johan interjects.

"Chong?"

"A goldsmith, an old friend of mine. If it's worthless, then it must be the heart-shaped symbol with the ancient writing that makes it valuable, worth stealing. The ancient miniature writing does give it a religious or mystical tang. Maybe like in the movies, she was the Chosen One, the one who will defeat the dark forces. The earring is the sign she's the Chosen One. The dark forces soldiers tracked her down, tortured her for the earring, then shoved it into her to weaken her power, making it possible for her to be killed," Johan conjectures proudly. "Not to let her identity be known, they erase her face and prints with acid."

Samsiah and Mislan laugh at Johan's screenplay hypothesis.

"The Chosen One is never killed—bashed to pulp, cut to pieces, shot full of holes, but never killed," Mislan mocks, bursting Johan's theory.

"Have you had the writing translated?" Samsiah asks, still smiling.

She's always glad to see her two officers going at it from every conceivable angle, even movie-bullshit angles. Both the investigators shake their heads.

"So, how do you know it's ancient writing?"

"It looks similar to that of the victim's tattoo of the Buddhist mantra."

"Looks alike, but it may not be. Tamil, Thai, Cambodian writing all look like Sanskrit. Why don't you get the crime lab to enlarge the writing and send it out for verification? If it's religious chanting, Jo, your theory may not be too far-fetched. Not the Chosen One crap but the religious artefact. Seemingly, a lot of people are now believers of dark, magical, or alien forces out there that want to take over the world." Turning to Mislan, she asks, "How's the composite coming?"

"Sai did the 3D thing and said he'd put in the data, which I'm afraid is not much to go by. Hopefully, he'll come up with something later today. Ma'am, are we going to the press with it?"

"If we have a composite we can use. Why, you've something else in mind?"

Mislan shakes his head. Samsiah senses something is bothering her lead investigator but lets it go for now. She knows he'll bring it up when he's ready.

"I'm thinking, and you don't have to decide now"—Samsiah utters the next words cautiously—"perhaps you may like to ask D11 for assistance."

D11 refers to the Sexual and Child Abuse Department. She is well aware that Mislan dislikes sharing cases with another department. Mislan opens his mouth to protest, but she holds up her hand, saying, "I don't need an answer now. Just give it some thought. Your vic is female and was probably a beautiful young woman. The angle of sexual aggression shouldn't be dismissed. At the same time, Jo, you may want to check with D7. The vice angle, just to cover all bases."

Mislan reluctantly nods his agreement.

"Why the Secret Society, Gaming, and Vice department?" Johan asks.

"You said the vic was dumped in Jalan Alor, a night entertainment hotbed. See if she is on vice section's radar."

———

As soon as Superintendent Samsiah steps around the corner, Mislan beckons his assistant to follow him.

"Where, D11?" Johan asks.

"Bring the earring along," Mislan instructs him.

Grabbing his backpack, he heads for the door while Johan keeps pace, throwing his boss cautious looks.

"Are we heading for trouble?"

Mislan responds with a grimace, and Johan laughs. At the lobby, Mislan punches the elevator call button, his eyes darting in the direction of Superintendent Samsiah's office. When the elevator door opens, he hastily steps in and repeatedly presses G. Once on the ground floor, they walk to his car in the parking lot and drive out.

"Where're we going?" Johan again asks.

"Forensics."

"Why? Ma'am asked us to check with D7 and D11."

"What can they tell us?"

"I don't know, but they may have something on their records or info that could be helpful. You never know unless . . ."

"You're one hell of an optimistic guy if I ever met one. You must've been frustrated often, right?" Mislan says, cutting him short.

"What do you mean?"

"I mean all the busted hopes," Mislan mocks, lighting a cigarette.

"It's better than being pessimistic."

"I'm not pessimistic," Mislan replies firmly, "I'm being realistic, pragmatic. Idealists and optimists are fairyland citizens who can't handle the real world."

———

Pulling into the Crime Forensics complex, the officers go straight up to Chew's office. Climbing the staircase, they bump into Saifuddin, who tells them he's on his way down to the canteen for a drink and smoke.

"How's the composite?" Mislan inquires.

"Not too good, I don't have much detail to work with."

"Maybe this will help," Johan suggests, dangling the exhibit bag in front of him.

Saifuddin squints. "What is it?"

"That's what you're going to tell us," Mislan grins.

"Can I have a drink and smoke first?" Saifuddin pleads. "Really need it."

"OK, be quick. See you in Chew's office."

19

CHEW BENG SONG IS at his workbench, bent over a microscope with his left hand turning and twisting the slide, while his right hand is busy scribbling notes on the notepad. *It must be one hell of a life looking through a microscope all day long for a living*, Mislan reflects. *You really have to be dedicated or into what you're doing. I don't think I'd last a day.*

"What's that you're looking at?" Mislan asks, stepping up next to him.

Startled, Chew pulls away from the microscope, ready to admonish the intruder, but manages to check himself when he realizes who it is.

"Inspector," he greet him, "something from another case. Yes, what brings you here?"

"I need you to take a look at what's inside the exhibit found in my victim."

Johan hands Chew the exhibit bag.

Extracting the exhibit he remarks, "This is an earring!"

"Yes, we all thought so, too," Mislan jests. "Thank you, now we've got an undisputed forensic confirmation."

"Funny. You said it was found in your victim. What exactly do you mean?"

"The pathologist found it in her stomach. I need you to look inside the earring: there's something written on the heart-shaped thing inside it. Can you put it under there and see what it is?" Mislan asks, pointing to the microscope.

"No, not this, it's not linked to the monitor."

Stepping to the next table, Chew places the earring onto the slide plate under the microscope and switches on the scope light. Instantly, the earring's image appears on the large mounted screen in front of them. Chew adjusts the lens, and the image on the screen sharpens.

"Can you turn it a little?" Mislan asks.

Chew does as requested, and the lettering on the pink heart-shaped symbol comes into focus.

"Another ancient writing," Johan offers.

"What is that word *Nadear*? Can you focus on that?" Mislan asks Chew.

Again, Chew manipulates the scope and the wording: เพื่อนกันตลอดไป *Nadear* appear.

"*Nadear*, what does it mean?" Chew asks no one in particular.

"Why is it written in normal writing with capital letter N?" Mislan asks. "It has to be something that has no ancient word for it."

"Like what?" Chew probes.

"A place, a deity, a temple, it could be anything," Johan says excitedly. "This is really getting more and more mysterious."

"It can't be, those things are ancient and I'm sure they would have words for them," Mislan refutes. "They cannot have something long ago and yet have no name or word for it."

"Chew, do you have a spare computer?" Johan asks.

"Over there, why?" Chew points to a desktop computer at the end of the room.

"Let's google the word *Nadear*. See if it's a temple, deity, or something in Buddhism."

"Is there a program that can read ancient words and translate it?" Mislan asks.

Chew shakes his head.

"I thought we had software for everything," Mislan sighs. "Jo, anything on Google?"

"Nothing."

"It looks like you need another visit to the Buddhist wat," Mislan tells his assistant. "Chew, can you print it?"

———

Walking to their car, Johan asks the inspector what his plans are for the day. Mislan says he has nothing planned and is heading back to the office.

"Why?" Mislan asks, looking at his detective sergeant inquiringly.

"Since you have nothing planned, why don't we go to the temple, I mean wat, together?"

Mislan picks up on the uneasy tone in his assistant's voice and turns to look at him.

"I just don't feel comfortable," Johan says, noticing the inspector's gaze.

"What do you mean?"

"I don't know how to explain it, but the wat, I mean the statues' eyes seem like they're following you around, watching your every move. . . . The high roof, hollowness of the building, the solitude, and chilly quietness of the hall really give me spooky vibes. It's like some unseen mystical beings or creatures are watching. And if you do or say something wrong, they'll emerge and pounce on you or put a crazy spell on you. You'll probably go bananas or get turned into a toad or something."

Mislan can't resist a hearty laugh. "Have you been watching reruns of *Indiana Jones* on Astro?"

"Have you been in a wat before?"

"No."

"OK let's go, then you tell me if I've been watching *Indiana Jones* reruns," Johan dares.

Mislan gives his assistant a smirk, accepting his dare.

———

Leaving the Crime Forensics building complex, Mislan makes a turn onto Jalan Sungai Besi and heads toward the old National Palace and down to the Federal Highway. Johan tells him to take the exit at the Employee Provident Fund building. Making a left, he gets onto Jalan Gasing, driving straight on until he passes the Chetawan Wat on his right. After about four hundred yards, he makes a U-turn at the traffic lights, heading back in the direction they came.

From several hundred yards away, they spot the towering yellow and gold colored wat set against the skyline. Driving into the compound, Mislan parks at the designated open lot facing the wat. From inside the car, the officers gaze at the astounding sight before them in silence. Neither is willing to make the first move to get out of the car. At long last, they turn to look at each other, both tight-lipped. Mislan jerks his head slightly toward the wat, gesturing for them to get going. Stepping out of the car, they stand by the door, giving the wat another silent gaze. It's clear that no one wants to take the lead.

The wat is indeed a building of magnificent architecture. Wide stairs leads to it, and beyond the staircase just before the landing stand five-foot brick walls with an opening in the middle. On top of the walls are sprawled two huge identical golden, yellow, red, and green dragons, one on each side. The top of their wavy scaled bodies is dotted with large spikes. The dragons stretch the full length of the front walls. With sharp claws on the forelimbs and their heads adorned with pointed horns and fearsome fangs, they guard the entrance. A menacing badass–looking dragon if they ever saw one.

Beyond the intimidating mystical creatures stands a majestic shrine that is yellow or golden depending on the angle of the sun. A glistening tower is on its top, reaching for the sky. Mislan has the impression that, on cloudy days, it could probably reach out to grab some of the clouds.

From where he's standing, Mislan has to admit the wat does ooze a mysterious creepy feeling. He feels his assistant's eyes on him and turns to him with a smirk. *All that's needed to make it a really spooky movie scene is clear-sky thunder and lightning.*

"Told you. It gets creepier inside," Johan warns as they close the car doors and walk up the staircase to the main gate.

The officers walk through the main gate, giving the two dragons a respectful glance. Mislan notices Johan giving them each a tiny nod of acknowledgment as he passes them, like he is seeking their permission or apologizing for intruding.

Approaching the top of the staircase, Mislan sees a couple dressed in ordinary working attire engaged in conversation at the main entrance. Mislan asks Johan if the man was the monk he met the last time he was here. Johan shakes his head.

As the officers walk up to the wat's entrance, the man stops talking and looks at them. Once they're within talking distance, he greets them and inquires in English if he can be of assistance. Johan introduces himself and his superior, asking if they can meet one of the monks.

"The *Phra*, sorry the monks are in evening meditation. Perhaps I may assist you," the man offers. "I'm Komkrit, the wat's administrator, and this is my sister Pagatip."

In greeting, Pagatip gives a lovely smile with deep dimples, which do not escape the officers' observation. She gives the *wai* to the officers and says, "*Sawadee ka.*"

Mislan is unsure of how to reciprocate and nods, while Johan proudly responds with a *wai*, saying, "*Sawadee kap.*"

Mislan gives his assistant a quick glance.

"That's the Thai way of greeting," the assistant whispers to the inspector.

Ignoring his assistant's explanation, he says, "We're investigating a murder and found some ancient writing, probably Sanskrit, on one of our victim's belongings. We're wondering if we could get one of the monks to explain what it means."

Johan holds out the printout of the wordings from the earring.

"May I?" Komkrit asks, extending his hand.

Johan glances at his boss, who consents with a nod.

"This's not Sanskrit or Pali. This is Thai," Komkrit says, handing it to Pagatip for endorsement.

"It means 'friends forever,'" Pagatip says. "Something the youngsters, normally girls, give this to each other."

"And *Nadear*, it's a person's name?" Mislan guesses.

"It is, though not a common Thai name. But nowadays, they all have English names or a combination of English and Thai names, the youngsters I mean."

The officers nod their understanding.

"It's very much the same here," Johan admits.

"May I know where this was done?" Pagatip asks.

"Why?" Johan inquires.

"My sister is an artisan. She's helping the wat restore some of its murals," Komkrit explains.

"The writing seems to be very fine and delicate. I'm just curious," Pagatip adds.

Johan takes out the exhibit bag containing the earring and shows it to her.

"May I take it out?"

Mislan nods.

Pagatip carefully takes the earring out, holding it between her thumb and index fingers. Lifting it above her eyes toward the sky, she closes one eye, examining the earring. The three men watch. After turning the earring several times, she hands it back to Johan.

"Have you located the seller?" she asks.

"You mean manufacturer?" Johan corrects.

"No, this is not manufactured—the workmanship is too fine. It was crafted, and usually the crafter is the seller. I mean of the artwork."

"Is there anything you can tell us about the artwork?" Mislan inquires.

"Well, this is just guesswork through experience and I may be wrong," Pagatip clarifies with a sweet dimpled smile.

Mislan nods his understanding.

"Grain or rice writing is said to have originated in India. It's a very old specialist craft, meaning only a handful of such crafters are around. As is the case with many other ancient crafts, the Chinese claim it to be their creation. Putting that argument aside, they, the Chinese, did further develop and master the techniques, applying it to other mediums apart from rice. However, examining the writing, I'd say the crafter is someone who is very familiar with Thai characters. I'm not saying he or she is of Thai nationality but someone who is very familiar with Thai writing. He or she didn't copy the characters from something that was written for him or her. If the crafter was to copy it from something written down, you'll be able to see some smudges of characters especially around the edges because the crafter didn't understand what he or she was writing." Pagatip pauses, smiling sweetly at the officers. "Am I making any sense to you so far?"

The officers nod.

"Good."

Again that sweet dimpled smile from her, and Mislan is thinking this woman really loves smiling. Perhaps she's aware she has a very lovely smile, so she gives it freely to brighten other people's days.

"I'm guessing this was done by a Thai crafter. I know there are a few of them in Chiang Mai who operate stalls in tourist spots. In my opinion, your best bet of finding the crafter cum seller will be there."

"Is it possible for you to assist us in locating the seller?" Mislan asks.

"I live in Hatyai, a long way from Chiang Mai. I won't promise you anything, but let me make some inquiries to a friend living in Chiang Mai. Perhaps he can assist."

"That's great. May I have your contact number or email to keep in touch?"

Pagatip hands Mislan her business card.

"Thank you, thank you for your assistance."

———

Back in the car, Johan comments that Pagatip is cute. Mislan agrees.

"You want her contact number?" Mislan offers.

"No thanks, cute but not my type," Johan declines.

"Surprising."

"She practically has nothing," Johan says, holding his chest.

Mislan gives his assistant a wry glance.

"Didn't you notice?"

"Unlike you, when I speak to someone I look them in the eyes, not the chest."

Johan lets out a cheeky laugh.

"You're a bloody sexist."

"No way. I'm not sexist. You think what? Women don't do it when they look at men?" Johan says, laughing. "You're so wrong. They look at your ass, your bulge, they study your lips, your abs, they give you more than the once-over when talking to you," Johan rebuts. "I look at everything that can be looked, at what they display, and *I* am a sexist?"

Mislan gives his detective sergeant a puzzled look but says nothing.

"So what's our next move, go to Chiang Mai? I heard it's nice there. Cold, since it's in the mountains, with all that the land of hot spicy tomyam has to offer," Johan remarks slyly.

"You wish."

20

THE TIME ON HER cell phone shows 23:21 p.m. as Dr. Safia zips her second suitcase. She turns dolefully to look at the almost-empty closet. Only a few dresses left hanging, including her favorite black negligee. The one they picked out together when they went shopping a few years back. The dresses will be taken later by her sister to be given away. A pair of slacks and blouse laid out on the bed, which she'll wear for the journey. She reminds herself there shall be no more tears shed. Yet she's unable to hold them back. Annoyed with herself, she snatches a cigarette and lights up. It was the cigarette, or to be precise, the act of lighting a cigarette for her by him that initially attracted her to him.

She had many men buy her dinners, drinks, gifts, or hold doors, push chairs, and all sorts of things men do to dazzle women, but never had one lit a cigarette for her. "Damn it," she says, extinguishing the cigarette in the ashtray. *There's really no one to blame. We made our own choices.* Yet somehow she feels the anger in her, like a time bomb. *What will happen when it explodes?* Angry at who or what, she herself doesn't know. *The cab is arriving soon. I should get dressed if I want to make it on time,* she tells herself, shoving the nagging anger aside for the moment.

As soon as she finishes dressing, her cell phone rings. It's the cab-driver informing her he's waiting downstairs by the guardhouse. She takes a deep breath and leaves the apartment.

Standing by the taxi's open door, she looks up at her apartment for a long final time, thinking about who will be the next person renting and staying in it. A single person or a family? Will they feel her ghost wandering about in it?

Tears begin to well up again. *What's wrong with you? The new tenants don't give a damn about you, the previous tenant. He, she, or they won't even bother to ask unless of course you hang yourself in it and make the news.*

The cabdriver sardonically asks if there is something wrong or if she has forgotten something. Dr. Safia ignores the driver's rudeness, taking her time getting into the cab.

"You pay hundred-fifty first OK," the driver demands.

"Why, wait-*lah* until we reach the airport," she protests.

"Reach airport already, you tell expensive, make a lot noise. There got many people see, also got police. You pay now, we go OK," the driver insists.

Dr. Safia knows he is overcharging, but she's not in the mood to argue. Opening her oversized handbag, she takes out one hundred fifty ringgit and hands it over. "Typical of our taxi drivers' attitude," she cusses under her breath.

As the taxi pulls out of the driveway, she leans back and closes her eyes, taking deep long breaths to blank her mind. Try as she might, her mind still turns the pages of memories, happy ones and painful ones.

———

At the airport, Dr. Safia checks her luggage, clears immigration, and looks for a café. She buys a cup of jasmine tea, finding a seat away from the concourse. She has two hours to kill before her flight. Sitting alone, she watches the faces of people passing by, some wide awake with excitement, some sleepy and zombielike. After a while she's able to categorize them—a couple is always excited, all chatty, while lone travelers are more likely to be zombielike. There must be something about traveling as a couple that adds to the excitement, she concludes. Especially so for young or newly married couples.

A family with two kids, a toddler on the father's back and a baby sleeping in the mother's arms, walks into the café. They all seem so happy and excited, apart from the baby, who is sound asleep. The toddler, probably three years old, is so full of energy even at this late hour. Dr. Safia smiles as she watches them, feeling happy for them. Suddenly, out of nowhere, she's overcome by anger. Agitated, she abruptly stands, striding off in the direction of the boarding lounge, leaving her tea untouched.

The boarding lounge has yet to open. Sitting outside, she finds herself alone as the call for boarding is a long way off still. The area is quiet and deserted, with nothing to observe to while away the time. She chides herself for not stopping to buy something to read upon leaving the café. Soon she finds herself indulging in a debate with herself.

"Maybe you acted rashly," says her heart.

"What do you mean, acted rashly?" her brain snaps. *"It's not like you decided this morning."*

"Yes, but you didn't give him a chance, didn't talk to him. I mean really, really talk to him."

"WHAT? Four years was not enough of a chance? Even the stupidest of a stupid man would've seen or sensed the chances. Don't fool yourself. And what good do you think it'll do you if you talked to him?"

"I don't know, but at least he would've known and if—"

"If WHAT? What if he says no, then WHAT? You think this opportunity, this LONG-DREAMED-OF opportunity is going to wait for you? Silly girl!"

"You should at least text him and let him know."

"Don't be silly, let him wonder, let him suffer. Do what he did to you and let him hang in limbo. He deserves it," the brain retorts.

Dr. Safia takes out her cell phone, scrolls through the music folder, selects "Say Something by Christina Aguilera," and sends it. Then switching off the cell phone, she angrily stuffs it in her oversized handbag.

21

MISLAN WAKES UP THE next morning to the blinking message indicator of his cell phone. The job trained him to be a light sleeper. The slightest of sounds would usually wake him up, especially a cell phone ringtone or beep. However, not this time—his training failed him. He must have been exhausted and slept like a log.

He reaches for the cell phone. It's a WhatsApp message. Another song sent by Dr. Safia. He knows she's into living her life by song lyrics. He has seen her sitting at home, working on her reports with earphones plugged in, listening to music.

As expected, there was no message only a song attachment: "Say Something by Christina Aguilera." Mislan pays no attention to it. Yes, he listens to music, but it's for entertainment and nothing more. Replacing the cell phone, he heads to the bathroom. "Idealistic," he says to himself with a smirk on his soap-covered face, remembering his conversation with Johan.

———

When Superintendent Samsiah dismisses the morning prayer, Mislan asks if he can have a few minutes with her. She nods, motioning for him to follow her to her office. Mislan stops by the investigators' office, signals to Johan to follow him.

As they're taking their seats, Samsiah asks what it's about.

"We've got a lead on the vic," Mislan starts.

"Good. I hope it's not one of the Chosen One theory leads," Samsiah teases.

Johan grins. "No, this is a down-to-earth lead."

"The writing or inscription in the earring is not Sanskrit. It's Thai and has nothing to do with religion. It's more of a modern-day teenage thing. Translated it says, 'Friends Forever Nadear."

"*Nadear* being a person's name," Johan adds. "It's not a common Thai name, but then again most young people nowadays are using English names. It's no different in Thailand."

"Interesting," Samsiah says, "and where did you get all this information?"

"An artisan we met at the Buddhist wat in PJ."

"Pagatip, she's helping the wat with some of their artwork. She's from Hat Yai and her brother is the wat's administrator. She said the earring is crafted, and she believes the crafter is Thai, probably from Chiang Mai."

"What led her to the assumption?"

"Something about the writing not having smudges or crooked edges or something like that. In her artisan's opinion it's something that can be quite obvious if the wordings were written down to be copied by the crafter. In this case it was all smooth, so she concluded either the crafter is Thai or someone familiar with Thai characters. But she was quite certain the crafter is Thai."

"That makes sense. Does she know whose work it was?"

"No, but she said she'll seek a friend's assistance living in Chiang Mai to check it out."

Samsiah nods. She knows this session was requested not just to update her. Mislan could have done it during the morning prayer. There's something her lead investigator wants from her.

"And your thoughts?" she asks, gazing at her investigator's face curiously.

Mislan responds by flashing one of his I-really-need-this expressions.

"Is it possible for us to go to Chiang Mai?" Mislan asks, bug-eyed.

"Us?"

"Me and Jo."

"Jo, hmmm. I heard Chiang Mai is a beautiful place. Is this a working or pleasure trip?"

"Of course work," Johan blurts out, blushing like a teenage boy caught kissing his girlfriend.

Samsiah laughs at her detective sergeant's face. "What do you think you'll achieve by going there? You've no lead, don't speak their language, and don't even know the territory."

The two investigators look at each other.

"You've not thought this through, have you?" Samsiah asks, her eyebrows arching.

Mislan nods. "I was hoping you could ask Dr. Sophia for assistance."

"Dr. Suthisa Ritchu?"

Mislan nods, "Yes, she."

"She's a behavioral scientist, a profiler, not a murder investigator."

"Yes, but I'm sure she has connections or at the very least she can direct us to the person we can work with."

"I can give her a call, but if we want to take this case there, it has got to go through D1, admin, and possibly Aseanapol."

"Aseanapol!" Mislan exclaims, unable to check himself, for which he receives a reprimanding stare from his boss. "Sorry. Can't we keep this within D9?"

"Have you looked at your authority card lately? Does it say Malaysia or World Police?" Samsiah chides. "You're talking about crossing international boundaries. There're protocols to be followed. You can't just simply hop into another country and conduct a criminal investigation, like in movies. Do you know their laws? What police powers do you have there?" Samsiah snaps. "I'll talk to Aseanapol and get their advice on how this should be handled."

"I was thinking more of getting Dr. Sophia's assistance informally. I mean, we go there and she, you know, sort of uses her police connections to lend us a hand."

"Then?"

"If there's anything to do with the law or arrests to be made, they, the Thai police can do it," Mislan says.

"You want to go on a private excursion financed by the department," Samsiah says, laughing. "You're becoming a true bureaucrat. Let me make some calls. In the meantime, figure out how you want to play this out."

———

Leaving Superintendent Samsiah's office, Mislan teasingly tells Johan off for not backing him up.

"You didn't tell me you were going to hit ma'am with the request," Johan replies. "Anyway, she was right, what are we to do when we get there? I agree with her, let Aseanapol handle it."

"How difficult can it be? Police work is police work, it doesn't matter where," Mislan insists.

Johan nods. "But the laws are different and so are the procedures."

Mislan lets out a grunt. Admittedly, he hadn't given his request a real think-through. Snatching his backpack, he signals for his assistant to follow him.

"Where to?"

"Look for more info as ma'am instructed."

———

Driving out of the contingent headquarters, Mislan circles to the back onto Jalan Pudu, heading toward Puduraya. He makes a right at the roundabout and cuts into Lebuh Ampang then onto Jalan Ampang, driving past the KLCC Twin Towers on his right.

"Where are we going?" Johan asks for the second time.

"Thai embassy."

"What's there?"

"Info, perhaps even answers," Mislan replies wryly.

Mislan's mode tells Johan not to pursue his inquiry any further. He knows they have a promising lead and, as usual, bureaucratic protocol is standing in their way. No way to chase it down without kowtowing to them, and that really pisses off his boss. Then again, his boss is not one who'll let bureaucracy stop him from getting closure. A find-a-way-around-it scheme is brewing in his boss's head, and Johan has a feeling it's not something by the book. If his boss were in the private sector, he would be seen as thinking outside the box—but his boss isn't, and he usually gets himself into trouble with the brasses.

———

In the meantime, back in the office, Superintendent Samsiah scrolls through her phone contact list. She finds the person she's looking for and presses the call symbol. After two rings, a woman answers.

"*Sawadee ka P*'Samsiah." The 'P,' pronounced as the letter itself, is a prefix in Thai for respecting an elder woman like an elder sister.

"Good morning, Dr. Suthisa, how're you? I hope I'm not interrupting."

"I'm fine, thank you. No, no, it's nice to hear from you. How are you?"

"I'm fine thank you. Can we talk?"

"Yes, I was just thinking of having a coffee break. Your call is an excellent reason for me to take the break now rather than later," Dr. Suthisa says, her voice sprinkled with light laughter.

"I don't want to keep you away from your work too long, so let me get straight to the point. I've a murder case. I know murder is not your field, but I thought I'd give it a go anyway. The victim, we believe, is a Thai national."

"Interesting."

"I said we believe, because we haven't been able to establish her identity, even until now."

"Her?"

"Yes, a woman or a young woman. Inspector Mislan is the lead investigator and—"

"Oh, how is he, still the, how shall I term it?" Dr. Suthisa interjects mid-sentence.

"Maverick," Samsiah finishes Dr. Suthisa's sentence.

The two women share a laugh.

"He's fine," Samsiah continues. "Anyway, he has just made a request to go to Thailand to pursue his investigation, and you know that's not something that can just happen. There're protocols and all the other G to G bureaucratic procedures. That can go on forever, and Mislan being Mislan, well, you know."

Dr. Suthisa laughs heartily, and Samsiah is drawn into joining her.

"May I ask what makes you believe the victim is a Thai national?"

"Two things: one is an earring with Thai writing, *Friends Forever Nadear*, and the second is her Buddhist Yant tattoo. The"—Samsiah pauses to check her file "—ahh, here it is, the Hah Taew Sak Yant."

"Hah Taew Sak Yant is indeed very popular among the women here, yes. Nadear, however, isn't a common Thai name."

Samsiah detects excitement in Suthisa's voice and pushes on.

"Let me email you the case brief, then you decide if you can assist, how does that sound?"

"Excellent. You still have my email address?"

"Yes, I do. Doctor, thank you so much for your time. It's really nice talking to you again."

"It is nice to hear from you and thank you for thinking of me. I'm looking forward to reading the case brief. Give my regards to Inspector Mislan, Inspector Sherry, and the rest of your staff."

Terminating the call, Samsiah makes a call to the D1, the Criminal Investigation Division administration in Police Headquarters, Bukit Aman.

22

THE ROYAL THAI EMBASSY is located along the stretch of Jalan Ampang popularly referred to as Embassy Row. It's sandwiched between the Spanish and Saudi Arabian embassies. Apart from its prime real estate, Jalan Ampang is infamous for its notorious all-day traffic congestion and lack of parking space.

Knowing the embassy's security can be real jerks about letting vehicles park within the compound, Mislan decides to bulldoze his way in. Driving up to the embassy gate, he asks Johan to flash his police authority card to the guard. Hopefully, the guard will allow them to park the car within the compound.

From inside the car, Mislan watches as Johan walks up to the guard and holds up his authority card. After an exchange of words, Johan animatedly points to the car and taps the top of his shoulder several times. Mislan assumes Johan is telling the guard that the person in the car is a high-ranking officer with several brass pips and stars. Whatever Johan says, it works. A guard emerges from the guardhouse and opens the gate, signaling for Mislan to drive in while pointing to a vacant parking bay.

One hurdle cleared, Mislan says to himself as he walks toward the main entrance where Johan is waiting. When they step into the welcoming air-conditioned lobby, the receptionist greets them with the familiar Thai greeting of *Sawadee ka* and a *wai*. A *wai* is the act of clasping the hands together with the tips of the fingers touching the chin or lower lips in a prayerlike gesture. Again, Johan response with *Sawadee Kap* and a *wai* while Mislan nods.

Johan again produces his police authority card, asking if they could meet with one of the embassy's officers for assistance in an investigation. The receptionist gives Johan a baffled gaze. Noticing the receptionist's expression, Mislan steps forward and asks if they have a PR officer. Using gestures, the receptionist invites them to take a seat while she calls for someone to attend to them. After several minutes a rather petite woman appears from the back office. She is in her mid-twenties, about five feet tall, with fair complexion and short hair, dressed in a white blouse, dark jacket, and skirt. She looks strikingly professional. She stops at the receptionist inquiringly before turning toward them.

Approaching the officers, she greets them with *Sawadee ka* and a *wai*, accompanied by a slight bow of the head. Again, Johan reciprocates and Mislan smiles with a nod. The woman introduces herself as Jutimapon, an officer akin to that of a general affairs officer. Mislan introduces themselves and asks if there is a place where they can talk in private. Nodding, she says *"Ka"* and leads them to a glass-walled discussion room without blinds next to the reception counter.

"How may I assist you?" Jutimapon asks with a touch of an American accent.

"We're investigating a murder."

Mislan pauses, noting the hiking eyebrows of Jutimapon.

"Ka," she says.

"And we have strong reasons to believe the victim is a Thai national," Mislan continues, going straight to the point.

"Murdered, here in Kuala Lumpur? You said believed to be Thai?" Jutimapon asks, wide-eyed.

It is Johan who nods. "We're still working to get a conclusive identification."

"When did this murder happen? How is it that we've heard nothing of it?"

"Miss Juti . . . aaa," Mislan says, groping for her name.

"Kung," Jutimapon says, smiling. "Call me Kung, that's easier to pronounce and remember."

"Miss Kung, we're still investigating and searching for answers. To answer your earlier question, we're unable to positively identify the victim as a Thai. However, we do have strong circumstantial evidence, or you may call them reasons, to believe she is. I guess that could be the reason why the embassy has not been officially notified." Mislan explains. "We came here to explore the possibility of the embassy assisting us in making the identification."

"In what manner is that possible?"

"We've gathered some physical evidence and are wondering if the embassy can liaise with the Thai police to track down the source of the evidence."

"May I view this physical evidence?"

Mislan motions to Johan to show Jutimapon the printouts. Johan hands her the Hah Taew Sak Yant and *Friends Forever Nadear* in Thai lettering. Jutimapon takes a quick look and puts down the Hah Taew Sak Yant printout.

"This's a very popular Buddhist mantra among the women. Most of our female staff here have one, too," she says, smiling, "but not me." Picking up the other printout, she stares at it long and hard.

"This Thai writing, is it also tattooed on the body?"

"No, it was inscribed in an earring found in the victim."

Jutimapon does not catch the second "in" and asks nothing of it.

"I think it is best if I refer this matter to my superior. Perhaps he may be able to assist."

Mislan immediately stands, ready to go with her to meet this superior who may be able to assist, but Jutimapon quickly stops him.

"I'm sorry, he's not here now. He's attending a meeting in Bangkok and will be back in a couple of days. I'll inform him then and get back to you." She notices the disappointment on Mislan's face and smiles pleasantly. "I'm sorry. However, if you tell me the nature of the assistance you require, perhaps I may assist you."

Disappointedly retaking his seat, Mislan asks, tapping on the earring printout, "Is it possible for this to go public, be posted in newspapers in Thailand?"

"Yes, that shouldn't be a problem. We can also put it on our social media if you think it'll help."

"Yes, I'm sure that'll be helpful, too."

"And what do you expect from it?"

"Someone to read of it and come forward with information. Should that happen, can you immediately contact us?"

"I can do that. However, it shall be done through our police, as the person with such information will probably contact the police. I really don't know how it works, but I'm sure the information will be forwarded to us, as we're the requesting agency. You've to excuse my ignorance, as this is the first time such a request is made of us. Usually, we deal with visa issues." She smiles sweetly.

"Don't you have a police liaison officer in the embassy?"

Jutimapon shakes her head.

———

Leaving the Criminal Investigation Division administration office after getting all the necessary information and forms for her officers to venture to Thailand, Superintendent Samsiah Hassan stops by Interpol (D12). The head of Malaysia Interpol, Assistant Commissioner of Police Soon Kam Hoon, or Peter to his friends, greets her warmly as she stands in the doorway.

"Sam, come in, come in, how've you been?"

Sam is what her squadmates called her during their training, and it has remained so among them and her close friends.

"I'm fine, thank you. How about you, and how's the family?"

"Fine, fine, thank you. To what do I owe this visit from the city's finest?" Peter asks jocularly.

Samsiah briefs the head of Malaysian Interpol on the case, seeking his advice on how she should go about it.

"The case hasn't made the news yet, has it?"

"Just a mention of a dead body found, not the full write-up, why?"

"It helps if the case has some publicity, creating public interest and all the hype. It makes spending taxpayers' money easier. I'm surprised your publicity-junkie boss let this case pass. What did he say of this request?" Peter chuckles, referring to Senior Assistant Commissioner Burhanuddin Mohd Sidek.

"I haven't discussed it with him yet. Thought I'll get all the information before, you know, going to bat with him," Samsiah replies with a guilty smile.

Peter Soon Kam Hoon lets loose a hearty laugh. "I've always wondered how crimes are solved in the city with him in the chair. Now I know how the city's finest are able to solve crimes . . . by going around him."

Samsiah blushes, embarrassed by her going-behind-the-back.

"I know it's unethical, but I suppose having Burhan as the supervising officer negates it all," Peter consoles her, adding another hearty laugh. "Right, back to your question, there has to be an official request."

"Of course, I got all the necessary forms from D1," Samsiah says, nodding. "Sorry, should I be talking to you or Aseanapol?"

"I'll inform Aseanapol. Anyway, they're a skeleton unit mainly tasked with arranging meetings and seminars for the brasses. OK, once the approval is obtained from D1, I'll contact my counterpart in Bangkok and also notify our senior liaison officer or SLO. The SLO'll make the necessary arrangements and introduction to the CIB, the Criminal Investigation Bureau, for attachment."

"I presume CIB is like our CID."

Peter nods. "How long will the paperwork take?"

"Depending on the case, it can be a day or never," Samsiah answers. "Any advice on expenses?"

"I suggest, put in the expected stay duration and budget, it'll come with the approval. Normally, it's more than enough. But if there're any official out-of-pocket expenses, the officer can put in their claims for reimbursement through the normal claim process. The key word is 'official.'" Peter smiles slyly.

"One last question: can I send two of them, the lead and his assistant?"

"Send as many as you need to wrap the case up. There're no hard-and-fast rules to the number of officers allowed on a single trip."

23

IT HAS BEEN THREE days since their visit to the Thai Embassy, and Mislan is getting restless. He has yet to hear from Jutimapon aka Kung. Nor had he heard from the dimpled, smiling artisan Pangatip. He checks his cell phone and makes a call from his office landline phone to see if it's in working order. There's nothing wrong with his cell phone; it rings just fine. Then a thought crosses his mind: he hasn't heard from Dr. Safia for quite a while, too, the last being the WhatsApp song. Instinctively, he dials her number and receives the mechanical female voice recording of "The number you've called is not in service." *She must be busy or really pissed off with me for not replying to her WhatsApp song*, Mislan assumes with a smirk. He tells himself he will call her later, after work, and perhaps go out for dinner. Just as he puts the cell phone down, it beeps, indicating an incoming WhatsApp message. He switches it on, and it's another song attachment—*Goodbye My Lover, James Blunt by Nikisha*—without any text from Dr. Safia. *Well, at least she's still sending me songs*, Mislan says to himself, grinning.

Pushing the cell phone aside, Mislan flips through the investigation diary of the murdered faceless girl. The photo of the earring begs his analysis. *Why am I in her stomach?* the earring seems to ask him. *How did I get there?* Mislan recalls that Dr. Safia said she didn't detect any trauma or injury to the victim's throat to indicate it was forced into her. That leaves only one other possibility: she must have swallowed it herself. *But why would she want to do that? Or what could've made her want to do it?* Mislan lets out another heavy sigh and rubs his eyes, tired from staring at the printout. He concludes that only Nadear, if she exists and can be found, could shed light on the reason.

He makes a call to Audi, the Astro Awani reporter. After two rings, she answers.

"Helloooo, Inspector, long time no hear. What's up?" Rodziah, or Audi, which is what she likes to be called, answers.

"Need a favor," Mislan says.

"No hello or how're you, just I need a favor," Audi chides. "Doesn't the police force teach their officers courtesy?"

"Look, do you want a story or not?"

"Lay it out."

"Need you to get a friend in the papers to report a murder."

"There're so many murders lately. What's special about this murder?"

"It's a Jane Doe, foreign national, but you can't use the foreign national part until we conclusively confirm it."

"Do you know how many foreign nationals got whacked here? I'm sure you heard of the Rohingya mass graves, right? What was it, 139 or more bodies were recovered and they're all John or Jane Doe, so tell me what's so special about your Jane Doe?"

"The killer or killers rid her of her identity."

"And that's special?"

Mislan laughs.

"What's so funny?"

"Nothing. Are you interested or not?"

"I'm always interested, but I don't think the press will be. What with the 1MDB and the 2.6 billion donation chaos. Even the 139 dead Rohingyas aren't getting any column space."

"OK, if you manage to generate interest, give me a call."

———

Ending the call, Mislan closes the investigation diary and heads for his self-authorized smoking area. Alone with his cigarette, his thoughts drift to his son Daniel, missing him. Every time Daniel goes away to be with his mother during the school vacation, he feels alone. A feeling he doesn't feel with the absence of any other people, not even Dr. Safia. Loneliness isn't something he's prone to, in fact he relishes being by himself. Counting the days, he smiles, comforting himself with *Kiddo will be home next weekend*. The emergency staircase door cracks open, and Johan steps onto the landing, handing a ringing cell phone to him.

"Mislan," he answers.

"*Sawadee ka*, Inspector Mislan, I'm Jutimapon from the Thai embassy," the caller announces. "Sorry for calling. Is it convenient for you to talk?"

"Yes, yes, Ms. Juuuu," Mislan answers excitedly, stammering her name.

"Kung, Inspector, just Kung. We ran an article on your case and a photo of the earring in the dailies and we got a positive response. An individual who recognized the earring came forward. "

"Great, where is this individual, when can I meet with him?"

"It's a 'her,' and I was advised by our police not to reveal her identity just yet, for safety reasons. I'm sure you understand. You can interview her whenever you wish. Let me know when you're going up to Thailand, and I'll make the necessary arrangements for you to meet with the officer in charge."

The line goes silent as Mislan digests Jutimapon's reply.

"Thailand? Not here?" Mislan finally asks. The disappointment in his voice is evident.

"Yes, in Hat Yai, Songkhla."

"Shit," Mislan swears, immediately apologizing.

"No need to apologize, we're quite used to such expressions, too," Jutimapon says with a chuckle. "I hope this development helps, and we await confirmation for your visit to Songkhla."

"I'll have to consult my superior and get back to you. Thank you."

Pocketing his cell phone, Mislan grimaces at his assistant who is watching him like a starving hyena. Johan's instinct is telling him— *trouble*. Mislan knows the case has taken a crucial upturn, but it happened by way of him going about it outside police protocol. Now he's caught and has to show his hands.

"Good or bad news?" Johan asks, studying his boss's face intently.

"Good gift-wrapped with bad," Mislan answers.

Johan follows his boss into the office, demanding, "Give it to me straight."

"Bad because we sought the embassy's assistance without going through protocol, good because they released a media statement and an individual came forward claiming she recognized the earring. She's in Songkhla, and they're waiting for us to go over there to interview her."

"Songkhla, that to me is good and better. The question is how the hell do we handle it?"

"That's south Thailand isn't it?"

Johan nods. "A seaside town or something, I haven't been there but heard it's beautiful."

"We could take leave, get into the car, and drive up," Mislan states casually, "or we can talk to ma'am."

"I prefer the second option," Johan stresses, keeping pace with him.

————

Superintendent Samsiah is finalizing the request for her officers to go to Thailand when Mislan and Johan knock on her door.

"Ma'am, you have a minute?" Mislan asks, stepping in before she can reply.

Samsiah turns her request form facedown. "What is it?"

Mislan updates her on the latest development, stopping short of asking for permission to go to Thailand. Samsiah waits patiently, but nothing more is said.

"That's it?" she probes.

Mislan puckers his lips then breaks into a silly grin. "Can we go to Thailand?" he asks coyly, "Songkhla, to be precise?"

"To investigate." This time Johan adds rather too quickly, keeping a straight face.

Samsiah grins at her two officers' comical team effort. She knows one of them is chasing for a closure, while the other is chasing for a closure and more.

"May I know how you came about this information?"

"Well, it's kind of a long story," Mislan says, trying to avoid answering. "Can we just say it came from a very reliable source that chooses to remain anonymous, like the 2.6 billion donor?"

Samsiah smiles at her officer's analogy of the 700 million US dollars banked into the prime minister's personal account, which it was claimed had been donated by an Arab donor who insisted on remaining anonymous. It had brought about a storm of public outcry over corruption at the highest level of government, and many people took to social media to ridicule the PM and his hardcore supporters. It became a nightmare for the enforcement agencies—police, attorney general, Malaysian Anti-Corruption Commission, and the National Bank. Some people lost their jobs, while others were transferred or consigned to cold-storage desk jobs. There was also talk that one person was murdered, but there was no evidence to support the claim.

"By that, you're telling me it didn't come through proper police procedures? Will I be expecting a call from, let's say, the OCCI or ISCD any time soon?"

Samsiah has just had one run-in with ASP Amir from ISCD over the complaint filed by the OCCI that she saluted a rank and file. She isn't looking forward to another. Come to think of it, her close association with Amir was brought about by her maverick investigator.

Johan turns to look at his boss quizzically as Mislan roguishly shakes his head.

"I'll take your word for it now," Samsiah says, knowing whatever her officers did will eventually come back to her. "Put up a report on your latest discovery and state the duration expected for your stay. Let me have it by this afternoon."

24

THE TWO DAYS FOLLOWING his meeting with Superintendent Samsiah were agonizing for Mislan. Waiting has never been his strong suit, and having to wait for the approval for his travel to Songkhla is driving him insane. He can't understand why it is taking the CID administrator so long to approve something they know is needed to solve a murder case. It's not like he is going for a holiday with the pretext of a study tour. Something he heard the bosses with their ass-kissing jesters and spouses go on every now and then. *Study tours my foot*, he says to himself angrily, sitting at the worktable in his bedroom. *No, not study tour, reciprocated visits*, he corrects himself. The Islamic agency under the Prime Minister's Department, it was recently disclosed, had funded such trips abroad with money donated for the poor. The excuse given was to study gay marriage in Paris.

He Googles Songkhla, Thailand, reading the blogs. Mislan has always believed blogs provide the kind of information that official web-sites shy away from or dodge.

Songkhla, or Singgora in the old Malay language, is the provincial capital city of the Songkhla Province. Spread along the sea front, it is also the administrative center. It is, however, not the largest city of the sixteen districts within the province. That honor goes to Hat Yai, some-times spelled as Hatyai. Hat Yai is one of the many popular destinations among Malaysian and Singaporean men for its glorious nightlife. Unlike Bangkok, Pattaya, Chiang Mai, or many island tourist destinations, Hat Yai has yet to be contaminated by the Westerners or *farang*, which is Thai word for foreigners, mainly used to refer to Caucasians. Hat Yai is most often a stopover for the *farang* before going down to Penang for visa runs. The recent spate of bombings targeting the city has done very little to keep the Malaysian and Singaporean sex tourists away.

Hat Yai is District 6 in the police zoning, and their criminal investigation division is called Criminal Investigation Bureau (CIB). Mislan couldn't find out what their detectives are called. Here in Malaysia, the term used to be *mata-gelap*, which means "dark eyes" and is still in use by the old-timers. But since the Malay language was bastardized with English words, they're now called "detektif." Searching the net, the closest to the word *detective* he can find in the English-Thai translation is *panak ngan suabsuan,* which means "investigator." There are so many things he wants to know about Thailand's police, but he's unable to find much online.

Quitting the search, he goes to YouTube in search of the song sent to him by Dr. Safia. He keys in "Goodbye My Lover" by James Blunt and listens to it. The usual boy-leaves-girl draggy ballad, he notes. Then he searches for "Say Something" by Christina Aguilera, but this time he listens to it with the lyrics prompt on the monitor. His interpretation of the lyric is she failed to get him to love her and she was saying goodbye. He pauses the music, dragging the cursor back to listen and reread the lyric. Crushing the cigarette, he lights another one, taking long drags and letting the smoke out slowly, repeating his action over and over again. Finally, he leans back heavily. *No wonder I couldn't get through. She's not taking my calls.* "Shit, what have I done this time to really piss her off?" he says in a low whisper. *Is she telling me she is dumping me? I've heard of SMS divorce; could this be the first breakup through song?*

Logging off, he stamps out the cigarette, turns off the lights, and gets into bed. Closing his eyes, the lyrics keeps playing in his head. The fervor of Songkhla and possibility of closure are lost for the moment. His yearning for his best-friend-forever, Daniel, and the mystery of Dr. Safia's sudden absence clogs his thoughts.

25

THE LOW-COST CARRIER THE officers boarded leaves Kuala Lumpur International Airport 2 (KLIA 2) at 1145 a.m. Malaysia time and lands at Hat Yai International Airport, Thailand at 12 noon Thai time. Thailand time is one hour behind Malaysia. In 1981 the-then prime minister brought forward Peninsular Malaysia's time by half an hour to make it the same as with the Borneo states of Malaysia. By doing so, he moved Malaysian time ahead of Thailand by an hour. In Mislan's mind, that was the one good and logical act by the-then prime minister for the country.

Hat Yai, pronounced Hut Yai, is the largest city in south Thailand. It is a district within the province of Songkhla and the most populous. As Malaysians, the two officers do not require a visa to visit the country. Producing their international passports to the immigration officer for stamping, they are given a thirty-day tourist entry pass. With only their carry-on bags, they walk toward the Customs checkpoint. Johan points out to the inspector the spiraling Thai writing on the signage. They share a smile over the private joke of ancient writing.

Passing through the Customs checkpoint is no hassle, probably because they're traveling light. Once through, Mislan stops in the middle of the concourse, suddenly realizing he has no idea where they're supposed to go. The officers look at each other questioningly and laugh at their predicament.

"Isn't someone supposed to meet us?" Johan asks.

Mislan nods. "That was what I was told by ma'am's PA. Someone from the SLO's office."

"Where?"

"She said at the airport, and I would expect over there, where the rest of the pickups are waiting."

"No one seems to be waving at us," Johan remarks anxiously.

"Let's go find a place to smoke. My brain needs stimulants."

Stepping aside, Mislan scans the lobby, trying to read the directional signs, searching for the way out of the building where he is confident he can light up. The Thai writing looks more like Tamil writing to him with its twists and curls, yet his ears are telling him they're not in the Tamil enclaves of Little India, Brickfields, or Klang.

His hearing tunes in to the buzz of voices. The Thais speak with a melodic rhythm in a rather high pitch, especially the women. His next observation: all meetings begin with a *wai*. Every sentence ends with *ka* or *krap*, which is pronounced without the r sound. The following *wai* signifies the parting. The unfamiliar language starts to make him feel uneasy.

Mislan spots a taxi sign and nudges his assistant, pointing to it. As they walk away, he hears someone calling 'Inspector' several times from the Customs checkpoint behind them. Turning around, he sees a smartly dressed woman walking hastily toward them, as fast as her medium-height heels permit without tipping over. Both of them gawk at the tall slim Pakistani-looking woman, elegantly attired in a business suit, with a white *selendang*, a real authentic long traditional Malay shawl, waving and smiling brightly at them.

The officers look at each other questioningly, a Pakistani woman in Thailand? They didn't notice any Pakistani woman on their flight. Mislan might not have noticed her if she was on the flight, but he's sure Johan wouldn't have missed her. She's in her early forties, with small, sleepy, inviting eyes and very graceful and feminine movements with an air of sophistication. Nothing close to what he expected in a woman police officer. Her smile is bright and sincere.

"*Sawadee ka*," the woman says with a *wai*. "I'm Naz Ghazali from the SLO's office. Sorry, I missed you at the Customs checkpoints."

Unsure if he is to extend his hand for a handshake or *wai*, Mislan does nothing but nod. Johan immediately takes over by imitating a decent *wai*, smiling broadly, and replying with a *Sawadee Kap*.

"I'm Detective Sergeant Johan, and this is Inspector Mislan."

Mislan, still unsure of how to respond, gives another nod accompanied by a smile.

"Pleased to meet you, and welcome to Thailand. I hope you had a pleasant flight," Naz says, catching her breath.

"Yes, we did, thank you," Johan replies.

"Is there a place I can smoke?" Mislan asks. "I'm dying for a cigarette."

"Yes, let's go to the car. You can smoke there before we leave."

Naz Ghazali leads the two officers, engaging Johan in small talk about Thailand, and in particular Hat Yai, their intended destination. Mislan has a quick puff before getting into the car, which is a black SUV with dark-tinted windows.

————

Leaving the airport, they drive to Songkhla, which is about twenty miles north. The road is a divided highway with heavy traffic in both directions, and unlike in Malaysia, it is toll-free. The landscape, with scattered brick and wooden houses surrounded by tropical fruit trees, brings back memories of his younger days—days before toll-highways, with trunk roads as the only link from north to south. Just like what he is seeing now, the roads back then were lined by wooden or half-brick half-wooden houses in the middle of large courtyards guarded by shady trees and palms.

Occasionally, they drive past a sundry shop and a row of roadside makeshift stalls selling fruits of the season. He notes on several occasions that when approaching tiny towns of even a single row of shop houses, there is a road sign saying CITY LIMIT. *How many cities do they have if all towns are deemed cities?*

Thai or Thai-registered vehicles, including the vehicle they're traveling in, for reasons known only to them, love driving on the right, in the fast lane. Thailand traffic flow is similar to that of Malaysia, that is, they drive on the left side of the road. However, trucks, vans, pickups, SUVs, and cars all hug, or hog, the right or passing lane at a leisurely speed. Passing is done on the left or the slow lane. Almost all vehicle windshields and windows are tinted, where the people inside cannot be seen from the outside. Motorcyclists and pillion riders don't wear helmets; three and sometimes four adult persons can ride on a single bike.

Johan occupies himself with learning essential Thai words like: *kop kun krap* for "thank you," *sabai dee mai* for "how are you." and, the most important of phrases, *khun suai mak krap*, which means "you are very beautiful," and *pom rak khun krap* for "I love you." Mislan, on the other hand, is silent, taking in the scenery and thinking about how he's going to handle the interview.

"Inspector, you're rather quiet. Have you been to Thailand before?" Naz inquires.

Distracted, Mislan turns away from the window to look at Naz sitting in the front passenger seat.

"Yes, a very long time ago."

Naz's inquiry brings back memories of him and his ex-wife Lynn vacationing in Kok Samui, an island resort in the Gulf of Thailand. They took the night train from Kuala Lumpur to Hat Yai, then got on a minivan to Surat Thani, where they took the ferry to the island. It was a long and tiring journey but filled with excitement and fun. They spent two nights at Chaweng beach eating, drinking, lounging on the beach, and enjoying the nightlife. They would rent a scooter and go sightseeing around the island. Those were happy times.

"But you don't seem excited to come again. You must be hungry then. It's 12:40 here but 1:40 in Malaysia, almost past your lunchtime."

Mislan remains quiet.

"We're close, and DSP Arif had asked for us to meet him at the restaurant for lunch. I hope you like tomyam." Tomyam, the spicy sour soup with seafood or chicken, is deemed a Thai traditional dish and supposedly loved by all, tourists included.

"I heard the tomyam here is different from the one we get in Malaysia," Johan chips in.

"You can decide for yourself after tasting it," Naz replies in a matter-of-fact tone, giving up on trying to initiate small talk with Mislan.

As they drive within the Songkhla city limits, Mislan fails to see Songkhla as anything close to the beautiful seaside town his assistant claimed it to be. The roads are lined with shophouses, heavily congested with vehicles that are mostly four-wheel, pickups, motorbikes, and *tuk-tuks*. *Tuktuks* are the locally modified minivan used as public transport. Watching the *tuktuks* weaving in and out of traffic without the slightest care or consideration for other road users, Mislan reflects on them with a smile, *The reincarnation of Malaysia's once-infamous minibuses.*

As they turn onto the coastal Chalathat Road, Mislan changes his view. *This must be where Songkhla gets its romantic seafront destination reputation from.* The road is a wide, divided boulevard. The streetscape is well-constructed, exceptionally clean, with huge modern government buildings and resort hotels lining one side. The coastal side is lined with specialty restaurants: Thai, Italian, French, and seafood. One of them is Islam Pai Deang Restaurant, where the senior liaison officer is waiting.

The restaurant is huge and beautifully decorated with Thai fabrics, drawings, and statues. To Mislan, it screams expensive. A restaurant he wouldn't consider having meals in, on his police salary. It has an indoor air-conditioned section and an outdoor patio overlooking the estuary, where the southern part of Songkhla Lake meets the Gulf of Thailand. It is picturesque, with small fishing boats on the water and seabirds in the sky.

At the restaurant, they are received with the traditional *Sawadee Ka* and *Sawadee Krap*, depending on the gender of the greeter, and ushered to a reserved table where the Senior Liaison Officer, Deputy Superintendent of Police Arif Rafhan Othman is waiting. Approaching the table, Mislan notices the SLO writing on a piece of toilet roll, commonly used in eateries here in place of tissue or paper serviettes. Taking his seat, he notes the writings are actually cartoon character doodles. Naz introduces them, noticing Mislan's quizzical gaze at the doodles.

"DSP Apan is a cartoonist at heart," she explains.

"Apan?"

"He's Apan the graphic novelist to us and DSP Arif the SLO to the police force," she explains, laughing, much to the amusement of the D9 officers.

DSP Arif Rafhan laughs bashfully.

"I've ordered for us, seafood *tomyam*, fish *kengsom*, which is like our *masak asam*, *yam tin khai*, that's chicken feet sour salad, and some mix veggies. Is there anything else you'd like to try?"

Mislan shakes his head. "May I smoke?"

"Here restaurants are no smoking, but go ahead. I know the owner, and since we're seated outside, I don't think he minds. ACP Peter of Interpol said to watch out for you, but he didn't elaborate. Need I?" Arif asks, gazing at Mislan.

Mislan gives him the what-the-fuck-are you-talking-about look.

"I guess I need to. Do you speak Thai?" Arif asks, then laughs. "What a stupid question, of course you don't. After two years here I can barely manage ordering my meals."

Arif laughs again at his own statement.

"He is being modest," Naz says, bringing a wide beam to the SLO's face.

"I've asked for CIB, that's Thai CID, to assign an English-speaking officer to you, but knowing the Thais, they probably won't do it, just to make it difficult for us," Arif says again, laughing at his own assumption.

Mislan and Johan look at each other with amusement, wondering which character they're sitting with—DSP Arif the SLO or Apan the cartoonist, or graphic novelist as they like to call themselves nowadays.

Lunch and the meeting with Arif or Apan turns out to be a disaster for PR, the very purpose the SLO office was established. The host tries to make small talk, but the inspector won't engage.

Mislan finally loses his patience when told the impending interview would be in Hat Yai and not here in Songkhla. The interview he had worked so damn hard to come to, the interview that kept him awake at night mentally preparing. The interview that made him come to this foreign-speaking land. Unable to hold back his annoyance, Mislan curtly expresses his wish to get moving back to Hat Yai, the place they drove from.

Arif reciprocates with, "Now I understand what ACP Peter was implying. Naz, call for the bill, then arrange for them to go to Hat Yai CIB. There's no need for you to accompany them."

Naz nods dismally, calling to the waiter, "*Kit tang na ka*," meaning, "May I have the bill please?"

Standing to leave, Arif gazes warily at Mislan.

"This is Thailand. They play the game differently here. I hope this experience will teach you to value the very few people that can and want to help. Your police powers and authority card don't mean a damn thing here, only your attitude and humility."

With these words of wisdom, Arif the SLO aka Apan the cartoonist exits the restaurant, leaving several of the Thai specialty dishes hardly touched.

26

THE ABSENCE OF NAZ Ghazali makes the twenty-mile journey back south to Hat Yai a gloomy, silent ride. DSP Arif had told her not to bother accompanying them in order to teach the ungrateful inspector a lesson in manners. *Let him grope in the dark, and hopefully he'll regret his attitude,* were the exact words Mislan overheard him telling Naz as he left.

Johan tries to engage the driver in conversation both in English and Malay, but the driver just shakes his head with a smile, indicating he doesn't understand the languages. Mislan is certain that, as a driver for a Malaysian organization, he must understand some English or Malay. He suspects the pissed-off SLO must have instructed him not to cooperate with them also.

After almost an hour of crawling with the flow of heavy traffic, the driver makes a left at the sign pointing to the city of Hat Yai. Mislan notices the change in landscape as they approach the city. Large modern structures line the road, with car dealerships for Toyota, Daihatsu, Nissan, Honda, and hypermarket Tesco Lotus taking the prime frontal real estate.

About a mile farther down the road, they're caught in a traffic crawl that reignites Mislan's almost pacified impatience. Johan, on the other hand, is taking in the sight of the bustling town with its massive development.

A police roadblock that has poison-channeled three lanes into a single lane, which is the cause of the crawl. The roadblock is heavily fortified, with red-and-white-painted forty-gallon drums, rings of barbwire on red-and-white-painted wooden tripods, sandbag posts, and two military marquee tents equipped with tables and chairs. Several uniformed military and police personnel, heavily armed with AR-15 or -16 rifles, are seated under the tent chatting or engrossed with their cell phones. No one is manning the roadblock or for that matter appears to give a damn about who is passing through. Without being stopped, vehicles still have to slow down to a crawl in order to maneuver the zig-zag channel, and Mislan wonders why the hell they have the checkpoint.

To his relief, once they pass the roadblock, traffic is smooth again. He starts to relax, knowing they're close to their destination. Like Songkhla, Hat Yai's inner town roads are narrow, with all sorts of vehicles parked at every available space. Double-parking seems to be an acceptable norm. Drivers and riders just go around them without a second glance, unlike where he comes from. In Malaysia, the air would be vibrating with honks, and probably a fistfight or two would break out. Malaysians are always in a hurry to go somewhere—though, in reality, the somewhere could be anywhere: they're just in a hurry. Another apparent difference to him is the numerous 7-Elevens, reflexology, traditional Thai massage outlets, and hotels. They're on every street, or *Soi* in Thai. He spots several traffic policemen, yet again none of them seem concerned by the maddening congestion and rampant double-parking. They seem content to be sitting under the shade of their traffic posts by the road junction, letting the users of the road work things out for themselves.

Hat Yai Crime Suppression and Police Station is located on Nipatuthit 3 Road in the heart of the city. Mislan notices the police insignia on the signboard as they turn into the compound. The driver drives up to the main entrance of a two-story office building and stops. Turning to his passengers, he points to it, uttering something in Thai that the officers interpret as "We have arrived." Using gestures, Johan asks if the driver is coming with them, to which he responds with a few shakes of his head, saying *mai krap* follows by a string of Thai words.

Johan turns to the inspector with eyebrows arched, concerned. "Now what do we do?"

Mislan opens the door and steps out, ignoring his question. Johan follows suit, and the driver leaves without even a goodbye. Slinging his backpack, Mislan steps over to the side of the main entrance, sits on the parapet and lights up. Johan stands in the middle of the entrance, looking inside, nodding and smiling to passersby who seem oblivious to his overt friendliness. A dead giveaway as the demeanor of a person lost in a foreign land. After a few minutes, Johan walks to Mislan.

"Is it me, or do you feel it's hotter here?"

The detective sergeant looks at him questioningly.

"The weather—I thought KL was hot, but this place is so damn hot."

"It's hot wherever you are. Your attitude caused the heat," the detective sergeant says, taking a swipe at his boss.

Mislan smiles at his assistant. "I'm the sun . . . the giver of sunshine," he says, chuckling.

"Yeah, right. What's your plan?" he asks.

"What else . . . we go in and ask around," Mislan answers offhandedly.

"Ask what? DSP Arif didn't even mention who to look for."

"He did say CIB, and we're at CIB. So we go in."

"Right, so we go in and where exactly do we go to?" Johan asks despondently, sweeping his hands across the entire complex. "Why don't you call ma'am? Perhaps she can direct us."

"My phone doesn't have roaming," Mislan says with a grin. "Why don't you call the Pakistani woman, Naz?"

"I don't have her number. I thought she was coming with us. Anyway, my phone doesn't have roaming, either," Johan says, laughing.

"I heard you learning Thai from her, so I guess we'll be fine," Mislan kids.

"Yeah, we'll be just fine with 'Hello' . . .' I love you,' and 'Thank you,'" Johan says with a chuckle. "And if we flash some baht to go with it, we'll probably get laid."

———

Stepping on his cigarette butt, Mislan beckons for Johan to follow him. Approaching the reception counter, Mislan introduces himself to the man behind it by producing his police authority card, repeating the words *Inspector* and *Malaysia* several times. The man gawks at him smiling, saying *krap* repeatedly. After several more *Inspector, Malaysia,* and *krap*, they both give up. Mislan turns around and announces loudly to passersby, "Does anyone speak English?" He receives several questioning stares and a lot of low murmuring, but no one steps forward.

Several tense minutes pass, and those walking through the lobby are making serious efforts to distance themselves from him, especially the women. After another agonizing minute of pestering passersby, Mislan catches sight of a woman emerging from the depths of the building. She is accompanied by a curly-haired man hastily walking toward him. Staring at the woman, he feels a sense of familiarity about her but can't pin it down.

The two of them make a beeline for him. Johan immediately steps closer to his boss. In his mind, they're done for—it's going to be so embarrassing when ma'am is informed that her officers have been arrested and detained for disorderly conduct in a police station. *Shit, we'll probably be sent back to KL in a Black Maria*, Johan says to himself. He racks his brain for a plausible explanation for his boss's behavior.

As the woman and man approach them, the woman greets them with, "*Sawadee ka* Inspector. I see you've already created a storm with your arrival."

It takes several moments for the D9 officers to figure out who she is—Dr. Suthisa Ritchu, the profiler. It was almost two years ago that they met and worked on a case dubbed UTube. She was then on an exchange program attached to the Federal Police Headquarters, Bukit Aman, when she heard of the case and made a request to observe and study it. To Mislan's recollection, she is a human behavioral expert specializing in serial rapists profiling or something like that.

In the UTube case, Mislan got all messed up inside and was too focused on getting closure before his impending suspension from duty for disciplinary reasons to take real notice of her. Now, in stressful but less traumatic circumstances, he notices her for the first time.

Her hair is browner and shorter than what he remembered. He notes she has sort of Mediterranean features, with a sharp nose and big eyes; she lacks in height but not in shape and curves. She walks with an ever-so-slight sway of her rounded bum, with a tiny skip now and then. Mislan has to admit she is indeed good-looking.

"Doctor Su-, Su-," Mislan greets her, making the connection.

"Sophia," she says.

"Yes, Sophia, boy, you don't know how glad I am to see you," Mislan admits. "You remember Detective Sergeant Johan."

"*Ka*, how are you, Sergeant?"

"*Sawadee krap*, Doctor. Fine, thank you," Johan replies with a *wai*, in gratitude to their savior.

Turning to the man with the shoulder-length instant-noodles curly hair, Sophia introduces him as Police Sergeant Surasuk Silasungnern. Noticing the pained expression on the officers' faces, she says, "I know Thai names are a mouthful to foreigners. You may call him A'sark."

With his curly hair, skinny jeans, keys hanging from a wide belt, and printed *Sadoa Bike Week* crew-neck T-shirt, Mislan thinks Police Sergeant A'sark looks more like a rock band's lead guitarist than a police officer.

"A'sark is from the Crime Suppression Division. He'll be assisting. By the way, unlike Malaysia, here the army and police use the same ranks and just add 'Army' or 'Police' before the rank," Dr. Suthisa explains, smiling.

"Is the informant here? When can I talk to her?" Mislan asks impatiently.

"Let's go to the office. We can talk there first."

Walking along the corridor, Mislan inquires as to how she knew of their presence. Dr. Suthisa tells them of her conversation with Superintendent Samsiah. Two days back, she was updated of the latest development and was asked if she could lend a hand. The timing was just right, as she was due for a break and decided to spend it in Hat Yai. She arrived yesterday and early this morning came to CIB to meet up with A'sark. While she was chatting with him, a policeman stopped in to inform them there is a crazy man talking loudly in English to passersby. Since she understands the language, she thought she might be of assistance to the crazy man.

"Thank God. Some of them were giving us intimidating stares, and I was ready to deny being with Inspector Mislan should they decide to put him in a loony jacket," Johan jokes.

"I would do the same if I were you," Dr. Suthisa agrees, laughing.

"Doctor, is it my imagination or do the people around here . . . seem standoffish and edgy?" Johan asks.

"Good observation. I'm an outsider, and so are you guys. The recent discovery of the Rohingya and Bangladeshi mass grave in Sadao and its link to human trafficking are still an ongoing investigation. The entire police force, particularly here in Hat Yai, is under close scrutiny."

"I read about it. The Thai police made several arrests and an arrest warrant was issued for a major general," Johan acknowledges.

"We discovered the same calamity with more than 130 bodies in Malaysia, yet nothing happened," Mislan says disapprovingly. "A few days of hoo-ha, a few low-ranking forest rangers roped in for questioning. No follow-up arrest was made, a lot of hot-air announcements by politicians, and that's the end of it all. So far, no one has been charged, and a smartass politician wanted to turn the grave site into a tourist attraction."

"Probably, he was hoping it would be operated by his children or family, cashing in on government grants," Johan adds cynically.

27

AT THE CRIME SUPPRESSION general office in the west wing of the building, the visiting Malaysian officers receive a curious ogling welcome. The room is crowded with tables and chairs taking up the entire space. The lights are low, and the air reeks of cigarettes. Johan nod-greets everyone he makes eye contact with without much reciprocation. The stares out of the corners of their eyes are laced with suspicion, making him uncomfortable. Hushed words and quick glances when they walk past tell him their presence isn't welcome. Johan cannot understand Thai, but he doesn't need to know it to feel the vibes. He notices Police Sergeant Surasuk Silasungnern, aka A'sark, furtively winking to some of his colleagues. Probably he's swaggering at being the one selected to assist their Malaysian counterparts or is telling them, *These are the assholes causing the ruckus up front.* Johan is almost certain it's the latter.

A'sark ushers them into a small discussion or interview room at the back of the building. Taking a seat, Dr. Suthisa asks if they would like a drink. Mislan says he can really do with a cup of black coffee and, taking out his cigarette, gestures to ask if he can smoke. Dr. Suthisa says something to A'sark in Thai and nods to Mislan, who immediately lights up.

"Is she here?" Mislan asks again.

"Yes, but we, A'sark and I, felt we should talk first," she answers calmly. "Firstly, I have to remind you I've seen how you operate back in Malaysia. Please don't get me wrong, I'm not judging your method, but I'd like to remind you, you're here on a tourist pass, therefore you have no legal powers of investigation. *Pi'* Samsiah cautioned me, you have the tendency to be blinded by your chase for closure and conduct yourself recklessly. I assured her I'd do my best to prevent that from happening, and I believe so will Detective Sergeant Johan."

She pauses, letting her words sink in. Johan nods at every word she says, while Mislan on the other hand is expressionless.

"A'sark will lead the investigation, and you'll have to piggyback on his powers of investigation. As for the young girl, Nadear, please remember she is a Thai national who came in voluntarily. Do treat her with respect. Can I have your word on it?" she asks firmly.

The officers nod.

"Good. Here's my cell phone number. May I have both your contact numbers just in case we get separated?"

"Ours are Malaysian numbers and not roaming," Johan offers.

"It's OK, we do have a lot of Wi-Fi hotspots here. We can *WhatsApp* or Line."

"What about A'sark's number?" Mislan asks.

"Yes, here, but he doesn't speak English. Your best bet for assistance is still me," Dr. Suthisa says, grinning.

She updates A'sark in their language on what was discussed, eliciting several *krap* from him, and he leaves. Mislan sips his black coffee, grimaces, and puts it down, asking himself, *What shit is this?* He lights another cigarette to kill the taste of the bland coffee.

———

A moment later, A'sark returns with a girl. Mislan puts her at around eighteen or nineteen. She's dressed casually in blue shorts and white T-shirt. She is quite tall and large-framed for a Thai girl, with an oval-shaped face with a nervous look. Her jet black hair is thick, cut to shoulder-length like most school-age teenagers. From her features and build, Mislan thinks perhaps she has some Caucasian genes.

Standing in the doorway, she politely gives the *wai*, mouthing her greeting. Dr. Suthisa immediately steps up to her, wrapping an arm warmly around the teenage girl, and leads her into the room. Holding her by the shoulders, she announces, "Gentlemen, this is Nadear."

Mislan and Johan nod in reply.

Switching to Thai, she tells her, "Nadear, these are the gentlemen we told you about."

The girl nods timidly and gives another *wai*.

Showing her to a seat, Dr. Suthisa continues, "I'd like you to tell them about the earring. You must speal slowly, as I need to translate for them."

"*Ka*," Nadear answers barely audibly, and immediately lowers her head, looking down at her hands resting on her lap.

Mislan practically has to bite his tongue to stop from firing off questions as Nadear takes her time to organize her thoughts. Unable to keep still while waiting, he toys with his lighter and instantly receives a reproving glance from Nadear, which makes him stop.

"The earring is mine," Nadear says at long last, translated by Dr. Suthisa.

As suddenly as she begins, she stops, tilting her head ever so slightly to Dr. Suthisa, who flashes an encouraging smile for her to continue.

"I kept one and gave the other to Jariya, my best friend."

Turning her head to the right, she pushes her hair to expose her ear with the earring, showing it to the officers. When the officers nod, she lets her hair fall back and assumes her original posture with her head bowed.

Another moment of silence ensues as the young girl reruns the memories of her best friend in her head. Her lips quiver, and she immediately tucks them in, biting them while tiny droplets of tears roll down her cheeks. Seeing her state, the usually obnoxious Mislan refrains himself from pushing on with the thousand questions running wild in his head.

After what seems like forever to Mislan, Nadear inhales deeply and bravely continues.

"I had the earrings made especially for us during my school trip to Beijing. When I returned, I changed the hook to the screw type here in Hat Yai."

Again Nadear turns her head to the side and pushes her hair to show the earring. Holding her ear lobe she twists it to show the screw lock.

"Why?"

"So it won't easily fall off and get lost. We visited the wat in our village and prayed for Buddha's blessing and for him to make us soul sisters. You see, in this life, I've no brother or sister. Then after I met and befriended Jariya, I believed we were sisters in our previous lives. I suppose that was why Buddha arranged for us to meet."

Mislan notes Nadear's conviction, and remembers that Buddhists believe in reincarnation. Unable to hold back the gust of questions in his head any longer, Mislan turns to Dr. Suthisa.

"Doctor, may I ask some questions?"

She relays Mislan's request to A'sark, who seems to give it deep thought before saying, "*Krap*."

"Nadear, can you repeat your full name please for my record," Mislan asks, jumping at the word *krap* which he understands to mean yes or something to that effect.

"Nadear Wimonlakha."

Mislan turns to Dr. Suthisa. "Can you spell your surname for me, please?"

"Her late father was Australian. He died in a car crash when her mother was carrying her," Dr. Suthisa explains. "Please avoid asking her anything related to it. She's already grieving as it is, and there's no need to aggravate it."

Johan nods his understanding for both of them. With the doctor doing the translation, Mislan starts his interview.

"What is Jariya's full name?"

"Jariya Praphasirat."

"How old is she?"

"About eight months younger than me."

"And you are?"

"I just turned nineteen."

"You went to school together?"

"*Mai ka,* Jariya *mai pie rongrian.*" Nadear answers before Dr. Suthisa translates the question for her.

"No," is all Dr. Suthisa replies to the inspector's question.

After several more questions answered with a "yes" or "no" in translation, Mislan brusquely stops the questioning. His inability to ask direct questions and understand the answers without being translated is making the interview process tedious and frustrating. He has come to the conclusion that Thais talk in a verbose way. For a simple short statement, they seem to use five to ten times more words. After a lengthy exchange, all he got back was a short translated response at best or a miserable "yes" or "no." He suspected that, for reasons known only to them, his questions and probably the answers were deviated or lost in translation. His frustration multiplies when he has to re-ask the same question even after a response was given.

Johan notices his boss's frustration and suggests they should take a smoke break. Having noticed the same, Dr. Suthisa Ritchu agrees. Leaving the interview room, the D9 officers head straight for the back courtyard, where Mislan immediately lights up, taking deep drags and letting the nicotine do its magic on his raw nerves.

"Take it easy, will you? You're doing great," Johan says.

"Great, my ass. It's so damn bloody frustrating," Mislan hisses. "I've got a feeling they're not translating the questions I asked."

"How do you know that? You don't understand the language."

"The answers I get tell me the questions weren't translated correctly for whatever reason or the answers weren't translated in full."

"Hey, we're talking about Dr. Sophia here, not the police. She came all the way from Bangkok just to assist us. What reason would she have to screw with us?"

Mislan doesn't respond, his expression knotted in deep thought. It's true what his assistant just said, yet he can't shake the feeling.

"OK, it's going to take us a little longer, but we'll get there. Be patient. We blew it with the SLO; please don't blow it with Dr. Sophia," Johan beseeches.

Mislan stamps out his cigarette and lights another.

"Shit, I'm all out," he swears, crushing the cigarette box.

"Don't you carry spare packs in your backpack?"

Mislan shakes his head.

"Thought I could get some at the airport, but there weren't any."
"We can ask A'sark to send someone to get some."

———

Returning to the interview room, they find Dr. Suthisa and A'sark chatting with Nadear. Nadear is telling them something in earnest, and Mislan's intuition tells him it's about his case. His anger rises back to a near boiling point, but Johan gives him a pat and a slow blink of the eyes, pleading for him to cool down. To his surprise, Mislan heeds him and calmly takes a seat, without protesting. Unbeknownst to Johan, it was actually Dr. Suthisa's sumptuous smile supported by Nadear's pleasing eye contact that calmed his boss down. Taking his seat, Mislan manages a brief smile to them, telling them to continue. Turning her attention away from Nadear, Dr. Suthisa begins addressing the officers.

"While you were away, A'sark and I asked Nadear some questions we thought would interest you. I'll narrate them and you list down what else you need to know or for her to elaborate. I'm sure we can speed up this interview and let the poor girl go. She has some campus activity tomorrow morning, so it's best that we let her off as early as possible."

Mislan agrees, much to the surprise of Johan, who has never seen his boss give in so easily. Flipping through her notes, Dr. Suthisa briefs the officers.

"As a foreigner, her father had started a business in Thailand using her mother's name to facilitate registration and business financing. When he passed away, the business accrued a huge debt, which her mother had to settle. The mother lost all her properties after she was taken to court, and from then on struggled to pay off the balance of debt. She had to work two jobs just to survive, so Nadear was placed in her aunt's care in Hat Yai. This also allowed her to be close to her daughter, and she would pop by to see Nadear in between jobs. During school vacations, she would send Nadear back to her grandparents in Khuan Khanun district, Phatthalung. It was there Nadear met the deceased, Jariya Praphasirat. The Praphasirat are a large family of poor village

168

people. Jariya didn't go to school, and Nadear took pity on her. She befriended Jariya, taught her to read and write. You must understand: Nadear is from a mixed marriage, so as a child she felt outcast. With Jariya, all that didn't matter. Nadear looked forward to school breaks, when she would spend most of her time in the village with Jariya. As the years passed, they evolved into the best of friends; in fact, they were like sisters. Nadear would bring gifts of girlie teenage things from Hat Yai, and they both would play pretend games till nightfall."

Mislan observes Nadear as Dr. Suthisa relates her life and relationships with the victim. He feels sorry for her. At a young age, she has already gone through two tragic losses, her father and her best friend. Taking into account the loss of motherly love while growing up would make for three tragic losses.

"About a year ago," Dr. Suthisa continues, "Nadear went to Beijing on a school trip. There she bought the pair of earrings and had them inscribed with the words *Friends Forever Nadear* on one and *Friends Forever Jariya* on another. After she returned from the school trip, they went to a wat and got a monk to bless the earrings and them as soul sisters. She gave the earring that had her name carved in it to Jariya, while she wore the one with the victim's name. They made a vow never to take it off or their friendship would break. It was on the same day outside the wat that Jariya told her she'd soon be making a lot of money. She was then going to buy a piece of land and build a house for her parents, where they would live together and never again be poor. Nadear did ask her how she was going to get the money, but Jariya told her it was better for her not to know. She promised to tell her everything when they met the next time. The following school vacation, when Nadear visited her grandparents, she was told by Jariya's siblings she had left to work in Phuket."

"When was that?"

"About seven months back, in April."

"Does she know where in Phuket?" Mislan asks.

"*Mi rue*," Nadear answers.

"No," Dr. Suthisa translates.

"You do understand English?" Mislan asks Nadear.

"*Nit noi*."

"A little," Dr. Suthisa translates.

"When was the last time you talked with the victim, I mean Jariya?"

"The day I gave her the earring."

"Never after that, not even a WhatsApp chat?"

"No. Jariya doesn't have a cell phone. She never had one when she was in the village. After she left, I didn't know how to contact her."

"I'm sure she had your phone number," Mislan says.

"I don't know, maybe not. I never gave her my number, and she never asked for it, I mean she had no phone, so why would she need my number?"

"Do you have a photo of Jariya that I can have?"

Nadear takes out her cell phone, searches for the photo, and hands the phone to the inspector.

After weeks of leading the investigation and many nights of imagining what his victim looks like, Mislan finally gets to see her. It feels strange, seeing her happy smiling face. He is more used to the agonized or shocked expression of a murdered person. She looks nothing like he had imagined her. Jariya is a pretty young girl, with long flowing hair, high cheekbones, and a beautiful set of white teeth, but sad eyes. The dress she's wearing seems a little loose, probably borrowed from or a gift by a best friend, Mislan supposes. He shows the photo to Johan, who looks at it silently for a long time before returning the phone to Nadear. Mislan asks her to WhatsApp the photo to him.

"One last thing. Do you know of any marking on Jariya's body?"

Nadear looks at the inspector questioningly.

"Like birth mark or tattoo?"

"She has a butterfly tattoo on her back, just about here," Nadear says, turning in her chair to point to her back, just above the panty line. "She wanted it, and I went with her to Phattalung to do it." Nadear scrolls her cell phone and shows the inspector the tattoo. "Jariya says it represents her life."

It is a blue-bodied butterfly with red wings.

"Meaning?"

"Jariya said her life started in an ugly state, I mean poor, without anything, but she'll be reborn and grow up being beautiful and free. It is symbolic, like an ugly caterpillar that became a colorful and beautiful butterfly."

"Any other?"

"I've seen the Hah Taew Sak Yant on the back of her left shoulder. That she didn't do with me."

"Can you WhatsApp me the butterfly tattoo? Thanks."

28

KHUAN KHANUN SUBDISTRICT IN Phatthalung is about sixty-six miles north of Hat Yai. By the time they reach Phattalung, it's almost dark. A'sark suggests they check in to a hotel, freshen up, and get some dinner before driving to Khuan Khanun, which is another ten miles north. He explains that Khuan Khanun is a small town and doesn't have suitable hotels for them. Despite Mislan's insistence that they continue on, A'sark, who is driving the SUV, makes a turn into Phatthalung. They stop at the Centric Hotel. Mislan glances at the SUV's dashboard digital clock. It's 6:45 in the evening but already very dark outside.

The Centric Hotel is in the center of the town, five or six stories high, and looks to Mislan like a three-star hotel. The lobby is large, with high ceilings, and its decor, fixtures, and furniture are in way luxurious or stylish. But the hotel employees are friendly and smile constantly. After A'sark checks them in, he informs them to meet back in the lobby at 7:30 p.m. to go for dinner.

———

Standing under the shower, Mislan has to admit A'sark's decision to check in to the hotel was a good one. The hot shower relaxes his aching muscles and at the same time washes away the stickiness of dried sweat. He turns the hot shower handle off, and the blast of cold water is vigorously refreshing. Stepping out of the shower, he finds the television on but Johan missing. He recalls seeing a sign for a massage center in the elevator and lets out a knowing smile. He's pretty sure his detective sergeant has gone to check it out. When his eyes fall on the bedside table, where a yellow Cricket lighter is waiting without its companion—Sampoerna Menthol—he curses under his breath. "Damn, I forgot to buy cigarettes." A quick look at the time on his cell phone says there is still time for him to run down to the 7-Eleven to get cigarettes and bottled drinks. Only then does he realize he has no Thai baht. "Damn Lan, you're hopeless," he swears out loud.

Confident the hotel would be able to change money for him, he slips into a pair of jeans and a T-shirt. Just as he's about to leave, though, the door opens and Johan appears, carrying a plastic bag.

"Been shopping, I see," Mislan says.

"For drinks and snacks. I also got us local SIM cards. Here," he says, throwing a packet of Dunhill menthol to Mislan. "They don't have Sampoerna here. I figured that would do."

"Thanks. Where did you change to baht?"

"KL, Sungei Wang Plaza. Our money is down by seventeen percent to theirs … 823 baht to 100 ringgit. It used to be 1000 to a 100," Johan whines. "The money changer said it was the bloody 1MDB scandal that's making our money float downriver. I bet the exchange rate is worse here."

"You can always depend on our politicians to fuck us," Mislan says offhandedly, lighting up. "I really don't understand why people vote, why they need politicians to manage their lives."

"If this continues, Malaysians will soon be illegal workers in Indonesia and Thailand," Johan offers.

"It's almost 7:30, why don't you get a quick shower and change before we go down," Mislan tells his assistant. "We don't know what the plan is and what time we'll be back."

———

When Mislan and Johan come down to the lobby, Dr. Suthisa Ritchu and Police Sergeant A'sark are already waiting for them. A'sark greets them saying, "*Pie*," and walks toward the main entrance. Dr. Suthisa follows him, saying to the D9 officers, "Let's go." The SUV is parked in the driveway right in front of the main entrance. After several minutes of driving through narrow streets, A'sark stops in front of a restaurant with a big sign saying MAKANAN ISLAM—Muslim Food. Dr. Suthisa explains that she suggested A'sark take them to a Muslim restaurant, as most Thai restaurants serve pork.

The restaurant looks nothing like the one they were treated to in Songkhla by the SLO. It's run-down, furnished with old folding tables and plastic chairs. The Thai population is mainly Buddhist, with pockets of Muslim communities scattered all over. The largest concentration is found in the southeastern tip of the country in Pattani and Yala.

"Because of that, you really don't find Muslim restaurants thriving except in tourist towns like Songkhla, Hat Yai, Phuket, Krabi, and so on, which cater to Muslim tourists mainly from Malaysia, Singapore, and Indonesia."

Mislan and Johan give an understanding nod.

"You'll also find the dishes prepared by the Muslims and Buddhists here are similar except the Buddhists will add pork to almost all dishes. Pork is more popular here than beef because of the Hindu influence."

Police Sergeant A'sark is given the honor of ordering, and when the food arrives, Mislan mulls silently, *Why do the Thais think all Malaysians like eating tomyam? Isn't there anything else?* He has heard people say the Thais are rich in culinary diversity, yet his second meal in this country is again *tomyam*.

The Malaysian officers suddenly realize they're ravenous, because of the disrupted lunch and the fact they have eaten nothing in between. Mislan's earlier plan of going to Khuan Khanun to seek out the Praphasirat family is temporarily shelved. He observes Dr. Suthisa and A'sark nibbling on their food and think they must be sparing their stomachs for pork dishes later. All through dinner, Johan and the doctor engage in small talk about Thailand, its people, and its culture. Mislan listens but is more interested in A'sark, who seems preoccupied with his cell phone. Now and then, he'll leave the table to take or make a call. It has to be a jealous girlfriend or lover asking his whereabouts, Mislan surmises. Perhaps conversations he doesn't want Dr. Suthisa to hear.

After the last call, A'sark seems to be in a hurry. He requests the bill without asking if they're done with their meal. Mislan wonders what's going on. A'sark says something to Dr. Suthisa in Thai, and she informs the D9 officers that the Phattalung police have picked up Jariya's parents and they're now waiting at the police station. Mislan springs to his feet with a what-are-we-waiting-for expression on his face. A'sark again utters, *"Pie,"* which the Malaysian officers later learn means "Go" or, in casual conversation, can also be used for "Let's go."

———

The police station is on the opposite side of town, but with A'sark's driving skills or recklessness it takes barely ten minutes to reach it through narrow and winding streets. The station is a single-story stand-alone building with the police signboard at the unguarded gate. Misan recalls that even the police station gate at Hat Yai was unguarded. Not like in his country, where all gates to police installations are guarded by heavily armed police. Stepping out of the car, the police sergeant hangs his badge around his neck and leads the rest of them into the station. The badge, or shield as the Americans term it, commands respect and acknowledgment of the power bestowed on its owner. Mislan takes delight in displaying his authority in such a manner, unlike what is mandated by Malaysia's police, which nearly cost him his job when he was investigating the UTube case.

A'sark stops to inquire with one of the policemen at the counter, who stands up, does the *wai*, and leads them to a room at the back of the station, leaving the counter unmanned. When the door is opened, two men and a woman hastily stand to greet A'sark with low bowing *wai*. The policeman guarding the couple introduces the man standing next to him as Sarawut Praphasirat and the woman as Sarawut's wife, Wipada Mookjai. A'sark thanks the policeman and asks him to leave them alone.

There are only four chairs, so Mislan and Johan lean against the wall while Dr. Suthisa and A'sark take their seats facing the couple. A'sark instantly dives into his police sergeant role. His voice transforms into a husky authoritative tone. Strings of questions and answers ensue, with *krap* being the only word the Malaysian officers can decipher. Dr. Suthisa tries her very best to keep up with the translation, but Mislan knows she's losing the race. Thais speak at a machine-gun pace, sounding like a hundred words per minute.

Dr. Suthisa narrates that A'sark asked if one of their daughters is named Jariya, to which they replied, she is the eldest of their three daughters. She is eighteen going on nineteen. According to the father, she had gone to Phuket to work in a restaurant. Jariya had last spoken to one of her siblings about ten or twelve days back. They're not aware of anything happening to her, and there was no reason for them to inquire. The father claimed she normally sent money for them to withdraw from the bank in Phatthalung between the twenty-fifth to twenty-seventh of the month, and that is about five to eight days away. If he hasn't received the money by then, it would be cause for him to inquire or be concerned.

Mislan grimaces, disturbed by the blunt admission by the deceased's father: only when there's no money in the bank by the end of the month does he think of his daughter.

The translation ceases when the police sergeant suddenly raises his voice threateningly at the father. Mislan is sure A'sark isn't satisfied with the answers given or believes he was lied to. Mislan steps closer to Dr. Suthisa, asking what is going on, and as A'sark badgers the father, she gives a running commentary.

"A'sark is saying the father is lying. He knows the daughter didn't go to Phuket to work. He's asking who took her to Phuket. The father said he was introduced to an employment agent by one of his friends from the coffee shop where he goes for his daily beers. He doesn't know the agent personally, but his friend does. He has seen his friend drinking with the agent many times before."

"Tell A'sark to tell the father Jariya was in Malaysia," Mislan asks.

Dr. Suthisa whispers it to A'sark.

When the police sergeant informs the father, he denies repeatedly with *"Mai dai, mai dai."*

"Tell him his daughter is dead . . . murdered," Mislan pushes on.

When A'sark reveals the information, both the parents stare at him disbelievingly. Mislan takes out his cell phone, scrolls for his victim's crime scene photos, and pushes the phone to the police sergeant. A'sark enlarges the photo of the faceless corpse and pushes the phone toward the parents.

With or without a face, a mother knows her child. She lets out a wailing cry and starts lashing at her husband. She grabs the phone, pressing it tightly against her bosom, trembling uncontrollably as she calls out her daughter's name. The father sits dumbfounded, biting his lips, staring fearfully at A'sark.

Mislan asks Dr. Suthisa if the mother can be interviewed separately. A'sark nods, as he recognizes and understands the police interview's breakthrough moment. Dr. Suthisa walks over to Wipada Mookjai, holds her by the arm and leads her out. The husband's half-hearted protest quickly dies off with one stare from A'sark. Mislan instructs Johan to stay with A'sark as he follows Dr. Suthisa, ushering the mother clutching the inspector's cell phone to her chest as they move to another interview room.

29

Sitting the grieving mother down, Dr. Suthisa coaxes her into returning Mislan's cell phone. She apologizes profusely between sobs, gazes longingly at the screen, and reluctantly hands it to her. Before Wipada is asked any questions, she spills her pent-up grief and suffering from the day her daughter was taken away. She is unstoppable. Dr. Suthisa makes a move to console her, and Mislan pulls her away.

"Let her grieve, just listen and translate for me," he whispers to her. "Her grieving may reveal all we need to know."

Dr. Suthisa understands his intentions. Sitting beside Wipada, she listens and translates as best she can the sometimes incoherent anguish mixed with prayer chants.

"From the very first time I laid eyes on the man my husband brought home, I knew he's not good," the mother says angrily. "The way he looked at my baby Jari . . . his slithering eyes when he thought I wasn't looking. When I asked my husband what they talked about, he got upset and told me to mind my own business. I'm not stupid. I've heard many stories from women at the market about young girls going away looking for work."

Wipada stops abruptly, lifts her head to stare at the doctor like something has just struck her mind.

Mislan whispers to Dr. Suthisa to probe more on the young girls the mother mentioned. She says something to Wipada as Mislan waits in anticipation.

"We're poor," Wipada admits with humility, "and can hardly provide our children with proper meals daily. But by the name of Lord Buddha, I'd never sell my baby . . . I would rather die than do that."

"Was Jariya sold?" Dr. Suthisa asks.

Dropping her head, she clasps her face with both hands, sobbing and nodding.

"To whom, the man your husband brought home?" Mislan probes. Another nod.

"What is his name? Do you know where he lives?"

Wipada shakes her head.

"My husband signed the paper."

"What paper? The sales paper?"

Wipada nods.

"What did the paper say?"

"I'm sorry I don't know. My husband refused to show it to me," she admits.

"Where's the paper?" Dr. Suthisa asks.

"I don't know. My husband kept it."

"How much was Jariya sold for?"

"I don't know," the mother answers, shaking her head. "My husband won't admit my baby was sold, so he never told me for how much. Yet a week after my baby left with the man, he bought a new motorbike and went out drinking."

Wipada pauses, breathing deeply. Then gazing directly at the doctor she says, "He insisted my baby went to work in Phuket. Work as what? My baby is not educated. The only reason a young uneducated girl is recruited is for ..."

Wipada stops short of saying the word every mother fears her daughter will turn into. Mislan and Dr. Suthisa know what she meant without her saying it. The room falls silent save for the heartbreaking sobs of a mother.

———

Mislan indicates to Dr. Suthisa that he's going next door to the father. Opening the interview room door, he signals to A'sark to step out.

When the police sergeant steps out into the corridor, Mislan points to the interview room, saying, "Father . . . papa," several times.

A'sark nods, indicating he understands.

"Sell daughter. He sold his daughter," Mislan says, gesturing by rubbing of his thumb with the index figure. He figures it's an international sign for money.

A'sark gazes at him blankly, probably thinking Mislan needs money for something.

Mislan pulls out his wallet saying, "Father." He then takes out some money, waving it to A'sark. Pointing to the interview room where the mother is, he says, "Mama said," then follows by cupping his breast uttering, "Jariya." Waving the money and pointing to the interview room, he says "Papa," extending the money like he is giving it away.

"*Chai, chai,*" A'Sark says nodding, saying he understands.

Mislan lets out a big sigh of relief, glad that this crude chicken-and-duck conversation has succeeded. He crosses his wrists, saying; "Father, papa, you need to put him under arrest."

"OK, OK, *krap.*"

Mislan reflects that that was the first real interactive exchange he's had with Police Sergeant A'sark, and it went rather well. Their shared police background must have helped make the sign language mutually comprehensible.

———

Returning to his interview room, Mislan finds the grieving Wipada has calmed down and appears to be praying. He asks if Dr. Suthisa can arrange for Wipada to be sent home to be with her children, whom he's sure must be hungry and worried by now. The doctor is touched by Mislan's sensitivity and assumes his departure earlier was to seek A'sark's consent for the release of Wipada.

Mislan rejoins A'sark and Johan while Dr. Suthisa makes the necessary arrangements to send the mother home to break the news to her other children. A'sark, flushed with anger, is standing in front of the father, whose chair is turned away from the table and is facing him.

Johan asks Mislan what is going on and why A'sark is behaving aggressively. Mislan updates his assistant about what the mother told.

"You mean sell like sell?" Johan asks disbelievingly.

"Yes, and the mother believes for prostitution."

"Shit."

The angry voice of A'sark is followed by a hard slap across Sarawut's face. Sarawut screams in pain, holding his cheek. Instinctively, Mislan positions himself to lean against the door. The police sergeant notices Mislan's collaboration and gives him a wink of appreciation. His tone turns grave, as he says something to the father, who is obviously denying whatever was leveled at him. In a single swift movement, A'sark grabs the back of Sarawut's head with his left hand as his right hand draws a Glock 19 Parabellum pistol, pressing its muzzle squarely on Sarawut's forehead.

A cold shiver shoots down Mislan's spine as he notes the police sergeant's index finger is on the trigger instead of the trigger guard. *Fuck, this guy is crazier than me*, he says to himself while throwing glances at Johan, who acknowledges with a concerned hike of his eyebrows. The police sergeant notices the exchange of glances between the Malaysian officers. He smiles at them as if saying, *Welcome to my world*.

Sarawut drops from the chair to his knees, head bowed so low it almost touches the cement, with hands above his head in a high *wai*, mumbling what the D9 officers assume are pleas for mercy. A'sark grabs the father by the hair, jerking him to a stand, pressing the pistol muzzle under his chin, and throatily hisses into the father's face. Although Mislan and Johan don't understand what's being hissed, they can feel the vileness of his words. Mislan's eyes are transfixed on A'sark's trigger finger, as he asks himself, *Is he pissed enough to blow the father's head off? More interestingly, can he get away with it?*

30

THE TIME IS ALMOST 11 p.m. when A'sark decides to stop badgering the father by shoving him to the floor. Mislan is relieved the police sergeant didn't blow the man's head off, yet at the same time he's disappointed. The man really deserved it. *For fuck's sake, the scumbag sold his daughter! How many more of his children is he going to sell?* He has no pity for the pile of shit slumped on the cold floor, crying, begging, and praying for his god's forgiveness.

A'sark leads the officers to another room, where food and beverages are laid out. Dr. Suthisa must have organized it, and she serves them coffee and a plate of the famous Thai sticky rice with deep-fried chicken. The police sergeant, probably starving from the hard work of whacking the victim's father, digs in. Mislan observes him ball the sticky rice with his fingers, dip it onto some fried shallot, then into the chili sauce, before putting it in his mouth. As he chews the sticky rice, he tears a piece of the deep-fried chicken, popping it into his mouth. His hand movements seem to be without thought as he updates them on the intelligence extracted from the victim's father.

Dr. Suthisa explains to Mislan and Johan that the father will lead them to the man with whom he signed the contract. The man he knows only by the name of A'chat.

"What contract, you mean the sales agreement the mother mentioned earlier?" Mislan asks.

"It's a sort of employment contract."

"What employment . . . prostitution?"

"I've heard of such papers to give a first-glance impression of legality for the sale of young women to prostitution syndicates, but I've never come across a case nor have I read one of these contracts. Perhaps when we retrieve the contract from his house later, I may be able to address your questions," Dr. Suthisa says, sipping on her tea. "For now A'sark is arranging for a few men from here to assist us in looking for A'chat. He's not familiar with the local geography, and without the local police assistance, we'd be going around in circles."

Mislan and Johan agree.

"Why don't you guys eat something? We may be out there the whole night. You should try the *kao ni'aw kai tot*, that's sticky rice with fried chicken. Some of my Malaysian friends come all the way here just for it," she says, chuckling.

"Doctor, is there a possibility of getting the parents to submit to a DNA test?" Mislan asks.

Dr. Suthisa addresses the question to the police sergeant, who looks at the inspector inquisitively.

"From what Neader describes of the victim's life, I doubt she has any dental records. I also doubt we can get anything from the house to test for her DNA. If we can get the parents' DNA, we can forensically identify the victim through parental DNA. As it is now, we only have circumstantial evidence of the victim being who she is."

A'sark nods. "I'll make the arrangements."

"Thanks. At the same time, we'd like to get a certified copy of her birth records."

A'sark nods again.

———

They leave Phatthalung police station in two vehicles. One is A'sark's SUV with Mislan, Johan, and the doctor, while the unmarked pickup is packed by three plainclothes policemen and Sarawut. Mislan glances at the dashboard digital clock; it reads 00:21 as they roll out of the police station. The town looks dead, contrary to the belief that Thai towns never sleep. Once they're beyond the city limit, the road is even more deserted. The night is pitch black with sporadic yellow lights from houses deep within the countryside. Mislan notices dogs running wild along and across the road. They seem to be everywhere.

A'sark tails the leading pickup, which is going at breakneck speed. After about fifteen minutes, the pickup reduces speed, making a left onto a narrower road with rice paddy fields on both sides. Another five minutes, and the pickup makes another left into a rubber estate. From the distance, Mislan sees bright lights coming from a wooden stand-alone shop in an open area.

As they approach the shop, he sees a group of men sitting around a table laden with beer bottles. Lit up by the pickup headlights, the men warily watch them approach like deer caught in headlights. A few of them stand, stepping away from the table. The pickup suddenly guns forward as though the driver intends to ram into the group of men, catching A'sark in the SUV by surprise.

The police sergeant swears loudly in Thai. Mislan and Johan anxiously lean forward from the back seat to have a better view. The pickup comes to a screeching halt a couple of feet away from the shop, scattering the group of drinkers. The driver and two other plainclothes policemen dash out from the pickup. They all seem to be after one of the men wearing a fedora, who is bolting into the rubber estate with one hand holding his hat in place.

A'sark expertly swerves the SUV through the narrow opening around the pickup, knocking over a parked motorbike and overtaking the chasing men. Gaining on the fedora man, he gives a slight jerk of the steering wheel, tapping the SUV's fender into him. The tap violently sends the fedora man crashing to the ground, making several rolls before agonizingly stopping by a rubber tree. A'sark jerks hard on the steering wheel, making a 180-degree spin. Before the SUV comes to a dead stop, he is already out with his Glock drawn, pointing and barking instructions to the fedora-less man groaning on the ground.

"What the hell just happened?" Mislan says, nonplussed, still holding tightly to the hand grip. "This motherfucker is crazy. I'm beginning to like him."

"Shit, I thought I was the crazy wannabe stunt driver," Johan declares. "Did you see how he slid through the rat's tunnel? He's good, really good."

Dr. Suthisa picks herself up from the footrest floor looking bewildered and flushed with anger. She bursts out of the SUV, screaming at the police sergeant with what Mislan assumes to be obscenities. He hears A'sark repeatedly say, "*Ko tot krap*," which, the doctor explained later, means *sorry*.

The plainclothesmen grab the hatless man, pulling him to his feet.

A'sark holsters his Glock 19, asking, "What's your name?"

"Tosakpon, Tosakpon Angdrekawanit," the hatless man answers, struggling free from the clutches of the three policemen and brushing dirt off his pants and shirt. "Where's my hat?" he asks, turning to search the surrounding area.

"Also known as A'chat?"

"*Krap*."

One of the plainclothesmen picks up the hat and hands it to him, and he immediately puts it on.

"What's this about?" he asks, more boldly now that he is again the fedora man, as the rest of his drinking buddies gather around.

"You're coming with us," A'sark instructs him, motioning to the plainclothesmen to bring the fedora man with them, and he turns to head back to the SUV.

"Why, what for?" A'chat protests. "Hey, hey, you're not from here are you, where are you from?"

Two unseen steps from A'sark are followed by a lighting *tomoi* backhand strike, and A'chat the fedora man's head spins to the left, blood coming out of his mouth. The three plainclothesmen standing next to him leap back, shocked by the suddenness of the blow. A'chat hits the ground like a ripe durian, this time not only losing his fedora but probably a tooth or two with it.

The unconscious A'chat is bundled up like a slaughtered pig for a feast and thrown into the back of the pickup. His drinking buddies, who held him in high regard as a man with powerful connections, watch agape. Two plainclothesmen climb into the back with him to stand or sit guard.

Mislan notices that even before the police team leaves the scene, the men are back at the table, continuing with their drinking. *Well, lives go on*, he says to himself, *why waste good beers over the arrest of one of them?*

31

DRIVING IN TO PHATTHALUNG police station compound, Mislan notices a group of three men at the main entrance. One of them in civilian clothing is flanked by two uniformed personnel with tiny stars on their shoulders. The man in civilian clothing looks like he's fuming with rage. The police sergeant parks his SUV next to the main entrance under the glare of the reception party. Mislan doesn't like what he's seeing. He senses a confrontation. A'sark steps out of the SUV, calmly walking toward them. Mislan, Johan, and Dr. Suthisa stay by the SUV, keeping their distance to observe. They watch as A'sark engages the man in civilian clothes, holding up his shield several times and pointing to the pickup where the fedora man is being unloaded. He then holds up his cell phone, offering it to the man in civilian clothing as if daring him to make a call.

Mislan asks Dr. Suthisa what's going down. She explains that the man is the head of Phatthalung police station, Police Captain Chakrii Phukimak. He heard of the arrest and is questioning the police sergeant about his probable cause.

"A'sark is challenging him to make a call to Crime Suppression if he's not happy with the arrest," she continues. "A'sark knows he's untouchable: Crime Suppression is above his level as a captain."

"News travels fast," Johan whispers to Mislan.

"Looks like it. Judging by the captain's manner, he's raving pissed."

"We're just a phone call away, isn't that what the telco says?" Johan jests.

"Just call my name, and I'll be there," Dr. Suthisa says, quoting a song.

"Why is the station head interested in the arrest?" Mislan asks. "Interested enough to be here at this hour? The suspect must really have strong cables."

Dr. Suthisa gives him a you-know-how-it-works look.

"Are we in trouble?" Johan asks.

"A'Sark knows how to take care of himself," she replies with a grin. "In a way, he's just like you, Inspector. He'll be fine."

Johan chuckles while Mislan hikes his eyebrows.

A'Sark turns around to signal for them to follow him and barks instructions to the plainclothesmen to bring the semiconscious A'chat to the interview room. Approaching the head of police station, whose face is flushed red, Mislan smells a strong stench of alcohol from his breath. *He must be pissed off at having to leave the karoake bar or pub and most likely the young woman he'd intended to land*, Mislan theorizes, smiling inwardly. Police Captain Chakrii flashes them a mocking smile as they pass by, saying something to his two uniformed personnel. Mislan senses it must be sarcastic and mocking.

Getting the same vibes, Johan offers a *wai* smilingly, saying in Malay, "*Kecik-kecik taknak mapus, dah besar menyusahkan orang.*" Basically meaning, Why didn't you die young and not grow up and cause trouble for others.

Police Captain Chakrii Phukimak and his two sidekicks think Johan is respectfully acknowledging them, and reciprocate with a *wai* and smile.

———

The semiconscious A'chat is slumped in a chair. The police sergeant grabs him by the hair, yanks his head back, and tilts his swollen lips upward. He groans in pain, resisting the yanking.

"Who did you sell Jariya to?" he asks menacingly.

A'chat blinks several times, flinching with pain as he tries to form a defiant grin with his swollen lips. It makes him look funny.

"Who did you sell Jariya to?" A'sark repeats slowly.

A'chat stares at the police sergeant with his funny-looking smile.

"You think you're protected? You saw me talking to Captain Chakrii just now. He came by just to tell me your protection has been revoked."

A'sark grins deviously, letting his lie sink in, watching his captive's expression change from arrogance and disdain to realization and fear.

"What do you mean revoked?" A'chat mumbles through his swollen lips. "That bloody *hi'ear* takes 20,000 baht for every bitch I recruit," he cusses. "How do you think I managed to operate all these years?"

A'sark smiles and moves behind A'chat. Before the suspect can turn to see what is coming, the police sergeant again grabs him by the hair, slamming his head onto the table, pressing hard.

"*Hi'ear*, you're the *hi'ear*, the two of you are *hi'ear*." Bending down close to his ear, A'sark whispers tauntingly, "And you know what we do to *hi'ear*."

The word *hi'ear* hissed venomously catches Johan's ears. He asks Dr. Suthisa what it means. She explains, *hi'ear* is the street word for monitor lizard. When said of a person in Thai culture, it's saying he or she is the lowest form of life.

"Why monitor lizard, why not snake or tapeworm?" Mislan asks, baffled.

Dr. Suthisa smiles. "It's like you Malays calling people pig, why pig? Here, pigs are loved by many. Anyway, you just need to understand our culture and Buddhism."

A'chat struggles to free his head. The more he struggles, the harder A'sark presses.

"You'll be coming with me to Hat Yai, and if you're lucky, you'll get there," he whispers, only for A'chat's ear. "But then my SUV may break down along the way on the dark deserted road. Who knows, you may take the opportunity to make a run for it and I'd be forced to shoot to stop you. It's dark and I'm a poor shot, instead of hitting your legs I might hit your head."

Releasing A'chat's head, A'sark swaggers across the table.

"You wouldn't dare," A'chat says, uncertainly.

"Try me," the police sergeant dares him with a grin. "These two men, they're Malaysian and after this, they'll go back. Who's to tell a different story?"

The fedora man stares at the police sergeant intently, trying to read his expression to call his bluff.

"There's the woman, she is Thai. She can speak for me."

"You stupid *hi'ear*, you fucking sold a girl . . . a teenage girl, and now the girl is dead, murdered. You really think the woman'll speak for you? She wants you dead more than I do."

———

After more skillfully administered Thai police persuasion, A'chat spills his guts. He's a free agent specializing in young girls. There's much more demand in this category and less hassle, he claims. A contract is signed by the parents, usually the father if the girl is under eighteen. It's done to legitimize the sale. The parents will be paid an agreed amount in one lump sum, upon the girl being handed over. The contract period is usually one year; there are instances where it is for two years but never more. In the case of Jariya, the father was paid 200,000 baht for a year's contract.

"That's not much, about 24,000 ringgit at present exchange rate," Johan chips in.

"To you, but to these village people that's an amount they never dreamed of having in one go," Dr. Suthisa explains.

"You mean it's all legit?" Mislan asks, infuriated.

"I'm afraid so," A'sark admits.

"Bull! It's bullshit!" Mislan says. "The father sold his daughter, and now she's dead. Tell me, how is that legit?"

A'sark, Dr. Suthisa, and Johan gawk at Mislan's livid outburst. Johan apologizes for his boss's flare-up and asks if they can take a smoke break. Dr. Suthisa agrees, saying it has been a long night and they all should call it a day, get some rest, and meet again tomorrow morning.

"Hold on to the thought, Doctor. We'll discuss it after we take a short break," Johan proposes.

———

Outside the station, Mislan lights a cigarette, and Johan asks for a stick. Mislan hands him the pack and lighter, then leans against the SUV.

"Why are you smoking?" Mislan asks his assistant.

"Need something to calm me down," Johan answers with a grin.

"Don't waste my cigarette."

Johan hands back the pack without taking one.

"We all know the victim was sold by her father for prostitution," Johan starts cautiously, "but if it's legal here, then it's legal."

"Jo, you don't get it, do you? This is not about prostitution: she was bought and sold. It's slavery, human trafficking," Mislan snaps. "Prostitution was forced upon her, what choice did she have? Did you read about the Middle Eastern girl who chose death rather than submit herself to ISIS as a sex jihadist or sex slave? Our vic was probably in the same position, and like most normal humans she submitted, she chose life. Not all of us are like the Middle Eastern girl."

"Yes, I do understand, but A'sark is doing his best. . . . His hands are tied. Anyway, ours is a murder case, and our victim was murdered in KL, our turf."

Mislan gazes at his assistant in silence.

"I think we should follow her trail and see where she ended up. If we can do that, we stand a better chance of finding out what really happened."

"I know," Mislan admits, stamping out his cigarette. "It just blows my mind when a father can legitimately sell off his daughter. What father does that?"

"I'm not saying it's right, but it happens elsewhere and in our country, too. I saw a documentary once, where fathers sell off their underage daughters for marriage in Europe, Middle East, India, and Malaysia. In Europe, the more skillful the girls are at stealing, the higher the price." Noting that his boss has calmed down, Johan continues, "We're guests here. Let's not criticize their laws. You can't right the world. The best we can do for our victim is to get closure. We won't achieve it by pissing off the people who are helping us achieve it."

Mislan silently admits his assistant is right. Making enemies of Police Sergeant A'sark and Dr. Suthisa Ritchu will only defeat their objective.

Rejoining the team, Mislan apologizes for his conduct and suggests they continue. Much to his delight, his police counterpart agrees. A'sark continues with his updates on his interview findings.

A'chat used to work as a recruiter for a flesh industry syndicate based in Bangkok. That was when he picked up the trade skills and contacts—the buyers. About four years ago he left the syndicate, returning to his hometown here in Phatthalung. Since then he has gone freelance, scouting the surrounding villages for potential. Whenever he recruits a girl, he'll send her profile to the buyers he knows. One of them is a woman he knows only as Aunty Sara. Interested buyers will offer a price, usually for the period of one year. The contract ranges between 300,000 to 500,000 baht depending on the merchandise features and age.

Once the buyer confirms the price, he'll then negotiate with the parents, usually the father. When all is agreed, a contract is prepared, whereby the parents sign off, allowing their daughter to work for an agency or individual for a period of one or two years. The agreed amount is paid in a lump sum, upon the girl being released to him. Should the girl run away or refuse to work as required by the purchaser, the parents are to repay the amount received, including interest. Failure to repay normally results in dire consequences.

In the case of Jariya, Aunty Sara bought the contract. She offered 300,000 baht for a one-year contract. The girl was taken to Danok, where he collected his agreed fee from the Aunty and the girl was handed over.

"Then what happened?" Mislan asks.

"The rest is arranged by the Aunty. He's not involved, but he knows she has immigration officers on her payroll."

"Malaysian?" Johan asks.

"*Krap*."

"Why does she need them?" Mislan interjects.

"They take the girls across without a passport. That's how they control the girls during their stay in Malaysia."

"What do you mean?" Johan inquires.

"Being illegal restricts their movements. There's always the fear of being picked up by the police. This is one way to discourage escape. You're illegal, where can you go for help? Even if you go to the police, chances are they'll take advantage of your illegal status for personal gain."

"That makes a lot of sense," Johan admits.

"And it's easier to get rid of them if the need arises. They'll just be a Jane Doe with no record of entry into the country," Mislan adds. "This Aunty Sara, how can we get to her?"

"A'chat says she looks like Malay but she could be anything—Malaysian, Singaporean, or Indonesian. She speaks fluent Thai without an accent, so he's not able to determine where she picked it up. She also doesn't stay in a particular hotel whenever she comes up, always changing. They always meet in a hotel room, never outside, so he really doesn't know if people in Danok know her. The meeting is always during late evening and by the next day she and the girl are gone."

"Danok is the border town between Malaysia and Thailand, right?" A'sark nods.

"Cowboy town," Dr. Suthisa adds.

Mislan turns to her. "What about this Aunty's contact number?"

"Malaysian number. You can get Malaysian cell reception in most parts of Danok. One of the reasons why it's popular with the Malaysians, especially the married men," Dr. Suthisa explains, laughing.

A'sark checks his notes and gives Mislan the cell phone number.

"I bet you it's prepaid with a fake name," Mislan sighs. "Can he set up a meeting?"

"Yes, but it'll take a few days."

"Can we use a plant?" Johan asks.

They turn to him like he just said something ludicrous.

"What?"

"Would you like to wire her, too?" Mislan mocks. "Get real, OK?"

"And where are we to find a plant?" Dr. Suthisa inquires.

"I noticed some pretty, young policewomen while we were in Hat Yai station," Johan suggests. "One of them could be a plant."

"An official plant will take a long time for approval by the bosses," A'sark explains.

"All right, silly suggestion," Johan confesses, chuckling.

"I'll just cook up a young girl's profile for him to bait the aunty," A'sark announces.

"In the meantime?"

"We take this whole thing back to Hat Yai tomorrow morning and work from there. Since the two of you are on a tourist pass, may I suggest you enjoy what Hat Yai can offer, and I assure you it has a lot to offer," the police sergeant says with a sly grin.

Detective Sergeant Johan reciprocates the grin.

32

WHEN THEY REACH HAT YAI, the police sergeant checks the Special Investigations officers into Lee Garden Plaza hotel, which is in the heart of the city and close to the Crime Suppression office. The first four floors of the hotel are a shopping mall, the next four floors are a parking garage, and reception is on the ninth. Next to the large circular reception hall is the coffeehouse where only breakfast is served for in-house guests. According to A'sark, other food outlets are in the shopping mall or outside the hotel. Mislan remembers the news some years back about the hotel getting bombed. He can't remember if there were any casualties or deaths. Not wanting to offend the police sergeant, he says nothing of it.

Dr. Suthisa tells them that, since they'll be having some downtime until arrangements can be made to lure Aunty Sara, Lee Garden Plaza is convenient for them. Almost everything is within walking distance. She, however, is staying at Novotel, just across the road. Mislan looks across to Novotel and notes that it definitely seems to be a few stars above their hotel. *Well, you're on a police budget, so don't start comparing,* he tells himself. Before the doctor leaves, Mislan asks if there's a place where he can change some money into baht.

"Drop your bags in your room and come down. I'll wait for you at the mall entrance and show you," she tells him.

When Mislan and Johan go down after depositing their bags, Dr. Suthisa is waiting for them at the stairs to the mall entrance.

"That was quick," she says in greeting. "The money changer is across the road to your left, over there. You can't miss it," she says pointing to the rows of shops.

"Thanks."

"And over there," she says, pointing to the right, "starting from six in the evening, it will be lined with food stalls. The stall next to the traffic light is a *nasi lemak* stall. It's nothing like those you find back home, but I'm sure it'll do just fine if you're already missing home-cooked food. Otherwise, you can sample some of our street food. I was told most of the food is *halal*, as they cater to Malaysian tourists."

Again Mislan and Johan thank her.

"Do you guys have any plans for later?" she asks.

"I don't know about inspector Mislan, but I feel like walking around and checking out the scene," Johan says, smiling coyly.

"OK, I'm calling it a day. Really need to catch up on my beauty sleep," she says jokingly. "I'll see you at A'sark's office tomorrow morning. If there's anything you need, give me a call."

Dr. Suthisa Ritchu parts, uttering the now ever-so-familiar *Sawadee ka* and giving a *wai*.

———

The officers stand at the curb, watching her cross the street and disappear into the shopping complex next to the Novotel. In unison, they turn to look at each other and smile.

"I'm going to change some money then get some rest," Mislan says, walking to where the doctor pointed earlier.

"You don't want to get a massage?" Johan asks, tagging along.

"Don't really feel like it, just feel like going back to crash."

"Oh, come on, we have slack time, and this is the land of massages. See there . . . Pink Lady Ancient Thai Massage," Johan says, pointing to a huge signboard across the road. "Let's check it out. I've never seen a pink lady before," he says, laughing.

"It's the land of smiles, not massages," Mislan says.

"I'm sure you'll be smiling after the massage," Johan jokes.

Mislan gives him a yeah-right look, proceeding on to the money changer. The going rate displayed on the board at the money changer is RM100 to 832 baht.

After changing a couple hundred ringgit, they cross the road to the 7-Eleven. Mislan is shocked to see the crowd shopping there. It is like a supermarket crowd, with long lines. *Not something you'll see in Malaysia.* Standing in line, Johan again inquires if they're checking out the Pink Lady.

"OK, but it doesn't necessarily mean I'm getting a massage," Mislan says, giving in.

"We'll decide once we check it out," Johan says with a grin.

The Pink Lady Ancient Thai Massage is located next to the 7-Eleven. The building is hidden by two rows of stalls selling fake branded T-shirts, Bermuda shorts, football jerseys, jeans, and so on. Walking through the rows of stalls, they climb the staircase to the second floor, where they're instantly greeted with a chorus of *Sawadee Krap/Ka.*

A short plump woman ushers them to a lounge with maroon sofas. The sofas are lined up facing a large glass room. The full width of the glass room is fitted with a red three-tier stadium bench against the back wall. On the benches are twenty-five to thirty women in tight-fitting uniforms in the vein of air hostesses. There are women of all sizes: tall, short, slim, not so slim, beautiful, so-so, and not beautiful. Each woman is provided with a small cushion, but none are sitting on it. Instead the cushions are used to cover their thighs exposed through the long slit in the uniforms.

A few of them eagerly eye the two arrivals. Most, however, are either playing with their cell phones or staring at nothing, and one is knitting. There is one thing they all have in common—all of them have a number pinned to their uniforms.

In broken Malay, the plump woman asks if they would like a drink, which both Mislan and Johan decline.

"Darling massat, ok," the woman asks. "Body massat, oil massat, Turkish bath?"

The officers remain quiet, scrutinizing the women in the human aquarium.

"What's your name?" Johan asks the woman.

"A'oo."

"What's Turkish bath?"

"Full package . . . massat . . . swimming."

"Oh."

"I recommend number twenty-two, she very good . . . all can."

Their eyes search for the woman wearing number twenty-two. She sits at the far end, a heavyset person with a big smile.

Johan looks at Mislan, grinning.

"Value for money," he says.

"If you're buying meat."

"OK, darling? Morning, morning girl very strong . . . boom-boom good."

Mislan gestures to Johan that he's going back to the hotel, and Johan can stay on if he wishes.

"OK my boss wants to go back first, I'll come back later," Johan tells A'oo, excusing themselves.

Walking out of the Pink Lady Ancient Thai Massage center, they stop at the rows of stalls. Mislan buys two pairs of Thai kickboxing shorts and a couple of Manchester United football jerseys for Daniel.

Back at the room, the inspector tells his assistant he wants to take a nap. Johan says he's bored and would like to walk around and see if there's anything interesting.

———

Walking the streets or *Soi* of Hat Yai and the bazaar, Johan understands why the town is a popular destination with Malaysians. For the women, there are knockoff branded merchandise, handbags, shoes, purses, Thai silk, and cosmetics. For the men, it's the same and more. Anywhere and everywhere you turn there are girls—smiling charmingly, alluringly inviting, and of course ever so lovely. The best part is that they all call you *abang,* older brother, no matter how ancient you are. After an hour or so of mooching about, his face aches from smiling to the girls, and he decides to stop for a drink. Taking a seat in a seafood restaurant, he orders iced coffee.

"*Arai na,*" the waiter asks, meaning "What?," and places the menu on the table.

"*Kopi peng,*" Johan repeats his order, then he says it in English, "Iced coffee."

The waiter points him to the menu and walks away. Johan scans the menu and notices they serve pork dishes. *Shit, it says "seafood" on the signboard, pigs aren't from the sea*, he says to himself, putting down the menu. *I guess the Thais don't know the difference between land-food and seafood*, he says, leaving the restaurant.

33

For two days, the Malaysian officers are tourists in Hat Yai. In the mornings, they check in at the Crime Suppression office. Dr. Suthisa informs them A'sark is still working with A'chat on baiting the buyer. They've made contact and are waiting for her to come back. A'sark isn't willing to push it for fear she may become suspicious. The officers agree with A'sark to let things take their course. Aunty Sara is the only link they have to Jariya's murder, and if she's spooked, they can kiss any chance of closure goodbye. Mislan just has to check himself and roll with the punches. It's not easy, but he knows he has to.

Nevertheless, after two days of a tourist-like existence, Hat Yai's vibrancy has faded for Mislan, though not for Johan. Mislan has had his fill of body massages, reflexology, *tomyam*, *somtam*, fried chicken with sticky rice, sticky rice with durian, cashew nuts, fake merchandise, free porno in the hotel room, and just about everything and anything to do with Thailand. Mislan figures his skin has thinned a millimeter or two from the massages and reflexology they've had every morning and evening. He just can't understand the hype. Most of the time the masseuses are soliciting through a combination of broken Malay or English, sign language, and subtle brushes of your groin area into having sex with them. The massage itself is basically pressing your body parts with her elbow or squashing your muscles with her clawlike hands. Perhaps it's the anticipation more than the actual act that lures men into the dens. As the saying goes, the excitement is in the chase, not the kill.

Waiting has never been Mislan's strong suit. Johan is at his wits' end trying to calm the inspector and in the end concedes to let him brood alone in the hotel room while he enjoys what Hat Yai can still offer.

———

The next morning, Mislan receives a WhatsApp message from Dr. Suthisa informing him Aunty Sara has taken the bait and they're required to come down to the Crime Suppression office. Mislan's excitement and impatience with the communication barrier compels the two officers to walk the half mile to the Crime Suppression building in the blistering heat of mid-morning instead of taking the *tuktuk*. The uniformed personnel manning the reception counter recognizes the crazy sweating Malaysians and points them to the interview room where Dr. Suthisa and A'sark are waiting.

Dr. Suthisa Ritchu and Police Sergeant A'sark stare at them quizzically. Johan explains their communication predicament with the *tuktuk* drivers resulted in them having to walk the distance. Done with their morning dose of laughter, courtesy of the two Malaysian officers, A'sark updates them on what went down last night with Aunty Sara.

"How do you want to do this?" A'sark asks.

"There is no girl, right, just a dummy profile?" Mislan reconfirms.

A'sark nods.

"What is A'chat going to tell the Aunty when he cannot produce the girl? She'll smell a setup and take to the wind."

"We can take her once we know which hotel she is staying in," A'sark offers. "The problem is we, by that I mean Thai police, have got nothing to hold her on, but you on the other hand do."

"That being the case, I'd rather we take her on Malaysian soil ... do away with extradition technicalities should it go to trial," Mislan suggests. "The challenge is to put eyes on her before she crosses over. My fear is, if she crosses over and smells a sting, she may not go back across into Malaysia immediately."

The room falls silent, and Mislan automatically lights a cigarette. No one stops him or protests.

"Didn't the informant say she'd drive up?" Mislan asks.

"Yes, it's the easiest means of smuggling the girl across. On leaving the Thai side she'll just say they're going to the duty-free complex. On the Malaysian side, she'll drive the girl through the immigration booth manned by the officer on her payroll," A'sark replies.

"I've heard of similar modus operandi by immigration at KLIA. The middleman or the go-between will tell the fake passport or visa holder the time and which counter to go to for immigration clearance," Johan says.

"Can the suspect spot her as she's coming in?"

"Which side?"

Mislan shrugs.

"Easier done on the Thai side because there's only one vehicle lane."

Mislan mulls over the situation. "I'd rather have it on Malaysia side to avoid technicalities. Let me talk to my boss."

———

Dr. Suthisa sets up her laptop and goes on Skype. A minute later, Superintendent Samsiah's face appears.

"*Sawadee ka*, *P'*Samsiah," she greets her.

"Doctor, nice to see you again," Samsiah replies, smiling. "I see you have my two officers with you."

"Yes, and this is Police Sergeant A'sark," she introduces him, touching the sergeant's shoulder.

"Sergeant, pleasure to meet you, and thank you for your cooperation and assistance."

A'sark offers that *wai* and greets her with *Sawadee krap*.

"Ma'am, we have a situation needing your long reach," Mislan cuts in with a grin.

"I'm listening."

Mislan updates Superintendent Samsiah on the latest developments and his game plan and desire to avoid international border technicalities. Samsiah agrees with her investigator: the takedown, if possible, should be done on Malaysian soil.

"I see you've all your bases covered. What do you need from me?" Samsiah asks.

"Our immigration checkpoint has several queue lanes. That makes it impossible for the suspect to be spotted. However, after the immigration, there's a police post that checks vehicle registration. About a hundred fifty yards beyond the post is still our soil. I'd like to put our spotter in the post. You think you can swing it?"

"When do you want this to happen?"

Mislan turns to A'sark questioningly.

"A'sark said the exchange is going down tomorrow. It usually takes place late evening around 7 p.m. Since the suspect is driving up, it would be good if we can put our spotter there in the morning," Dr. Suthisa explains A'sark's suggestion.

"What're the chances the suspect is already in Thailand?"

All eyes turn to A'sark.

"According to our informant, she doesn't hang around in Danok for long. She checks in, does the exchange, and leaves."

"We'll arrange a backup plan," Mislan butts in. "If our informant gets a call from Aunty Sara for the exchange, A'sark will go with the informant as an associate or apprentice to lay eyes on her. From then on, A'sark's team'll keep her under close surveillance until she crosses onto our soil, where Johan and I will take her into custody."

"But you just said there is no girl to be exchanged," Samsiah points out, poking a hole in his contingency plan.

"A'sark will come up with a believable excuse," Mislan says, turning to the police sergeant with a wink.

"You just came up with that, didn't you?" Samsiah says. "Sounds like a good plan. I'll make some calls and get back to you. Doctor, Sergeant . . . pleasure talking to you, and thank you very much for all your cooperation."

The screen goes back to the Skype logo, and Mislan lets out a long sigh, lights another cigarette, and returns to his seat. Three pairs of questioning eyes are on him. A'sark flashes him a tiny smile of acknowledgment and respect. He knows this inspector from Special Investigations had just assumed his role as the lead investigator. From here on, he will be making the call.

Through Dr. Suthisa, A'sark suggests they move their operational base to Danok. Having heard so much about it as a cowboy border town, Johan eagerly agrees. Mislan, on the other hand, is skeptical.

"Can we not involve Danok police in this?" Mislan asks. "We really don't know if this Aunty Sara has any protection from them."

"I'm not involving them," A'sark agrees. "I don't trust those guys, either. Don't worry, only Crime Suppression men will be involved."

With A'sark's explanation, Mislan breathes easier.

"I made reservations at the Siam Thana Hotel. It's more convenient for you. The rate is reasonable, and there's a lot of Muslim food just in front of it."

"I'd like to check out the immigration and police checkpoints when we reach there."

"I'll take you," A'sark offers. "We'll go to the duty free."

"Great, I hope they have my brand of cigarettes. I really can't smoke these," Mislan says, lifting up his cigarette. "Where will the informant be?"

"With my team in a different hotel. I don't want him seen with us."

"Good planning," Mislan compliments him with a smile. Turning to Johan, he says, "Let's go back to the hotel and check out."

"We're taking the *tuktuk*," Johan insists. Walking out he asks, "How do you know so much about the immigration routing? You been there before?"

"WhatsApp-ed a friend who's based in Alor Star, and he told me the normal way up to Danok is through Bukit Kayu Hitam. He provided me with the information I needed."

"When did you figure out the takedown plan?"

"At the tiger show last night. To be precise, when the girl was showering in the bathtub," Mislan says, laughing heartily.

———

Johan fully takes advantage of the thirty-one-mile drive south to Danok for a Q&A session about the town's reputation. Dr. Suthisa and the police sergeant confirm what Johan has heard of the town—a men's paradise. Danok is the country's southernmost territory and is within the district of Sadao in the province of Songkhla. Like most border towns, it's quite independent of administrative rules imposed by its provincial master. After the Hat Yai bombing incident, the Hat Yai flesh trade catering to Malaysians particularly from the neighboring state of Kedah moved down to Danok. Johan supposes, like the saying goes, if Muhammad cannot go to the mountain, the mountain comes to Muhammad. The advantages are: it's a stone's throw from Malaysia; it's within Malaysian telecommunication coverage, so the wife wouldn't know you're in Thailand; and no passport is required for a quickie crossover—at least for those who know how to go about it. Kedah has always been ruled by strict Syariah compliance. For the alcohol-, entertainment-, and sex-craving Kedahans, they cross over after office hours and cross back into Malaysia before the gate closes at midnight, Malaysian time. It's estimated 80 percent of Danok businesses is made up of hotels, massage parlors, karaoke joints, pharmacies, restaurants, and food stalls, of which the first three businesses provide sex services. The rest of the real estate is 7-Elevens, fake merchandise outlets, and rice wholesalers.

As they pass the Customs complex while making their way into the town, Johan notes the large number of Malaysian vehicles on the roads as well as those parked along them.

"Shit, if I didn't know better, I'd think I was in Malaysia," he remarks.

"You're right in many ways," Dr. Suthisa jests.

Checking into their hotel room, Mislan recalls what the doctor said about Malaysian telco services being available in Danok. He immediately checks his cell phone. Seeing two signal bars, he straightaway makes a call to Daniel. After several rings, his son answers.

"Hey kiddo, how are you?"

"OK . . . where are you, Daddy? I can't hear you clearly."

"Daddy's in Thailand. Miss you, kiddo."

"Thailand, what are you doing there?"

"Miss you, kiddo," Mislan repeats, knowing his son won't say the same if his mother is close by. "Miss you, too, Daddy," he says, teasing Daniel.

"Hmmm," Daniel answers, making Mislan smile. "Bye, Daddy, I'm going out with mummy."

"Bye kiddo, have fun, love you." Then, laughingly he says, "Love you, too, Daddy."

The brief chat only flames his longing for his best friend forever.

"How's Daniel?" Johan asks.

"Fine, he's going out with his mummy."

"Good. How's Fie?"

Mislan shrugs. He hasn't heard from Dr. Safia since, since . . . *Damn, you can't even remember since when*, he chides himself.

The room's in-house phone rings, distracting Mislan from his thoughts. It's Dr. Suthisa inviting them for lunch. She and A'sark are already waiting for them in the lobby when the officers come down.

"I heard you're bored with *tomyam*," she says, greeting them with a laugh. "I'm sure by now you're already missing home food. So today, we've decided to treat you to one of your local foods."

"You mean mixed rice?" Johan asks.

"Nothing like it at all. *Pie*, I'll explain when we get there."

Getting into the SUV, Johan asks if it's far away.

"No, it's just down the road at *Soi* 9 or the post office *soi*. A friend of mine just opened her kiosk called the Roadside Cafe. Don't worry, it's *halal*. Her husband is Malay."

The proprietor greets Dr. Suthisa warmly, and they immediately talk about old times with giggly chat while the rest wait patiently. At long last, the proprietor steps behind the food counter.

"What would you like, they have *nasi lemak*, noodles, or prawn cakes. Satay is only available in the evening."

"I'll try the noodles," Johan says, "I'm sure Inspector Mislan will have the *nasi lemak* with chili-fried squid and fried egg."

Mislan nods.

"Drinks?"

"Iced coffee, thanks."

While he's enjoying his favorite meal, Mislan's cell phone rings. It is a WhatsApp call from Superintendent Samsiah.

"Yes, ma'am."

"I've made the arrangements for your spotter to be in the post. Call DSP Razman Mohd Noor from Jitra Police and he'll arrange the necessary. I'll WhatsApp you his number."

"Thanks, ma'am."

"Lan, I know you and Johan aren't armed. I asked Razman to assign a detective with you for the takedown. It's a precaution, should Aunty Sara or anyone with her be armed. Should you need to reenter Thailand for whatever reason, the detective shall not, I repeat the detective shall not go with you. Do you understand me?"

"Clear as a bell."

"Lan, please don't turn this into an international circus," Samsiah stresses. "I mean it."

"I won't."

"Good, make sure you drag Johan back," she says, laughing. "He's probably thinking of staying in Thailand permanently by now."

———

Mislan receives the number from his boss and makes a call. After explaining what he requires, they agree to meet at the Zon Duty Free entrance at 4 p.m. Malaysian time. A'sark motions to the wall clock, which reads 2:25 p.m., and tells them they should be making a move.

"It's only 2:25. We still have an hour and a half to go," Johan comments. "The border is, what, five minutes from here."

"It is 3:25 Malaysian time," Dr. Suthisa reminds him. "We're one hour behind, remember. Your contact is referring to 4 p.m. Malaysian time. Yes Johan, it can be five or fifty minutes depending on the jam at immigration. I agree with A'sark, let's make a move." Waving to the proprietor, she calls out, *"Kit tang na ka,"* asking for the bill.

Johan notices her paying one hundred and forty baht, which is about seventeen ringgit, for the lunch, and thinks, *Damn bloody cheap.*

———

The road leading to the Thai immigration checkpoint is clogged with queuing trucks stretching about a mile long. Due to ongoing road upgrade work, a real mess by any standard, light vehicles are allocated a very narrow passage on the left, barely enough for a car to squeeze through. Again, the Malaysian officers marvel at the police sergeant's driving skills, as he squeezes the SUV through the narrow opening between motorcycles, roadside peddlers, and pedestrians. After what seems like endless stop-go-stop-go driving, they reach the immigration checkpoint. A'sark lowers his window, flashes his badge, says something to the security guard, and they're waved through the VIP lane, which is actually the truck lane.

Immediately after Thai immigration, Mislan notes they're already on Malaysian soil—without valid travel documents. The Malaysian immigration checkpoint is still about a mile farther south. The land between the Thai and Malaysian checkpoints is Malaysian soil, but it's like a no-man's-land. There is a duty-free complex, an army camp, a police camp, and even a golf course. So, in reality, a Thai national doesn't need to have a valid travel document to enter Malaysian soil if you're coming from Danok. A'sark makes the illegally legal incursion for another five hundred yards before cutting right into the Zon Duty Free complex. Again Mislan notes the numerous Thai cars, pickups, vans, and especially motorcycles parked there. Walking up to the main entrance, he sees the people are mainly Thais. He scans their faces but doesn't spot anyone who could possibly be his contact person. He tells Johan to look out for DSP Razman while he goes in to check out the cigarettes.

Entering the spirit and tobacco section, he spots his brand of cigarette, Sampoerna Menthol. Making a quick dash to the shelf, he grabs two cartons and goes to the checkout counter. The cashier asks if he is going into Thailand or back to Malaysia.

"Thailand."

"Thailand OK, if Malaysia can buy only one carton," the cashier says indifferently.

While paying, he observes the people browsing. Some are carting bottles of whiskey, crates of beer, and cartons of cigarettes. *Who is this duty free for? Malaysians or Thais?* He even observes the cashiers are all fluent in Thai. Seeing the confused expression on his face, the cashier tells him laughingly: "The Zon Duty Free is Malaysian-owned Thai hypermarket."

"Isn't the Zon Duty Free owned by Datuk' K, the guy married to Siti the singer?" Mislan asks.

The cashier looks at him blankly, holding up the plastic bag containing his purchase.

———

Walking to the main entrance, he sees a man talking with Johan, Dr. Suthisa, and A'sark. As he approaches, the man asks, "Mislan?"

"Yes, DSP Razman Mohd Noor? Sorry, I went in to buy some cigarettes," Mislan apologizes.

"Superintendent Samsiah said you needed assistance."

"Yes, I do, I need to go into the post and see if I can have a clear visual of car drivers from inside it."

"Sure, I don't think it's necessary for everyone to come along. You don't want to attract attention, do you?" Razman says.

Mislan tells the rest to wait for him, and he walks with DSP Razman the three hundred yards to the post.

———

The police post is a bottleneck for all vehicles exiting Malaysia into Thailand. There is a lane for motorcycles and pedestrians and another for other vehicles, including trucks. The lane for cars, vans, buses, and trucks is jam-packed and crawling at a snail's pace. Malaysian drivers are required to lower their window and produce a copy of the vehicle registration for inspection. Farther up the road, about four hundred yards from the police post, is the paramilitary General Operations Force (GOF) base camp.

"Your spotter can sit in here," Razman points to a spot in the post by the window, "and observe through it."

Mislan takes up the position in the main post and observes. It's not as easy and straightforward as he initially thought. Disappointed, he notes that he's able to see the driver's face clearly but not anyone sitting in the front passenger seat and definitely not those in the rear passenger seats, as the rear window isn't required to be lowered. At the same time, he notes that not all vehicles are stopped and asked to produce the registration card by the policemen manning the post. Some vehicles are casually waved through.

"Is there a random selection of vehicles for checking?" Mislan asks Razman.

"No . . . why?"

"I see some of the cars just drive through."

"Some are regulars, the men know them," Razman replies, grinning. "Usually the Kedah plates . . . They normally cross over to buy supplies—rice, eggs, and so on."

"Is there a position from where the spotter can see the front passenger, too?"

"You said the suspect is driving," Razman states.

"That's the info we got, but I'm not willing to chance it. What if the suspect is driven, you know, like by a driver-bodyguard?"

Razman looks around the area, thinking, then says, "Unless your spotter is stationed outside the post, I don't think so."

"Not possible, I can't risk the suspect spotting the spotter. How about in that post?" Mislan suggests, pointing to the motorbike checkpoint. "Station another man on the passenger's side and get him or her to lower the window, too."

Razman steps out of the post and gives instructions to the corporal in charge. He motions for Mislan to follow him across to the motorbike checkpoint. Mislan stands under the cover of the post and observes. He's able to get a clear view of the passenger and the driver for positive identification.

"Can we make sure your men insist the passenger lowers the window for every car?" Mislan asks.

"I'll give the instruction. Why don't you station your detective sergeant here to make sure it's done?"

"Good suggestion, I'll do that," Mislan agrees. "Can we take the suspect and the car to the General Ops camp for the arrest formality? I really don't want to do it out here."

"Yes, I'll inform the guardhouse. Your spotter will be here at 10 a.m. tomorrow?"

"Yes, with Jo. I'll position myself at the entrance of GOF base camp."

They arrive back in Danok around 5 in the evening Thai time, and A'sark suggests they go for a relaxing traditional body massage to be followed by dinner before retiring. Johan instantly agrees on behalf of the rest, and A'sark heads for Mutiara Spa 2. After a brief exchange between the police sergeant and the woman at the counter, he makes the payment. Johan asks if he can get a masseuse who speaks English or Malay. Mislan on the other hand prefers one that does not. Dr. Suthisa makes the necessary arrangements. To the detective sergeant's disappointment, his masseuse is an elderly woman who speaks fluent Malay, while the inspector is given a lovely young woman who only speaks Thai but smiles a lot.

They are all ushered into a room each. The spa is quite well-outfitted and much better than those they visited on their own in Hat Yai. The girls or women are well-attired, friendly, and charming. Mislan was later told by A'sark there is a chain of four Mutiara spas under the same owner. The husband of the proprietor is a police officer and an old friend of his.

By the time they're done with the massage, it's dark outside. Dr. Suthisa suggests they go for a Thai-Western dinner for a change. After a short drive, A'sark parks the SUV in front of Skyline Thai & Western Restaurant. Earlier at the duty-free complex, Dr. Suthisa bought a bottle of Johnnie Walker Black Label, saying she feels like unwinding with some drinks and live music. She also says she knows the band leader, who plays a mean lead guitar.

The restaurant is packed with Malay Malaysian men accompanied by lovely young Thai women. Alcohol consumption is prohibited in

Malaysia for the Malay Muslims, and prostitution is illegal. But Malays are human, too, and Danok is just a short drive away. Dr. Suthisa notices the inspector looking at the customers.

"Here they're referred to as 'working girls,'" she says with a tiny smile. "Unlike in your country, here they're not looked down upon."

Mislan turns to her, nodding.

"Here they're respected, well maybe not respected but certainly not frowned upon. They're what spur the economy, the attraction of tourists that bring in the money so that businesses like food, pubs, clothing, and others can flourish. Without them, this town, for example, is dead."

"I never would have thought of that."

"Most of them are from remote villages from up north where there is nothing for them to earn a living. They work for a period of time until they can save enough money to go back and start a new life."

Mislan nods without saying anything.

"I don't know if you can understand this: it's not what they want to do, but it's what they need to do. When it's all over, they'll ask for forgiveness from Lord Buddha and erase the sins and memories of this life forever."

Skyline's band takes the stage after their short break. The band consists of three musicians—the lead guitarist, a Thai, who is Dr. Suthisa's friend; Mus, the bassist; and Man, the drummer. Mus and Man are Malaysian Malay with unofficial Thai wives. Their repertoire ranges from evergreen oldies, ballads, to slow-rock and hard rock. The instrumentation is tight and the vocals listenable. True to Dr. Suthisa's words, the lead guitarist is excellent, his scaling and finger work superb. By the time they adjourn from the restaurant, they're relaxed, chatting cheerfully and laughing. For the first time since setting foot in Thailand, Mislan is in good spirits.

34

INSPECTOR MISLAN AND DETECTIVE Sergeant Johan are up early in the morning, feeling rejuvenated. The exhaustion, fatigue, and body ache are gone, rinsed away by the body massage, great music, wonderful company, and an early restful night. They meet for breakfast, and the police sergeant gives them the latest update. According to his men, nothing has changed from their last plan with the Aunty.

Yesterday at dinner, Dr. Suthisa suggested that Mislan and Johan check out and leave their passports and luggage with her. To facilitate the border crossing with their travel documents, the police sergeant will drive the team across, and he'll return to Danok. That way, should they pick up the suspect, to avoid immigration clearance complications, they need not reenter Thailand with her. Dr. Suthisa and A'sark will clear their passports for them at Thai immigration and hand them over, together with their luggage, at the General Operations Force base camp.

By 10:02 in the morning, the team is in position. A'chat the fedora man, now labeled the spotter, is safely tucked away in the motorbike checkpost with Johan outside supervising the policemen at the car lane. Mislan is idly sitting on a parked motorbike in front of the General Operation Force camp, smoking. A'sark and Dr. Suthisa are waiting in their hotel rooms, ready to spring into action should contingency support be needed.

By noon, Mislan is feeling restless: two hours have passed and nothing. Not even a false alarm from his assistant. He thinks of calling the police sergeant to check if he's in contact with the spotter. To ask if the spotter has received any call from the Aunty telling him of her whereabouts. He decides against it. He, however, cannot stop from playing devil's advocate, asking every imaginable *what-if* question that could screw up his plan. *What if she decides not to come, and instead sends her rep, who isn't known to A'chat? That's not possible, because then A'chat might not want to deal. She won't take that chance. What if she is already in Thailand? But the arrangement has only just been made. Why would she already be in Thailand? Anyway, the call was made to her Malaysian number, so she has to be in Malaysia. What if A'chat pulls a double cross on them? Lets her go in without telling them, then when she calls, he tells her to disappear. Not a chance, his cell phone is with the police sergeant's men. Shit, Lan, stop screwing with your brain, it's just been two hours . . .*

To restore his confidence, Mislan again makes a call to his assistant.

"Yes?" Johan answers.

"How's it going?" Mislan asks, ignoring his assistant's annoyed tone. "Are the men instructing the passengers to lower the windows?"

"Yes, yes. They even asked all the occupants to step out of the car and do the cha-cha-cha," Johan answers, joking. "This is the hundredth time you've called. Relax, OK? It's only noon. Even if she leaves KL immediately after breakfast, she won't be here at least until teatime. It's a five-to-six-hour drive."

"Sorry, I'm just bored," Mislan says.

"Go for a massage, it's two hours. You can be done with a lot of time for a happy ending and still make it here before she arrives," Johan teases.

"Yeah right, that's all you think about. Jo, no lunch break, OK? I'll buy you guys something. What do you want?"

"No need, thanks. I'll get one of the men to buy something for us. And don't call, I'll call you when we spot her."

———

Mislan whiles away the time by trying to eyeball drivers and passengers in passing cars. He pays particular attention to cars with Kuala Lumpur and Selangor registration plates. There are a lot of aunties, mainly as passengers and wearing the hijab. *She could be wearing the hijab to disguise herself and elude attention . . .* Not knowing who he's looking for, all the aunties look suspicious to him. The minutes crawl by slowly, but to him it's like they aren't ticking at all.

Mislan glances at his watch; it is 3:17 in the afternooon. His body is feeling sticky from the heat and perspiration. He walks to the drink seller on the tricycle cart and buys coconut juice. Thai young fresh coconut is smaller than that of his country but the juice is sweeter. Malaysia's tastes a little sour, and the seller normally adds a sugar solution to it. Perched on a parked motorcycle, he lights another cigarette and realizes there are only two sticks left. *Shit, I should have brought a spare pack.*

His cell phone rings. It's Johan.

"Yes," he answers in anticipation.

"We got her. . . . The men are asking her to pull over to the side. I'm letting the spotter go. I don't want her to see him."

"OK, hang on, I'm coming over."

———

Literally trotting to the checkpoint, Mislan makes a call to Dr. Suthisa, informing her of the development and to bring their passports and luggage over. Approaching the police checkpoint, he sees Johan standing on the driver's side of a white Toyota Vios bearing Selangor registration plates, with several uniformed policemen surrounding it. The driver's door opens, and a woman steps out while speaking to Johan. She appears to be in her mid-thirties, dressed in blue jeans and a simple pastel blouse. She's about five feet three inches tall, slender, with a light brown complexion, rather pretty, with short hair. She has the exotic features of a person from a Malay-Indian mixed marriage.

"Can I see your authority card?" she demands condescendingly.

Johan shows her his authority card.

"It doesn't say you're from here."

Johan smiles. "Because my powers extend all over the country."

"Where're you from again?"

"KL Police, D9—Special Investigations Unit."

"KL!" she yelps. "KL . . . you don't have power here!"

"I just told you, my powers cover the entire country, and you're in Malaysia still, aren't you?" Johan asks.

"Yes, I've not crossed over yet," she answers smugly. "So I've not done anything wrong. I know my rights. You cannot arrest me for not stamping my passport. I'm still on Malaysian soil."

"Where are you heading to?" Johan asks in mocking tone. "Duty free is back there."

"I made a wrong turn, and now that you've kindly pointed out my silly error, I'll be making a u-turn up there, which is still Malaysian soil, and go back," she taunts back. "Give me a break, please. I'm sure you're exhausted working in the hot sun. Here, let me treat you and the men to drinks." She pulls out her purse.

Johan gives her a nice-try grin.

"Put it away. Pull the money out, and you'll be wearing these beautiful bracelets," Johan says, pointing to the handcuffs on one of the policemen's belt.

She makes a face at him but shoves the purse back into her handbag.

———

Mislan arrives at the scene, introduces himself, and takes charge. Unfalteringly, he tells the suspect to shut up and get back into the car. He instructs Johan to get into the front passenger side, while he slides into the rear seat, telling the suspect to drive to the General Operations Force base camp. Mislan introduces himself to the policeman guarding the main gate and tells him DSP Razman has given them permission to bring the suspect to the camp. The policeman acknowledges he has been told that and tells the inspector to park the car at the main building and check in with the duty corporal there.

At the main building, the inspector again goes through the motions of introduction and asks the corporal on duty for a room he can use to interview the suspect. He is directed to a room next to where the corporal is seated. Mislan informs him to expect Dr. Suthisa and A'sark to arrive in about half an hour.

"Please direct them to me."

"Yes, sir."

"Thank you."

Once they're by themselves in the interview room, Mislan goes straight for her jugular.

"Listen, you have barely twenty minutes before the Thai police arrive. Either you submit yourself to us, or we'll hand you over to them. I'm sure you've heard stories about what Thai prisons are like."

Mislan pauses, lights a cigarette, and lets his lying threat sink into the suspect. He knows the suspect, in her line of business, must have known or heard horror stories about Thai prisons. He sees a flicker of fear in her eyes, but then it immediately vanishes.

"Here is the deal," he presses on. "If you submit to us, we'll take you back to KL."

Mislan suddenly realizes he hasn't made any transfer arrangements for the suspect or themselves. He and Johan have return flight tickets, but they're from Hat Yai, and there's nothing for her. At the same time, he's not about to reenter Thailand with the suspect and risk a diplomatic complication. He backtracks.

"You'll consent to us taking you back to KL in your car. Otherwise, we'll have to keep you here in the lockup for one or two nights to make transfer arrangements, and your car will be left by the roadside. It may well disappear into Thailand once we're done with you."

"What am I arrested for?" the suspect asks boldly.

Mislan examines the suspect's identity card.

"Syazreen Sara Sukor, age thirty-three, born in Penang. You're known as Aunty Sara to flesh traders. . . . Do I need to tell you what you're being arrested for?"

Mislan again sees the flicker of fear in her eyes when he mentions the name *Aunty Sara*. Like before, it quickly disappears, and her arrogance returns.

"Why the aunty moniker? To throw the authorities off your age?" Johan asks.

Sara stares at him, tight-lipped.

"I'm sure the Thai police will be very interested to get their hands on you for selling their young girls. We, me and Jo, are only interested in one of the girls you sold. Although I'm sure our Anti-Trafficking in Persons & Anti-Trafficking in Migrants Department will be happy to talk to you after we're done."

It was agreed earlier between the two D9 officers that the murder of Jariya is not to be mentioned until she's in their custody at Special Investigations office in Kuala Lumpur. Mislan doesn't want her to clam up and play her I-want-a-lawyer card.

"I help the girls find jobs," Aunty Sara tries to justify herself. "These are poor people and—"

Mislan raises his hand, stopping her mid-sentence. "Don't give me that crap, I have all the statements needed to put you away forever," he snaps.

———

The arrival of Dr. Suthisa and A'sark with his badge around the neck clearly terrifies Sara. This time the panic in her eyes stays, and she is shaking. Mislan grabs the moment to introduce them, emphasizing on the Crime Suppression Division. Sara murmurs a greeting in Thai, giving them a bowed *wai*. Mislan pulls Dr. Suthisa and A'sark out of the room and out of Sara's hearing. He explains what he had laid on the table for the suspect. A'sark nods, indicating he'll play along.

Returning to the suspect, A'sark says or asks her something in Thai to which she repeatedly answers *mai* something something and a submissive *koh tot ka*. Thai words or phrases that by now the D9 officers know to mean "no" and "sorry." More admonishments or threats or advice from A'sark, with the word *hi'ear* and *Rohingya* thrown in several times. Each time Aunty Sara answers with a timid *ka*. Johan likens the unfolding scene to a prayer session where the congregation utters *Amin* to every Arabic verse recited by the imam.

Dr. Suthisa explains that Sara is one of those Malaysians living in two countries, a Malaysian of Thai origin. Although she is officially Malaysian, the crime originated in Thailand, and should the Malaysian officers decide to surrender her to them, they would gladly accept the gift.

The explanation and interest expressed by the Thai police shake her to the core. She immediately tells them she had agreed to submit to the Malaysian police.

"Protective custody for now," Mislan corrects her, "because we're riding back to KL in her car."

"Right . . . protective custody. When will we be leaving?" Sara asks anxiously.

"Soon."

"Better make it quick, because by the time we reach KL it'll be late night," Sara says, eager to get away from the Thai police.

Dr. Suthisa explains what just transpired to A'sark. Mislan and Johan step closer to them with tight-lipped smiles. They know their adventure together has come to an end.

"You got my number, keep in touch. Love to know the outcome of your case," Dr. Suthisa says.

Mislan nods. "I will."

A moment of awkward silence shrouds them. Finally, Dr. Suthisa opens her arms, giving Johan a big hug, saying it has been a pleasure. She does the same to Mislan, asking him to give her regards to *P'Samsiah* and to take care of himself. Johan offers the *wai* to A'sark, saying, "*Kon kup mak.*" Mislan proffers his hand to him, and as A'sark takes it, he pulls the police sergeant in for a manly hug.

"Thank you for all your assistance, and I apologize for my behavior," Mislan says sincerely. "We couldn't have done it without both of you."

A'sark nods, smiling, saying, "*Mai pen rai,*" "you're welcome" or "no problem." Another hugging session ensues before Dr. Suthisa and A'Sark take their leave, to the relief of Aunty Sara.

Mislan experiences both sadness and gladness on seeing the two Thais leave. Sad that they are parting ways, not knowing when or if they will meet again. Glad that he is going home and able to continue chasing his closure under his own steam and terms.

Johan, on the other hand, is just sad that they are leaving the Land of Smiles, for he hasn't had the chance to experience all the country has to offer.

35

With Aunty Sara's permission, Johan takes over the wheel for the drive south to Kuala Lumpur, with all expenses for gas and tolls gladly borne by her. The inside of her car is exceptionally clean and smells fresh. She sits in the front passenger seat while Mislan sits in the back. Once they drive past Malaysian immigration, Mislan notices she is more at ease. She is cordial and chatty, and he even sees her smile warmly to his assistant as they engage in small talk.

Johan asks where she learned to speak Thai. She tells him that after college, she started her own business selling Thai-made knockoff sports shirts, handbags, and women's accessories in the night bazaar along the Batu Feringgi main road. It's a tourist area with resort hotels lining the beach road. Business was so-so, competition was cutthroat. When the Pakistanis and Middle Easterners started muscling in, business was hit hard. She sold off her stall spot and with the money she ventured into supply and distribution of knockoffs. To have a bigger margin, she bought directly from Thailand. Her business expanded, and she started supplying to night bazaar stall operators in Kuala Lumpur, too. The increase in volume demanded that she spend more time in Thailand to visit more suppliers. She also needed to be friendly with the Malaysian and Thai customs and immigration personnel to facilitate bringing in the volume across without paying tax or having her merchandise seized. Thais are usually monolingual, so she needed to master the language if she wanted to deal effectively with the suppliers and authorities. As usual, when there is money to be made, many other players started to join in, and they became better financed and connected. As a small player, she was again sidelined. That was when she heard of poor young girls looking for work to help support their parents and a chance at a better life.

Mislan listens to her narrative and sneers at how she avoided saying "buying the young girls to be sold in Kuala Lumpur." "That's very noble of you," he mocks.

Sara turns to him with a glare.

"Tell me, how did you help the girls?"

"Through friends and acquaintances, I asked if any of them have job openings for the girls. If they did, then I talked to the girls about it. If everything worked out, I handed the girls to be under the care of the employer."

"In return?"

"In return, I get a small token for my efforts. Not much, just enough to cover my expenses for picking the girls and a little pocket money for myself. I, too, need to live, don't I?"

Mislan pokes a little more but is careful not to mention the murder. If it is to come into the open, he wants for her to be the first to mention it. That would allow him to implicate her through her knowledge of the crime. Mislan notes that Aunty Sara is no novice. She answers all questions without giving away anything that can be used to incriminate her. She is always the savior, always doesn't know the hidden agenda of the people she assisted, although she admits to being paid or, to use her term, *reimbursed for her expenses*. Mislan can't wait for them to reach Kuala Lumpur and for him to seat her in one of Special Investigations' interview rooms.

"Why are you called 'Aunty'?" Mislan asks, curiosity getting the better of him. He remembers the question was unanswered when Johan asked it.

Sara turns to look at him, puzzled by the change in subject.

"I mean, you're certainly not in that age category to the public, perhaps to your nephews and nieces yes but not to the general public, not yet."

Sara laughs heartily. "Dear, oh dear, are you hitting on me, Inspector?"

Hearing Sara's response, Johan burst into laughter. "Boss, earlier when I told you to go for a massage and a happy ending, you declined, and now you're hitting on our—"

"Like hell I am," Mislan snaps. "I'm just curious, OK?"

The matter is put to rest when Sara insists they stop for a nature's call break. As they're not able to follow her into the female washroom in a rest area to ensure she doesn't bolt, the request is denied. When they approach the Tapah rest area, Sara threatens: Either they stop or she will pee in the car.

"I'm not kidding, my bladder is bursting," Sara declares, unbuttoning her jeans.

"OK, OK, just hang on," Johan says, chuckling.

"Not the rest area," Mislan instructs. "Make a detour to the Tapah police station. I'm not taking any risks."

"If you don't stop in ten minutes, you can forget the detour. I'm doing it in here," Sara threatens.

"Oh, shut the hell up, will you," Johan snaps. "It's your bloody car. Do it if you want to, you think I care?"

Sara stares at him, making a face.

"Jo, pull over here. Let her pee by the roadside. I'm not sitting in a car smelling of urine for the next two hours," Mislan instructs. "If she tries to escape, just shoot her," Mislan bluffs, knowing they don't have their sidearms with them. "And if you don't want to shoot her, you have the honor of going after her."

Johan pulls into a petrol station at the rest area. He tells Sara to leave her handbag in the car and follow him. At the main entrance to the female washroom, he tells her not to do anything silly. Other users of the washroom stare at them as they walk past.

"Like what? Escape through the toilet bowl?" she snaps.

"You got five minutes," Johan says sternly, trying to stop from laughing at her remarks.

"And if I'm not out by then, what are you going to do . . . come in after me?"

"I'll do more than that, I'll come in, cuff you, and drag your sorry ass out."

Sara laughs, "Huuuu, I like that."

———

With Sara's bladder emptied, they continue the journey without further unpleasant events. As they approach Rawang, the border district between the state of Selangor and Kuala Lumpur, Mislan notices Sara's nervousness. She suddenly becomes very quiet and constantly looks out the window, paying a lot of attention to cars that come level with them. *What is she afraid of? That someone might recognize her car and see us with her? Is she supposed to rendezvous with someone on coming back from Thailand with the merchandise?*

"Where are we going?" Sara asks, without taking her eyes off the window.

"Told you, IPK," Johan answers.

Sara is again quiet. Mislan thinks she is probably trying to decipher the initials IPK, which is Malay for police contingent headquarters. Without warning, she turns around to face him, her expression serious and colored with fear.

"Am I in trouble, I mean really like trouble trouble?" Sara blurts.

"Trouble definitely . . . Really trouble trouble, depends," Mislan replies, reading and probing her fears.

Sara gazes at him questioningly.

"Depends on, how shall I put it . . . how cooperative you're going to be," Mislan hints.

"Going to be! What do you mean by that, have I not been?" Sara frowns. "*What*, tell me what you want, and how more cooperative you want me to be?"

Mislan notes her sudden desperation with interest. Something about Kuala Lumpur or being in their company in Kuala Lumpur is making her nervous. He feels this is as good a time as any to put the pressure on and not wait until they are in a D9 interview room.

"Tell me about your up-liner," he asks, still cautious and skirting around his case.

To capitalize on the save-your-butt ticket, Sara spills the beans on her flesh trafficking contact. *Better him than me*, she decides. Her contact is known to her as Zamly, a guy in his late thirties, a stout individual about five feet six inches tall, with dark brown skin, straight shoulder-length hair, and a wide ear-to-ear smile. He claims to be connected to high-profile individuals and never fails to drop names whenever they talk. Whenever she receives a girl's profile, she will forward it to Zamly, who will then forward it to his circle, details of which she swears she is not privy to. If the merchandise is wanted, Zamly will get back to me, usually within two to three days. The contract is normally for one year and ranges from fifty to a hundred thousand ringgit, depending on the girl's looks, figure, age, whether she is used or unused, language ability, origins, and so on.

Once agreed with Zamly, she'll negotiate with the seller, which in her case was A'chat the fedora man—one of three recruiters she works with. She only handles girls from Thailand; it's much easier to transport and manage. When a deal is struck, she will pick the girl up herself and bring her into the country. She will also make the necessary arrangements with her immigration contact for the girl to come in without valid travel documents. This is Zamly's specific requirement for the girls—no legal entry, meaning no record of the girl's existence in the country, so no hassle with monthly entry endorsement or overstaying.

The girl is usually kept in a five-star hotel to avoid unnecessary harassment from the religious police and prying eyes. Upon satisfactory examination by Zamly of the merchandise, she would receive her payment in cash. From then on, she doesn't know what happens to the girl.

That must be it, the reason for her nerves. She must have made a deal with this Zamly and he's expecting to view the merchandise, Mislan figures. *Since she doesn't have the girl as agreed, she anticipates trouble.*

He probes, "I find it strange that you don't try to find out what happens next. I imagine an ambitious businesswoman like you would be very interested to know, for future advancement. Escalate yourself to the next level, where I believe the money is more. Anyway, the contract is only for one year, isn't it?"

Sara nods.

"Then I'm sure you'd like to know what happens to the girls after their term expires. . . . Perhaps the chance to recycle the girls and make some easy money."

Sara gazes at him intently, telling herself: *Fuck, this guy is shrewder than I give him credit for. I should offer him to be my partner.*

"Well," Sara says hesitantly, "I did hear a little of this and that."

"Which was?"

"He sells the contract for a premium to another person who runs a, how do I describe it . . . online bidding." She pauses in thought.

"Online, you mean like eBay?" Johan asks.

"Yeah, sort of, but with exclusive membership for high-profile individuals. I heard these people have girls from Mongolia, China, Indonesia, and some Eastern Europeans, too. Now the Mongolians are the most popular."

"What's the website?"

"I don't know. . . . I just heard talk. Maybe you should ask Zamly, he might know about it?"

They reach Kuala Lumpur Police Contingent Headquarters minutes before midnight. It's too late for Mislan to call Superintendent Samsiah for instructions on handling protective custody. He knows that letting Aunty Sara off with the promise to return to the office tomorrow would be foolish, yet to place her under arrest now can prove to be technically dicey. After a private consultation with Johan, it is agreed she is to be persuaded to stay the night in the office.

Aunty Sara is shown to the detectives' room, where she'll be spending the night. While Sara tries to make herself as comfortable as possible, Johan pulls the standby woman detective Kamelawati Ibrahim aside.

"She's our guest for tonight," Johan says.

"Yeah right, what's she in for?" Kamelawati asks.

"Protective custody."

"Informer or witness? Which case?"

"Soulless," Johan says, for the first time giving their case a name. "Kam, you watch her closely, don't let her out of your sight even for a second for whatever reason. Also don't be taken in by her threats or sweet talk."

"Soulless, which case is that?" Kamelawati asks.

"The faceless girl . . . the Jane Doe."

"Why 'Soulless,' why not 'Faceless'?"

"The faceless girl was caught in a web of soulless people."

Kamelawati looks at him blankly.

"Never mind, it's a name I just came up with. Kam, remember what I told you: do not let her out of your sight."

"Is she one of the soulless? Shit, why not send her to the lockup? What if I have to go out on a case?"

"Excuse yourself. Say it is per Inspector Mislan's instructions."

———

Mislan showers and changes into a pair of shorts, feeling fresh and grateful. *It's so nice to be home—no, it's so nice to be back in your country.* He makes a cup of coffee and switches on his laptop. Surfing the net, he searches for websites offering sex for hire or sale. To his surprise, hundreds of sites appear from all over the globe, mainly Russia, Ukraine, USA, China, Vietnam, Philippines, Pakistan, and Thailand. "Shit, it's an open market out there," he exclaims. He needs to narrow his search to Malaysia. He stares bug-eyed at the screen, surprised at what he is seeing. There are pages and pages of them with obvious names like Hadiah4u, Climax2u, Condom69, Domdom, Sexywawa, KLcondom, and many others. It's true what they say—sex sells.

He clicks on one at random but finds it to be a site promoting sex toys for both genders and performance-enhancement pills and gels. After several more sites, Mislan is convinced he needs more information if he is to identify the modus operandi and the targeted website. Switching off his laptop, he slides into bed and is soon lost in an exhausted dreamless sleep.

36

THE MORNING PRAYER IS perky with sexual innuendos as Mislan walks in. One of the officers even playfully feels Mislan's knees as he takes his seat.

"Do they impose GST on boom-boom?" Inspector Reeziana jests.

"Serious question," Inspector Tee asks Mislan, "were you given a happy ending allowance?"

"You're a bunch of *hi'ear*," Mislan remarks, laughing.

The officers gawk at him, and at that moment Superintendent Samsiah Hassan steps in, taking her seat.

"Glad to see you're back in one piece," she greets Mislan good-naturedly. "I received some rather unpleasant feedback from ACP Peter Soon Kam Hoon, the head of Interpol, on your un-officer-like conduct toward the SLO, DSP Arif. I'll deal with you later on that," she says with a tired sigh. "Let's hear how business was the last twenty-four hours."

Business was brisk as usual, with reports by the outgoing shift's investigating officer—two murders, three armed robberies and one fake kidnapping. The two murders are believed to be gang-related and are being handled by Anti Gambling/Vice/Secret Society (D7), while the armed robberies were basically muggings, which are being handled by the respective districts' IOs. The fake kidnapping was the usual Malay-teenage-girl-escapade: she ran off with her boyfriend, and the parents lodged a police report. As soon as the outgoing shift investigating officer finishes, all eyes including Samsiah's turn to Mislan.

"What?" Mislan asks.

"We'd all like to hear of your adventures," Samsiah says. "I'm sure you've something to share."

Smiling, Mislan says, "It was purely police work, no R and R involved."

His reply is greeted with hums of disappointed *ahhh* from the rest.

"No worries, we'll get it out of Jo," Reeziana says, to the laughter of the rest.

————

Not seeing Johan at his desk, Mislan stops to peek into the detectives' office, only to find one of the detective's desks covered with packs of nasi lemak, fried noodles, roti canai, and drinks with Aunty Sara holding center stage. The detectives, including Kamelawati, who ended her shift hours back, are seated and standing around, mesmerized by her tales of *tomyam* land. Johan is perched on a desk and enthralled by her charm, which hides her true soulless self. Mislan supposes this is what the unsuspecting girls saw in her—the caring Aunty Sara, until they were sold and forced into living a nightmare. Only then would they realize how evil Aunty Sara and the rest of the human traffickers were, but it would be too late.

Mislan taps Johan on the shoulder, motioning him to tag along. Coming off the desk, Johan asks, "Where to?" with a tiny tilt of his head.

"Ma'am's office. I need to update her. By the way, she mentioned she received complaints about us."

"What did we do?" Johan asks, gazing at him.

"She didn't say, but we'll find out soon enough," Mislan chuckles. "We always do . . . don't we?"

"It has to be the ruckus you made at Crime Suppression's reception," Johan sighs, "tarnishing the image of the Malaysian police."

Mislan laughs, shrugs, and arches his eyebrows, pooh-poohing it off.

Superintendent Samsiah puts her reading glasses down, gesturing to the two officers to take their seats. Glancing at her watch, she says,

"I have approximately ten minutes before I have to attend a meeting upstairs, so let's hear it."

"Most importantly, the suspect Aunty Sara is yet to be informed of our case," Mislan starts. "She's of the impression she is detained, sorry, under protective custody for her cooperation with us against the human trafficking syndicate for prostitution."

Samsiah furrows her eyebrows and purses her lips. "Go on," she says.

"I didn't want her to go into a frenzy in the car. She's already crazy as it is, so I decided to hold on until we're back here. Anyway, she's a small fry in the whole scheme. Her go-between is a man she knows by the name of Zamly. Once the girl is handed over to Zamly, she is out of the loop."

"She and Zamly are not a team then?"

"No, she believes Zamly has several others supplying girls to him. She only trades in Thai girls. Usually it's for a one-year contract."

Mislan pauses, searching for ways to continue.

"Can she give us Zamly?" Samsiah asks, picking his brain.

"We may have to do a sting to draw him out," Mislan sighs, glancing at his assistant for support.

"She was supposed to bring in a girl for him. She said this Zamly will examine the girl once she's here. Can we use that to lure him?" Johan suggests.

"We can, but I don't think she'll do it."

"Why not?" Johan asks.

"Then Zamly will know it was she who set him up, gave him away, and I don't think she wants that. We could be putting her life in danger."

"I agree with you," Samsiah says. "Think of other ways to lure him without exposing her."

Mislan nods. "The challenge is to go farther up the ladder."

"Why is that?" Samsiah asks, with Johan also showing interest.

"For one, Zamly may not be as cooperative as Aunty Sara. Two, he may be well protected, being higher up the ladder, and three, he may not know who is two or three steps up on the ladder."

"Go on."

"Aunty Sara said she heard the girls were sold online, like on eBay. The difference is this is exclusive to a specific group of people, high-profile, politicians and the country's elite. I did some surfing last night. There're lot of websites offering sex services, toys, performance enhancement pills and gels. I don't have the IT skills needed to search for the specific site."

"What about the forensic IT tech, Saifuddin?"

"I'll inquire. Coming back to the case, my theory is the vic, by the way her name is Jariya, was most likely murdered by the contract owner or by the person at the top of the ladder."

"Theory based on?"

"It's more of a gut feeling." Mislan smiles. "The vic was viciously tortured before she was killed with a blow to the back of her head. My feeling is that she screwed up big-time, and this could only happen with the contract owner or top guy."

"I don't get you," Johan butts in.

"Aunty Sara said she heard the contract owners are basically high-profile individuals. These people cannot risk their identity being linked to such girls or activities. If the vic screwed up big-time, the only way to erase the evidence was to get rid of her. She couldn't be allowed to walk away, the risk of exposure would be too great for them."

Samsiah and Johan remain silent, encouraging Mislan to continue.

"On the other hand, if it were those down the ladder, they'd have just recycled the vic and squeezed more money out of her. The contract owner or top guys have got more than money to think about. I suppose, those who can afford such a contract are already sleeping on money."

"Let's say your gut feeling is right. Who're we talking about here?" Samsiah asks.

"Politicians," Johan offers.

"Possibly, could even be corporate leaders or public figures," Mislan adds.

Samsiah lets out a tired sigh, gazing at Mislan unblinkingly. "Don't discuss this with anyone until you get me more concrete evidence. What's your plan with Aunty Sara?"

"I'm hoping I can hold on to her for a little longer before turning her over to ATIP."

"Two days, that's all. With the recent Rohingya death camp still in the air, I don't want to have to justify the delay to him," Samsiah says, jerking her head sideways and upward, indicating the OCCI.

Mislan stands to leave, but she waves him back to his seat.

"I thought you said you've a meeting to attend," Mislan says, knowing she wants to talk about the complaint.

"I've a few more minutes," she says, holding back a smile. "ACP Peter of Interpol informed me you were rude to the SLO. He went out of his way to receive you, to accommodate you, but instead you displayed impatience and lack of appreciation."

"I'm sorry," Mislan submits.

"I don't want your apology. You should apologize to DSP Arif and his assistant Naz." Samsiah looks long and hard at her maverick officer. "Lan, police officers have long memories. You may be good at what you do, maybe even be the best, but it won't get you anywhere if you keep making a career of pissing off others. To advance, you need friends and allies, not enemies, especially in the force."

"But—" Mislan opens his mouth to defend his conduct.

"Lan, look at where you are and where your squadmates are. Most if not all of them outrank you now. Are you telling me you want to be an inspector for the rest of your career? Think about it."

37

MISLAN SITS IMPASSIVELY ACROSS from Aunty Sara. After a few muted minutes, Sara starts to feel uneasy. She turns to Johan, her forehead creasing in question, rolling her eyes toward the inspector. Johan responds with a tiny shrug, further testing her unsettled nerves. Mislan's cell phone rings, startling the edgy Sara, who immediately turns to face him. He sedately retrieves the phone from his pocket, looks at the screen, and places it on the table, letting it ring. With every ring, Sara imagines it getting louder and louder until she can't bear the ringing any more.

"Aren't you going to answer the damn phone?" she cracks.

Mislan merely looks at her, letting the phone ring.

"Damn it, what's going on?" Sara barks angrily. "What's with this silent treatment? You said I'm under protective custody—well, screw your protection. I don't need protection, and you've nothing to hold me with, otherwise you would've thrown my lovely ass in the lockup last night. Right? . . . Right?" she demands smugly. "I'm leaving, and you can't stop me."

The ringing stops, and tense silence rules again. Mislan notes Aunty Sara is not backing her threat to leave with action. She hasn't made any move to leave. *How much can I trust this piece of shit to reel in Zamly?* Mislah asks himself for the tenth time. *Once ATIP gets their hands on her, it'll be the end of the road for me, unless I get Zamly first.* Mislan lets out a couple of long sighs, stands and signals for Johan to step out.

"What was the silent treatment back there?" Johan asks.

"Er," Mislan says, unable to relate Johan's question to his passive behavior in the interview room.

"Just now with Sara, what was that about?"

"Nothing, I was just lost in my thoughts. Get Jeff to sit with her, then come join me at the smoking area," Mislan instructs him, walking toward his self-designated smoking area.

————

At the emergency staircase landing, behind closed doors, Mislan lights a cigarette, leaning on the handrail and looking into the well. A moment later, Johan joins him.

"Want to tell me what you were thinking back in there?" Johan asks.

"How much of what she told us do you believe to be true?" Mislan starts.

"Is this a trick question?" Johan asks, laughing. "If it is, I'm not answering."

Mislan laughs.

"Why?"

"We need this Zamly fellow to get to the top of the ladder," Mislan says, mulling the matter more than explaining it to his assistant. "And we've got two days to do it before she's handed over to ATIP. The only way to get Zamly within these two days is to crack her. My gut tells me she knows more than she's letting on."

"What makes you think so?"

"She's smart, streetwise, greedy, and hungry. A soulless person like her won't be satisfied with just being a low-level player. She wants to rise, to cut the big deals herself. And where protection from the top is readily available. At her level as a freelance supplier, the money is small and she has to fend for herself. If she's higher up, by now we would've received several calls if not visits from the top people."

"You think so?"

"I know so. When someone close to the top gets nabbed, those at the top get nervous . . . very nervous because they can be fingered or the probability of them being fingered is high. Their first action is to ensure self-preservation, save their asses by securing the release of the nabbed person. Or at the very least, send a message to the nabbed person: *Hang on tight, we're working on your release.*"

Johan puckers his lips, nodding in agreement.

"We need to work on her," Mislan continues, lighting another cigarette. "We need to dig more intel on the online sales MO she mentioned. I did some net searching but am not getting anywhere."

"You checked with Sai?"

Mislan nods.

"He's saying the site is probably on the deep or dark web, whatever the hell it is. It's not their area, it's MCMC."

"I've heard of it. You need to get on the Onion Route or TOR to search for them. Traditional search engines like Google or Yahoo won't be able to," Johan offers.

Mislan looks at his assistant with the expression of how-do-you-know-this? "I say our best bet is that soulless woman in there. On second thought, we should've stayed in Thailand and let A'sark work on her. I bet you five minutes with him and she would be singing like a karaoke hostess."

Johan laughs. "Can I take this case and reach out to a friend?"

"What can this friend do?"

"He's into all these deep and dark IT things."

"We need ma'am to OK it. Talk to your friend and find out as much as you can without revealing the case. Once we're sure he can give us something, I'll speak to ma'am."

———

Reentering the interview room, Mislan finds Aunty Sara gaily indulging Jeff in his quest for knowledge of Thai women. Their conversation ceases instantly with Mislan's admonishing stare.

As planned, Johan enters the room with a serious face, nodding to Mislan saying, "Done."

"Good, when is the handover?"

"They'll be here tomorrow by noon."

"Get the front desk to complete the paperwork before they arrive tomorrow."

Aunty Sara and Jeff gawk back and forth between Johan and Mislan as they continue talking, ignoring their presence. Johan motions for Jeff to leave and takes his seat beside the inspector.

"Who's coming? What handover?" Sara asks tremulously, her eyes darting between the two officers.

"He's already on it, will get ma'am to sign them before she leaves," Johan says, ignoring Sara's questions.

"Good . . . I'm really tired. Can you get a detective to send her to the lockup until they arrive?" Mislan says, standing to leave.

"What's going on?" Sara pleads. "Where the hell are you going?" she asks, terrified, standing up to block Mislan from leaving. "Who's coming? Is it the Thai police? Why are they coming?"

Mislan stares intently at her. Turning to Johan, he allows himself a minuscule smile at the accomplishment of their sting. Johan instantly plays the role of good cop in the good-cop bad-cop interview technique—the oldest and most effective.

Johan bends down close to Mislan and pretends to whisper something into his ear. Mislan nods once, then twice, and retakes his seat.

"Sit down," Johan tells Sara. "I'm sticking out my neck for you here. My boss has a problem with your story but agrees to give you another chance. For some inexplicable reason, I like you, and I really hope you take this chance seriously."

Sara nods continuously like a chicken pecking padi grains as Johan speaks.

"I don't have a problem," Mislan corrects Johan. "She has a problem."

Johan chuckles at Mislan's interjection.

"What problem? I've told you everything," she says.

"My boss believes you're holding back on us," Johan states. Instantly, Sara opens her mouth to dispute him, but Johan retorts, "Listen! Don't get into something you'll regret."

Sara blows a childish raspberry.

"We checked the phone number and gmail address you said belong to Zamly and both are registered to phony names. So, we're back at square one and that's you."

Johan pauses, letting it all sink in. He notes the change in her expression, although she tries hard not to show it.

"Inspector Mislan and I agree, you know more," Johan continues deliberately. "For some reason you're not laying it out. It could be out of fear of him, but we think it more likely you and Zamly are a team. Not business associates as you claimed, but partners."

"*No!*" Sara rebuts angrily. "No, no, no. I only provide him with girls. I already—"

"How did you get to know him?" Mislan sneers, stopping her from ranting on. "I'm sure he didn't take out an advertisement saying *I need people to supply me young girls for prostitution.*"

Sara leans back, blinking rapidly, caught off guard. Mislan seizes her fuzzy moment to go in for the tight squeeze. He places his cell phone with the photo of his victim Jariya on the table. Sara cannot hide the look of recognition on her face.

"She is dead, tortured and murdered," Mislan growls menacingly, swiping his screen to the gruesome mutilated photo of Jariya from the crime scene.

Sara flinches, turning her face away.

"If you're not giving me Zamly, I'm pinning this murder on you," Mislan threatens.

"You can't do that. I didn't kill her. Hell, I didn't even know she was killed. And what reason do I have to kill her . . . Why? She was sold to Zamly, and I don't know what happened after that."

"I don't know your motive, and I don't care. You think I can't do it? Just watch me," Mislan dares. "You're the last known person with her, that's more than enough to put you as the prime suspect. My theory, she refused to submit herself, and the contract owner demanded the return of his money. You and Zamly tortured her to get her to submit, and when things got out of hand, you killed her."

"You're fucking crazy, no, no, a fucking lunatic. No fucking judge is going to buy your story!" Sara says.

Mislan laughs, joined by Johan.

"What's so funny?"

"You're right, no judge here will buy my theory, but who's saying you'll be prosecuted here?"

Sara's face suddenly goes pale. "Noo, you wouldn't," she manages to squeak.

Mislan and Johan smile.

38

A MEETING WITH JOHAN'S shady dark-web surfer friend is arranged at Calipso restaurant in Taman Melawati. Johan takes the inner roads through housing developments to avoid the Middle Ring Road 2 (MRR2) traffic crawl. The Taman Melawati commercial hub, in the northwest of the city, is another area where parking is murderous. The area is lined with rows of shophouses with only roadside parking managed by the city council, nowhere near enough to cater to the volume of vehicles. *Town planning with no planning* is what Mislan used to term it. After driving around the area twice, they still can't find a parking spot.

"Why the hell do we have to meet him here?" Mislan grumbles.

"Because he wanted to meet here," Johan replies. "He must have his reasons."

"There, there!" Mislan says, pointing excitedly.

Johan swerves the car right, causing Mislan to bump his head on the window as he squeezes into a tight spot.

"Shit," Mislan swears, rubbing his head.

"That's one of the reasons they installed safety belts in cars," Johan says, laughing.

They somehow manage to struggle out of the car, which is sandwiched between two closely parked ones. Mislan shakes his head in disbelief at the tight squeeze.

———

From the restaurant's main entrance Johan spots his friend Abdul Mukmin Burhan Tajuddin sitting alone, engrossed in his tablet in the alfresco section. Mislan gives him a once-over: he is in his mid-to-late thirties, rather large-sized, perhaps five feet eight in height, balding at the front with a ponytail and thick glasses.

Taking their seats, Johan introduces his boss. Mukmin, or Min to Johan, raises his eyebrows in acknowledgment but offers no handshake. Mislan takes Min's response as either oooh-shit-trouble or geek-style greeting and settles on the former.

"Sorry I couldn't tell you much over the phone," Johan starts. "My boss is interested to know more about the dark web. I'm hoping you can assist him."

Mukmin indicates *no problem* with a slight slant of his head. "What do you want to know?"

Johan gestures to the inspector to take the lead.

"We need to know if you can do two things: one, track a cell phone, and two, identify a website," Mislan starts.

"The first one is easy, use Friend Finder," Mukmin says, chuckling. "The second, just do a search using the keyword for the activity the site is into."

"The phone belongs to someone we're not friends with. We checked. The listed owner's name is fake, and the site we believe is on the dark net."

"You're the police. Can't you go to the telco? I'm sure they would be only too happy to help you out."

"Too many protocols," Mislan says, shaking his head. "Jo said you're good at all this shit," he says, challenging him, hoping it will provoke the geek to show off his talents.

Mukmin hikes his eyebrows at Johan questioningly.

"Can you triangulate the phone location or something like that?" Johan asks.

"Anything is possible if you have the right infra and tools," Mukmin brags.

"You can!" Johan exclaims excitedly.

"This is all legitimate right … like authorized police work?" Mukmin asks, gazing at Mislan warily. "I'm not like going to be arrested or go to prison after this, right?"

"Yes, we've got our boss's clearance," Johan replies.

Mislan nods, endorsing Johan's statement.

"OK, not here . . . let's go to my place. The Wi-Fi here is third world."

————

Johan pays for Min's drink, and they walk back to the car. Mislan asks Johan to back the car out as it is impossible for the big Mukmin to squeeze into it. Driving out of the commercial hub, Mukmin directs Johan to their destination. Hitting the main road, he tells Johan to make a left at the traffic light. They drive deeper and deeper into the housing development until they come to its fringes. Johan tells his friend they're running out of road. Mukmin tells him to slow down and, after the next bend, take the gravel road. On both sides of the gravel road is secondary jungle, bushes and scrub. A few yards in and the development is blocked from view. Mislan begins to wonder where the hell his assistant's friend is leading them. After about fifty yards, he sees a cluster of four stand-alone single-story houses. Mukmin points to the last unit, telling Johan to park at the front yard.

Stepping out, Mislan scans the area and realizes they're actually at the end of the dead-end road. Beyond the clusters of houses, a range of hill-covered primary jungle looms. Mislan thinks it is probably the water catchment area. The houses must be on government reserved land, the boundary between the development and the catchment area. The house pointed out by Mukmin is basic, brick-and-mortar walls, wooden doors and windows with no security grille. It gives the impression of an abandoned house, with no human occupancy. There are no satellite discs at the front of the house or transreceiver antennas protruding from the roof or CCTV monitoring the surroundings. The only glaring distinction between Mukmin's and the other houses is it really needs a fresh coat of paint.

As Mukmin unlocks the front door, Johan asks whose house this is.

"My late father's," he answers nonchalantly.

Stepping in, the officers notice the gloominess of its interior. With the windows shut, the air is stale from spoiled food and soiled clothing littered everywhere. Mukmin is the only one among them not disturbed by the smell and thrown-about decor.

"You live here alone?" Johan ventures the question.

Mukmin nods and heads toward one of the rooms at the back.

"What about your wife?"

Mukmin throws him a glare, saying nothing.

"Girlfriend?"

Mislan gives his assistant a nudge, gesturing for him to shut up. Mukmin disappears into the room and the lights come on, followed by swearing.

"Is everything OK in there?" Johan asks, heading toward the room.

"Yeah, yeah, stay there, don't come in until I call," Mukmin commands.

The two officers look at each other with inquiring eyes.

"Logging off illegal hacking programs," Johan speculates, "probably 1MDB or Sarawak Report."

Mislan gives him a glare.

"What? I heard from a hacker friend . . . A lot of hackers were approached by one or the other camp's recruiters to work for them. Big money offered, depending on how good you are."

"To do what?"

"Monitor, extract, distort, destroy, troll, depending on which camp you're working for."

"Any of your friends take it up?"

Mukmin calls for them to come in, saving Johan from snitching on his friends. At the doorway, Mislan abruptly stops, awed by what he's seeing. Johan pushes past him into the middle of the room, wide-eyed and speechless. The room is freezing cold. Half is crammed with electronic equipment. On one side, there are all sorts of IT gadgets linked to monitors of various sizes displaying running programs. Against the wall behind them are stacks upon stacks of equipment with blinking or running LEDs in red, orange and green lights. On the opposite side is an L-shaped table with several desktops and laptops. Two swivel chairs complete the setting. Cables coil under the tables and through every available opening like mating snakes. Mislan feels like he just stepped into a movie scene of a nerdy character with headphone and mic in a dim basement room full of monitoring electronics.

Mukmin allows himself a smile, seeing the looks on the officers' faces.

Damn, this guy must be doing some serious shit, Mislan says to himself. He steps closer to one of the monitors, reading it.

"Please don't touch anything," Mukmin cautions. "Right, what's the number you want to track?" he asks, taking a seat in front of a desktop.

Johan gives him the number.

"Celcom, I'll need to set it up. Once done, I need you to make a call to the number. Keep him on until I say 'done.'"

"How long is that?" Mislan asks.

"One minute, give or take a few seconds."

Johan pulls the spare swivel chair next to Mukmin, his eyes glued to the monitor like a hawk tracking its prey. Every now and then he asks a question. Most of the time Mukmin replies with *ummm*.

"Your handle is SquareBean?" Johan asks amusedly.

"What's wrong with the name?" Mukmin answers with a question.

"Nothing, what does it mean?"

Mukmin turns to stare at him, and his fingers momentarily stop running over the keyboard. Johan grins sheepishly. Mukmin continues working the keyboard, eyes back on the monitor. To every prompt he replies with a string of commands as if he is chatting, but in a language only he and the machine understand.

Mislan steps away from the two of them to make a call to Inspector Reeziana.

"Yana, can you get Sara's phone from my desk and take her to an interview room?"

"In your drawer?" Reeziana asks.

"Yes, top left. Stand by for a call from me. . . . When you get my call, ask Sara to use her phone to make a call to Zamly."

"OK."

"She needs to keep Zamly on the line for a minute or so until I call you. Yana, you listen to every word she's saying, and if the conversation sounds suspicious, terminate the call immediately."

"OK."

"Get two teams of standby detectives ready to move."

"I'll get Reeze to arrange it."

"Good. When we're ready here I'll give you a call."

"Where are you?"

"Some weirdo's house," Mislan answers, terminating the call.

———

After several minutes, Mukmin heaves a sigh of finality and announces he is ready to go. Mislan makes the call to Reeziana, giving Mukmin the thumbs-up. A red blip appears on the monitor. Mukmin keys in several commands and an orange line emerges from the red blip, extending outward. Then a second and third orange line emerge slowly, extending outward. The three lines terminate at three telecommunication towers, forming a triangle that cuts across the blip. Mukmin keys in more commands and a location map appears in the background, showing building, road and location names. He zooms in on the blip.

"Your guy is at Meno Café, Plaza Mont Kiara," Mukmin announces.

Mislan makes a call to Reeziana, repeating the location. "No, no subject image. Dispatch the team there and stay loose. I'll try and pass on more details as I get them. Yana, I may need Sara to make another call. Stand by, I'll call back."

"Can you tag him?" Mislan asks.

Mukmin keys in several commands.

"Done, GPS and A-GPS ... whenever he is on the phone I'll know his location."

"What's A-GPS?"

"GPS uses only satellites. A-GPS uses both satellite and telco transmission towers."

"Is there any way to get an image of him, like a Google satellite image?" Johan asks.

"I can try but it'll not be what you expect. The location image will be a delayed image from the previous orbiting cycle."

"Try it anyway," Mislan insists. "Mukmin, can Johan bunk here with you to monitor his movements until we get him?"

The second request makes the two of them look at the inspector as if he just let loose an explosive smelly fart.

"I need him to be the eye on the target until he's picked up. Is it OK with you?" Mislan explains.

Mukmin shrugs, indicating it's fine by him. Johan on the other hand stares at his boss intently, as if asking *are you serious*?

"Thanks, it's all settled then," Mislan states, ignoring his detective sergeant's stare.

Johan shakes his head, disliking the decision.

39

Mislan pulls Johan aside, reminding him of their second objective and urging him to get his friend started on it. Johan nods and steps back next to Mukmin.

"Min, can you go to the dark net?" Johan asks.

"What do you want, child porn, drugs, guns, contraband?"

"Sex for sale sites?"

"There're hundreds of them on the traditional net, why the dark net? What specifically are you looking for?"

"Not the usual one game or one-nighter sex. More of an exclusive sex contract for a year or something like that. And can you confine your search to Malaysia?" Mislan asks.

"Sure, anything specific that I can use as a search key?"

"How about sexual contracts for sale?"

Mukmin pushes his chair to face another laptop and starts tapping on the keyboard. After several commands, he tells the rest he is in the dark net. The two officers peek at the monitor, confused.

"It looks like an ordinary search and site to me," Mislan remarks.

"What're you expecting, a sinister-looking site? The dark net is similar to the traditional net. It's just an alternative," Mukmin explains.

"So how do you know you're in the dark net?" Johan asks.

"The vehicle of getting there, and when you go there you'll know," Mukmin says with a laugh. "See this," he says, pointing to the monitor, "it's not dot com, it's dot onion. You use TOR—the Onion Route—to go into the dark net."

Johan nods like he fully understands what was explained.

"Can you look for the site?" Mislan asks.

"I just did, but it'll take a while. My search request will be encrypted and bounced around like six thousand times before it reaches the target. That's to ensure my IP is anonymous to watching eyes."

"Like the FBI?" Johan asks.

"And others. Here it's the MCMC or people like you," Mukmin sneers.

"I read they have a chatroom, too," Mislan says. "Can you go there to inquire?"

Mukmin logs on to another desktop and goes into one of the numerous dark net chatrooms using his handle SquareBean. After several minutes he starts chatting with a handler, SeeingEyes, about sex contracts for sale.

SeeingEyes: heard of it but not my scoop.

SquareBean: site names.

SeeingEyes: sorry cant't remember. Bro, you heard of the shooting of a Mongolian woman with a Datuk in a car? Heard it's them.

SquareBean: what do you mean it was them?

SeeingEyes: heard the Datuk didn't return the merchandise so they took her out. Could be them you're looking for?

SquareBean: could be. Why take her out and not the Datuk?

SeeingEyes: don't ask me man. If it were me I would take the bastard out and send the woman home.

"Because the Datuk won't talk, too much to lose, the woman is just disposable merchandise," Mislan explains. "By now the Datuk would've learnt his lesson and is most likely in their back pocket."

"By the way, what did happen to the case? It just went off the air," Johan remarks.

"Ask him if he has heard of a trader name Zamly," Mislan asks Mukmin.

SquareBean: know of a Zamly?

SeeingEyes: the journalist who goes all over war-torn countries in Central Asia, why?

Mukmin turns to Mislan inquiringly. Mislan shrugs.

"There could be something there," Johan interjects. "Traveling freely to war-torn countries in Central Asia under a journalistic cover to establish contacts and recruit potentials."

"Ask him if he has a photo of Zamly," Mislan suggests to Mukmin.

SquareBean: got photo of him?

SeeingEyes: go traditional man, check out his podcast.

SquareBean: ☺

Mukmin logs out of the dark chat and searches the traditional net for Zamly's podcast, which leads to Juicy Fact Media. Zamly's photo appears. He is in his mid-thirties with shoulder-length hair and a big smile.

"Can you enlarge the photo?" Mislan asks, taking out his phone.

He snaps the photo and WhatsApps it to Reeziana, then makes a call. "Ask Sara if that's Zamly," he tells her. "Call me back."

"You think it's going to be that simple?" Johan asks pessimistically.

"You said it yourself: he has all the needed cover. People in war-torn and poor countries are desperate for a better life. The best hiding place is in the open, and money is a powerful motivator," Mislan replies.

His cell phone rings.

"Yes, that's your man," Reeziana confirms.

"Where're the men?"

"At the location."

"Ask Sara to make another call and wait for my instruction."

"Roger that."

The blip reappears on the laptop screen. Mislan WhatsApps the photo to Detective Jeff with instructions to pick up the suspect. He pulls Johan to one side.

"Jo, you stay here, I'm going back to the office. Keep him here until we know where we're going with all this."

"Here, take the car. I'll find my way back," Johan says, handing him the keys. "Don't do it."

"Do what?"

"Beat the shit out of him."

"Isn't that illegal?" Mislan says, laughing.

40

WHEN MISLAN REACHES HIS office, Reeziana informs him the team is on its way with the suspect. He asks for Aunty Sara to be placed in the detective room until she's called. He walks over to Superintendent Samsiah's office.

"Ma'am," he says, standing at the doorway beaming. "We got Zamly."

"Well done, where is he?"

"On the way here . . . Like to sit in?"

"Why, are you expecting complications?"

"Not expecting, but I'm damn sure. This guy is supposed to be a journalist covering war-torn countries specifically Central Asia. Even has a podcast. I'm pretty sure he's connected in some way."

"In that case, get Reeziana to sit in. At least she can be your witness should any allegation arise. I'll fend things off from here."

"Thanks."

———

Stepping back into his office, Mislan informs Reeziana of the boss's instructions that she babysit him in the interview. She laughs, saying, "Why do you always catch the nasty cases?"

"Cos I'm a honey badger and honey badgers don't give a shit," Mislan says with a swagger.

The team arrives with the suspect, and Mislan instructs them to put him in Interview Room 1.

"Let's go," Reeziana says.

"Not yet . . . let him wait and sweat a little," Mislan says, heading to his private smoking area. "Tell Syed to frisk him, take away his cell phone, and make sure no one speaks to him. Tell Jeff to check his records."

Reeziana goes off to give the instruction then joins Mislan at the emergency staircase landing.

"Spare me a stick," she says.

"Thought you quit," Mislan says, handing her the pack.

"I thought so, too. Where's Jo?"

"Babysitting a geek."

"The weirdo?"

Mislan grins.

"What's wrong? You look muddled? Is the case messing you up inside? I mean your vic was sold by her own father for prostitution and . . ."

Mislan remains silent.

"You should know better," she advises, lighting the cigarette and handing him back the pack. "Don't let it get to you. Humans are humans. They'd sell their own mother if they could get the right price. We're born with a soul, but greed made us soulless."

Mislan allows a tiny grin but remains silent.

"Soulless. I heard that's the name Jo gave the case . . . fittingly. These people are soulless, feeding and getting rich on the suffering of others."

Mislan extinguishes his cigarette. "Come. Let's see what this asshole's got to say."

———

Heading to the interview room, they bump into Detective Jeff, who informs them Zamly is clean. Mislan hears his name being called from the hallway. It is Superintendent Samsiah waving for them to wait up.

"What's up?" Mislan asks.

"Just got a call from OCCI asking about the arrest. I've got a feeling he's on his way down."

"That was superfast," Reeziana hisses disgustedly.

"What did he say?" Mislan asks.

"Asking why we made the arrest, and if we know who the suspect is, the usual things. OK, let's go in. You conduct your interview, and I'll sit in just in case he pops by."

Entering interview room 1, they're greeted by a smiling Zamly, the war-torn-country journalist. Mislan thinks he looks more like an Amazonian than a local. Samsiah returns his smile but not Mislan and Reeziana. Taking a seat across from him, Mislan introduces Superintendent Samsiah, Inspector Reeziana, and himself. Instantly, the suspect asks why he was arrested.

"We're investigating the murder of a Thai woman," Mislan answers, looking directly at his face to read any sign he may give away. "And we've evidence that you knew of her prior to her murder."

"I know of many Thai women," Zamly answers condescendingly. "It doesn't mean I murdered them or was involved in their murders. That's of course if they were murdered," he says, laughing at his own statement.

This asshole actually laughed, Mislan tells himself, *arrogant bastard*. Samsiah notices Mislan's angry expression and decides to take over.

"Yes, I'm sure you knew many Thai women, what with your good looks and all. However, we're only interested in one particular girl: the murder victim in our investigation. She was unfortunate enough to have met you . . . or should I say been bought by you?"

Samsiah's last statement wipes the smile off Zamly's face.

Before she can capitalize on her advantage, the door bursts open and Senior Assistant Commissioner Burhanuddin Mohd Sidek, the OCCI, steps in, accompanied by a man in office attire complete with necktie. Samsiah immediately stands, stepping between them and the suspect.

"Sir, would you and your friend or guest here care to step into my office?" she says before Burhanuddin can say a word. Then turning to Mislan and Reeziana she says, "Carry on and update me later."

She grabs the doorknob and ushers the two intruders out of the interview room. Caught by surprise, Burhanuddin and his guest follow her like lost lambs.

———

In her office, Samsiah walks around the table and sits in her chair, offering the OCCI and his guest the visitors' chairs—declaring her domain. *This is my office, and you're guests in my office: bloody behave* is the message she's sending.

"Sir, would you like to introduce your friend?" Samsiah asks.

"Eh, oh yes, this is Mr. Nurul Hafiz from Nurul Hafiz & Partners law firm—"

"Mr. Nurul Hafiz, pleased to meet you," Samsiah cuts in. "How may I assist you?"

"I'm appointed by Mr. Zamly—" Nurul says.

"Oh really, when and why?" Samsiah asks, cutting him off. "We just brought him in for questioning. I really don't see how he could've engaged you in the very short time that passed since we brought him in."

The room falls silent. Nurul the lawyer and Burhanuddin the OCCI look at each other.

"Would you like to discuss the matter between the two of you and try again?" Samsiah says mockingly.

Burhanuddin's face flushes with anger at being mocked in front of his guest. Standing abruptly he says, "I want a full report of the interview by tomorrow morning . . . a full report."

"I'll inform my officers of your request," Samsiah replies calmly. "In the meantime, it's best if we let the officers do their job without interference."

"You and your officers really don't have any clue what or who you're dealing with," Nurul hisses.

"Enlighten me, please."

Nurul stares at her intimidatingly.

"Is there anything else you wish to discuss, Mr. Nurul Hafiz?" Samsiah asks with a smile.

"I'll have you know the man in there has connections you can only dream of," Nurul asserts.

"A young girl was murdered, her face and hands were mutilated with acid, and her body covered with torture marks. And you stand here threatening me to release the only man who can help us solve the brutal murder? We have direct evidence putting your so-called client as the last person with the victim." She pauses to let her last remark take effect. "How dare you come into my office and threaten me?"

Burhanuddin, rendered speechless by Samsiah's comeback, only manages to gaze at her.

"Sir, I suggest you take your guest out of my office before I decide to lodge a report for intimidating a public servant in discharging her duties."

Samsiah watches, holding back her anger as the two men, now with their tails between their legs, scamper out of her office. She takes several long deep breaths, asking herself, *Why are there so many creeps in this world who all seem to stand by each other? Why can't decent people stand by each other like them, against them?* She picks up the phone and makes a call. After two rings Inspector Tee answers, "Yes, ma'am."

"Tee, I need you to go to the guardhouse and check the visitors' IC. There's a Mr. Nurul Hafiz who visited the OCCI. Take down his address in the IC, and I want you to scramble two teams together and put a tail on him. I want to know who he meets on leaving here. Get photos if you can, and vehicle registrations."

———

Samsiah opens the interview room door just as Mislan is heading out of the room, holding a cell phone to his ear.

"Jo, hang on, let me step out," he says into the phone.

Samsiah closes the door behind them and stands outside with Mislan.

"Jo, I'm putting you on speaker. Ma'am is with me. OK . . . go ahead."

"We got the site, I mean Min got the site. We're in it now," Johan says excitedly. "You won't believe the things in here. I tell you, it's like nothing I've seen before. It's like something you only see in movies."

"Jo, calm down, take a deep breath and count to ten," Samsiah says. The line goes silent.

"Jo, are you still there?" Mislan asks.

"Yes, yes, counting to ten."

"Good. Tell Min to copy everything he can from the site, names, contact numbers, records of contracts if any," Mislan instructs.

"OK."

Samsiah and Mislan hear muffled sounds of Johan talking to Mukmin.

"OK, he's doing it now."

"How did he get in?" Mislan asks.

"Min cracked Zamly's password and used it to get in."

"Isn't that dangerous?" Samsiah asks. "What if someone chats with him, what's this Min going to say?"

Suddenly, Samsiah and Mislan hear swearing in the background.

"Jo, what's happening?" Mislan asks anxiously.

More swearing in the background ensues.

"Jo, what's happening?" Mislan repeats with more urgency.

"Min said he's being tagged."

"What does that mean?"

"I don't know what it means, but Min is panicking and shutting down. A prompt just came up on his computer, saying, *This is Techman, you're a fake and you're trespassing.*' Then the wordings sort of started bleeding."

"What are you talking about?"

"Wait, there is another warning prompt. It says: *No one fucks with Techman and gets away with it.* Shit, the wordings just exploded. I mean in animation."

"Who's this Techman?" Mislan asks.

"Min said he heard of this guy. He's like a legend in their world."

"I thought you said Min is good."

"Yeah, but I'm no geek, so Min to me is like damn good. Min's a geek and if he's saying this guy is a legend, I guess he must be bloody damn good."

"Does he know who Techman is in person?" Samsiah asks.

Another muffled conversation continues in the background.

"Not in person, only by reputation," Johan says.

"Tell your friend to burn whatever he has into a disc or copy it to a thumb drive and bring it back with you," Samsiah instructs. "Jo, tell your friend to find out what he can about this Techman. I mean anything in real life as a person . . . not virtually."

41

REENTERING THE INTERVIEW ROOM, they find Zamly leaning back with his arms folded, a silly grin plastered on his face and shaking his legs. Before Samsiah and Mislan take their seats, he asks sarcastically, "Trouble?"

"What makes you think there is?" Samsiah asks with a smile.

Zamly grins broadly. "I guess by now you know who I am and—"

"Look at my face," Mislan says, cutting him off. "Do I look like I give a fuck?"

"If you know what's good for you, you should," Zamly replies smugly. "So, when are you sending me back to my car?"

"When I feel like it, you can find your way back to your car. In the meantime, you're a guest of the Royal Malaysia Police."

The grin disappears from Zamly's face. He leans forward and is about to say something when Mislan leans forward a couple of inches away from his face.

"Listen, asshole, you bought this girl," Mislan hisses, pressing his cell phone with Jariya's photo onto Zamly's right eye. "You're the last person with her, and now she is dead." He swipes the screen with his thumb and presses the phone with the photo of his gory victim back to the suspect's eye. "Her blood is on your fucking hands."

Mislan shoves Zamly away, plonking him onto the chair.

"You think your people are going to protect you? Think again. Ma'am just told your high-price-suit we can pin this on you. What do you think he is going to tell your people?"

Zamly stares at Mislan, but the grin is absent, just perky lips and narrowed eyes.

"That's right . . . now you got it," Mislan says. It's his turn to grin. Making a gun with his fingers, he points it to Zamly's forehead and pulls an imaginary trigger saying, "Bang, just like the Datuk."

The suspect's eyes dart from him to Samsiah to Reeziana then back to him.

"What's the matter Mr. Smartass . . . trouble?" Samsiah asks sarcastically.

———

Johan hands the thumb drive to Mislan, saying Mukmin managed to copy or download a few pages before he was prompted by Techman. From that moment on everything seemed to stop, as if the entire system got overtaken and cut off remotely.

Mislan plugs the thumb drive into his desktop and waits. After a few seconds, a file appears and he clicks on it. The first two pages are lists of usernames or handles, mostly acronyms. One of them is FJ.Med, which Johan was told by Mukmin is Zamly's handle. The third page contains four photos of white teenage girls named Mera, Darly, Barbee, and Marylyn.

"Is that all?" Mislan asks disappointedly.

"Just about twenty seconds or maybe less after Min started downloading or copying, the Techman prompt came up, and Min went into panic mode."

"What's the site's name?"

"I forgot to ask. . . . I meant to ask Min after he was done, but then everything went chaotic and I forgot," Johan says apologetically.

"Where is he now?"

"I don't know. We left together and he said he was going to check with his friends on crazy Techman. You should've seen him. He was terrified, his hands were literally shaking, and he was swearing nonstop. I've never in my life seen anyone in his state of fear. I mean this guy Techman was not even there. It was just a prompt."

"In the geeks' world, virtual reality is reality," Mislan says.

Mislan prints the first two pages containing the usernames or handles and walks to Superintendent Samsiah's office together with Johan. Samsiah, who was clearing up to leave for the day, stops and invites them in.

"Jo, I see you survived the scare," she says, smiling. "What've you got there?"

"Mukmin managed to get only three documents, these two contain usernames or handles," Mislan says, handing her the printouts.

"FJ.Med is Zamly's handle," Johan says. "That's the name Min used to go into the site."

Samsiah examines the list silently. Mislan notes her eyes widen in recognition or excitement as she reads the list.

"See anyone you know?" Mislan asks.

Samsiah doesn't answer. Her eyes remain fixed to the list.

"Ma'am, you know anyone on the list?" Mislan asks again.

"No, no, just shocked to see so many of them. What, eighty, a hundred of them?"

"I didn't count, could be."

Shifting her focus from the list, she asks, "Is there any way these can be deciphered?"

Mislan turns to Johan, who shrugs.

"Check with your friend if it can be done," Samsiah instructs him. "Also check with the forensic IT guy, what's his name . . . Saifuddin, and MCMC, too, if needed."

Everyone is silent, like they are suddenly being weighed down by a national issue.

"What about this Techman guy, any real-life info on him?" Samsiah asks.

"Min has gone to ask a few of his friends," Johan answers.

"So, this Techman is the key master?"

Mislan and Johan look at her askance.

"The gatekeeper," she says, laughing at her mistake. "Lan, arrange for Zamly's remand tomorrow. I'm sure there will be a lot, and I mean a lot, of heat from the top. But do it anyway. We'll work on him once we get the remand order."

Samsiah gathers her bag, indicating the discussion is over. Walking them to the door, she says, "Cool down the next time you interview him. I don't want to see black eyes and bruising."

———

Saifuddin is driving home when he receives a call from Inspector Mislan to meet up. He makes a detour back to the city, back into the infamous Kuala Lumpur crawl that he has just clawed out of. Mislan is impatiently chain-smoking and Johan is on his second iced tea when Saifuddin pulls up to the roadside stall behind the police contingent headquarters.

"Sai, thanks for coming," Johan greets him. "Can I buy you a drink?"

"Iced tea without milk, what's up?" Saifuddin asks edgily, taking a seat. "If it's about the composite, it's still not there yet."

"We already know who she is. Here," Johan says, showing him the photo of Jariya stored on his cell phone.

"She's so young and pretty," Saifuddin says. "Then what's this about?"

"Sai, if I give a username or handle can you find out who he or she is?" Mislan asks.

"Handle?"

"OK, username."

Saifuddin lights a cigarette, deep in thought. Mislan lights his fourth cigarette and waits. Saifuddin takes a sip of iced tea, puts the glass down then takes another sip.

"Yes, it's possible, but it's a lot of work or rather time. It's called social engineering."

Mislan and Johan look at him with smiles.

"Great, how much time?" Mislan asks.

"Depends. Depends on how active the person is on social media."

"You mean what, Facebook?" Johan asks.

"Facebook, Twitter, Instagram, WeChat, these are the more popular social media here, but there're many others. If the person uses the same username on most of the social media, yes it's possible to pin him or her down."

"Here is a list of usernames I need you to pin down the real identities of," Mislan says, handing him the two sheets of paper.

"All these!"

"Mm hmm."

"It'll take months."

"I got two days, so you got two days, that's all."

"Two days! You're kidding, right? Even if I'm on it twenty-four hours, I'll probably pin down two or three of them. That's if I'm lucky."

"Good, that's all we need to start with."

42

AT 9:20 IN THE evening, while Johan is at home, he receives a call from an unknown landline number. Answering the call, he doesn't recognize the terrified whispering voice. The caller is rambling uncontrollably about how he is a dead man, that they have tracked him down, the house is in ashes and he's lucky to still be alive. Only then does Johan realize it's his friend Mukmin.

"Min, Min, slow down. Why are you whispering? Where're you?"

"Somewhere," Min answers, frightened.

"Somewhere where?"

"Not over the phone, they may be monitoring."

"This is a landline . . . where are you calling from, and who're they?"

"How the hell do I know? You're the one asking me to track them. Who the fuck are these people?"

"OK, OK, don't panic. Do you remember where we first met? I'll be there in fifteen minutes. Once you see me, come out from wherever you're hiding to meet me."

"How the fuck do I remember where we first met, I can't even remember where I first met my ex-wife. Shit, now that you brought it up, I do remember."

"Good, you get yourself there, give me a call to tell me where, and I'll meet you there within half an hour, tops."

"Where I met my wife? Fucking hell Jo, no way can I be at Pelangi Mall, not at this hour."

"Where's Pelangi Mall?"

"Penang of course, where the fuck else could it be? That's where I first met my ex."

Johan laughs. "Go to the nearest police station, get them to call me, and stay put until I arrive."

Terminating the call, Johan calls Mislan to update him. He informs Mislan he doesn't know the full details as Mukmin was in panic mode and was rambling about they somehow got to him and his house was burned down.

———

Johan receives a call from Cheras police station, saying a man by the name of Mukmin Burhan Tajuddin is there waiting for him. Johan tells the station he'll be there in twenty minutes and to not let the man leave. He calls Inspector Mislan to meet them there.

When Johan arrives at the station, he finds Mukmin sitting in the visitors' area. He is wearing a baseball cap with its visor pulled down over his face and his head bowed low, staring at his feet. Mukmin's hands are shaking, and every once in a while his body lets out a tiny shiver. Johan walks quietly, sliding into the chair next to his terrified friend, putting his arm around his shoulder. Mukmin almost jumps out of the chair.

"Easy, easy," Johan says, soothingly. "You're safe here."

"Shit, Jo, you nearly gave me a heart attack. Jo, what's happening? Who are those people you asked me to track? My house is totaled, all my babies toasted. I'm so dead, Jo. When this news gets out, all my clients will drop me . . . no, no they won't even bother dropping me . . . they'll just ignore me."

"Look Min, I'm really sorry for what happened. We never for one minute thought things would turn out this way. If we suspected you would be in any kind of danger, we would never have approached you. We're just hunting and never figured we would be hunted."

Mislan arrives and inquires if they can use the back room. He signals Johan to bring Mukmin along. Mislan gives one of the policemen some money, asking him to get drinks for them. Once they're in the room by themselves, the inspector asks Mukmin to relate everything from the moment he left the house.

"Like I told Jo, I left to chat up a few friends to see if they know who Techman is. After dinner, I drove back and found my house was totaled. All my babies are dead and I'm fucked."

"Didn't anyone call to inform you when your house was on fire?" Mislan asks.

"Who? No one knows me there. . . No one even knew I was living there," Mukmin says.

"No one?"

"*No!* Except you guys."

"You said you've got clients, and I'm pretty sure these are not your run-of-the-mill web design clients, right?"

"What're you getting at?" Mukmin asks, staring at the inspector.

"I'm thinking, could any of your clients or their adversaries have done it?"

Mukmin gazes at him, puzzled.

"What my boss is saying, you're into some shitty things, maybe the people you do it to, did it to you. You know, revenge or to shut you down."

Mukmin's face contorts. He takes off his baseball cap and runs his fingers through his long hair. "Possible, but why only now?"

"What do you mean?"

"I've been doing this shit for years. Why only after my encounter with Techman? Anyway, my engagement is only in monitoring roles— monitor and report. I'm not into all that shit like hacking, stealing, manipulating, or disfiguring, just monitor and report."

Mislan lights a cigarette, gazing at him, trying to figure if Mukmin is telling him the truth.

"What I did for you guys, well, it's something I've not done for a long, a very long time, I swear."

"OK, we believe you. We need to stash you somewhere until we can get to the bottom of all this," Mislan says. "Jo, any suggestion?"

"We can throw him in the lockup," Johan suggests.

Mukmin stares at him, wide-eyed.

"I'm kidding," Johan says, laughing. "I've got a spare room. You can bunk with me."

———

Johan takes Mukmin back with him, and Mislan drives to Wangsa Maju Fire Station. The inspector introduces himself and asks to see the fire investigator who attended to Mukmin's house fire. The fire investigator says it is too early to determine the cause of the fire. However, from the amount of electronic equipment and air conditioners found in the ruin, the probability of overloading being the cause of the fire is high. The fire investigator will revisit the site tomorrow morning to continue his investigation in the daylight. Mislan gives his contact number and asks him to call him once he has concluded his investigation.

"Do you by any chance know of the owner?" the fire investigator asks.

"No, not really, a friend of the occupant asked me to inquire as a favor."

"Can you ask your friend to inform the occupant to come and see me? I need to ask some questions. I've never seen so many electronics in one single room in a house before. What is the occupant's job?"

"I don't know," Mislan says with a straight face. He is not actually lying.

"There's also something puzzling about the fire."

"What's that?"

"We got the call at 2020 hours and first responder arrived at the scene at 2037 hours. By then the entire house was burnt to ashes. We asked around, and the neighbors said they heard nothing and only realized the house was on fire when they felt intense heat. They all described the flame to be very bright and whitish, not like what they are used to seeing."

"What does that mean?"

"My tech guy did some sample reading on site and found traces of magnesium."

"What does that mean, I mean in terms of fire?"

"Extreme heat."

"Could it be from the electronics?"

"Initially, I thought so, too, but the reading was too high. Well, we'll know more when we revisit the site tomorrow."

"Is there a possibility of arson?"

"Can't say until we complete the investigation, but the discovery of high traces of magnesium is rather peculiar. You see magnesium in any form is very combustible, so we're not ruling arson out just yet."

"Sorry, I failed my chemistry, so I wouldn't understand any of that," Mislan says as the fire inspector tries to explain more to him. "I'll leave it in your good hands and please let me know your final findings."

————

Driving home, Mislan updates Superintendent Samsiah and is told to watch his back. She says if these people can get to Mukmin with just one intrusion into their domain, they have the technology and unscrupulous resources to do more than just burn a house.

43

INSPECTOR MISLAN ARRIVES VERY early at the office and is surprised to find his detective sergeant already at his desk. A plastic bag containing two packs of *nasi lemak* topped with chili fried squid, fried cow's lung, and bull's-eye egg is on his table, accompanied by two packs of iced black coffee.

"What's the occasion?" Mislan asks, motioning to the food.

Johan smiles, picks up the iced black coffee and walks to the make-shift pantry. Mislan joins him, where Tee the outgoing shift investigator is having breakfast.

"How was business?" Mislan asks.

"The usual stuff. Nothing special that would interest you," Tee says.

Mislan ignores Tee's jesting, takes a seat, and unwraps his fragrant rice.

"Now, this is what a breakfast should be. Not the sticky rice with fried chicken or the other stuff they have in Thailand. They don't even have precooked fried noodles or *koay teow*. The *roti canai*, or a poor attempt at it, is thin like worn-out underwear and the curry is so sweet they might as well call it sweet curry."

"You and your *nasi lemak*," Tee mocks.

"*Nasi lemak* and black coffee," Mislan corrects him, laughing. "With the American cops it's donuts and coffee but here in the land of food, it's *nasi lemak*."

Inspector Reeziana joins them, and Mislan asks if the remand team has gone.

"Yea, bumped into them downstairs. You friend Zamly was giving me the I'll-get-you stare," she says, chuckling.

"I'll get him before he can get anyone," Mislan says earnestly.

———

The morning prayer is short and sweet. Tee updates the rest, and when no issue is raised by other investigators, it's adjourned. Superintendent Samsiah signals Mislan to follow her to her office.

"Bring Jo along," she says, walking off to her office.

Mislan updates Superintendent Samsiah on last night's incident, with Johan filling in the gaps.

"So Mukmin is safe for the time being," she says, letting out a sigh of relief.

Johan nods but says nothing.

"He believed it was his encroachment into the dark web site that got his place torched," she says more as a statement than question. "What do you guys think?"

"I tend to agree with him," Mislan says. "Remember the 21 Immortals case? When the hacker we got to snoop into the Indian geek's site got tagged?"

Samsiah and Johan nod in sync.

"It could be the same. This Techman tagged him and obtained his location. Then he, and most probably he sent someone, torched the place as revenge or warning. Johan said Techman did send a prompt to Mukmin: no one fucks with him and gets away. So he backed up his words."

"Jo, you said Mukmin inquired with his friends about Techman's identity. Did he find out anything?"

"Mukmin said one of his friends knew of an IT guy named Ted something, but he doesn't know if he's the same person as Techman. According to him, this Ted used to work for an IT company called the Virtual Screen or something that sounds like it, but he left quite some time back and hasn't been heard from since. There were rumors saying he's like a virtual man, like in *The Matrix*, where he's able to step into the virtual world and live there."

Samsiah and Mislan look blankly at the detective sergeant.

"That's a movie. I say he could well be our man," Mislan says.

"No one just drops out of sight, especially a professional. If they do, either they're dead or have gone underground. Get Tee to track him down. I think your Mukmin may have something there," Samsiah says.

Mislan and Johan agree.

"By the way," she continues, extracting some photos from an envelope and handing them to Mislan. "Recognize any of them?"

Mislan and Johan scrutinize the photos.

Mislan shakes his head.

Johan taps the photo of a woman standing behind Nurul, the lawyer, and some men.

"Isn't that Raja something, our ex–home minister's daughter?"

"Sharp eyes, Jo," Samsiah comments. "Raja Eszura Raja Ibrahim, or Raja Esz to her close friends."

"Jo knows all women," Mislan mocks, "especially the young and available."

"Weren't there some rumors about her being her dad's bagwoman when he was home minister? The talk was she brokered protection to gambling operators, brothels, loan sharks, and organized crime syndicates, anything and anyone who needed protection from the law. A lot of talk, but as usual nothing happened to her. The rumors died immediately after her father was dropped from the cabinet."

Samsiah nods.

"What's she doing with him, I mean the lawyer who claimed he represented our suspect?" Johan asks.

"Where did you get these photos?" Mislan asks.

"I, too, was an investigator, remember? I do have a few tricks up my sleeve," Samsiah boasts. "To answer your question, Jo, I'm asking myself the same thing."

"Ma'am thinks she's involved?" Johan ventures.

"I don't know, but until we know for certain one way or the other, assume she is. If not directly, then by association."

The officers ponder their boss's statement.

"Lan, I received a call from ATIP, ASP Tina Isaac. She's asking when Sara can be handed over to them."

"I guess with Zamly already in our custody, ATIP can have her anytime they want."

"OK, I'll let them know."

———

Johan asks the inspector if he can visit Sara before ATIP picks her up.

"Why?"

"I don't know, I just feel sorry for her. I'm hoping all these experiences will kick some sense into her. I believe underneath all that hardness there is a good person."

"I'll say it again Jo: you're too trusting."

"I'll see if she's willing to work with ATIP and maybe cut a deal with them."

"I wish you luck, but don't get yourself suckered by her charm."

"I'll tell her you said hi," Johan says with a smile.

———

At 11 a.m. Mislan is informed by the front desk that Zamly has returned from court after being remanded. Mislan tells the front desk to send him to Interview Room 1. Waiting for the suspect to be brought to the interview room, Mislan asks his assistant how it went with Sara.

"She didn't say much but seemed remorseful."

"They all do when arrested," Mislan says.

"But she was sincere. Anyway, she gave me her word she will give ATIP her full cooperation."

"Well, I hope it works out well for her."

"She says hi back to you."

Their conversation stops when the suspect is escorted into the interview room. Once inside, the detectives turn him around to remove the handcuffs.

"Leave them on," Mislan instructs him. "Take them off only when you send him to the lockup."

Zamly throws the inspector a veiled stare, hissing, "*Mafakas*, you're one prick I'm going to enjoy taking down."

"The feeling is mutual." Turning to Johan he asks, "Jo, do you know what *mafakas* is?"

"Motherfucker, I think. His journalistic version of it," Johan replies. Mislan laughs.

"You know the hip local way of saying it is *mak lu punya nonok,* which means your mother's cunt."

Zamly glares furiously at him, biting his lips.

"Sit down, *mafakas,*" Mislan barks using the suspect's term and shoving him into a chair. He laughs louder, joined by Johan, with the intention of provoking Zamly into uncontrolled anger to loosen his tongue.

"You think you're a big shot with your police badge," Zamly rebukes him angrily. "One phone call and you're out on the street."

"You really don't want to do that, because if I'm on the street, I'll have no choice but to muscle in on your action. You don't want me as your competitor. I eat people like you for breakfast," Mislan says, continuing to laugh, "without chili sauce."

"Fuck you," Zamly cusses, spitting at him. With a dry throat, his miserly saliva lands halfway across the table.

Johan who is standing next to him instantly grabs Zamly's head, slamming his Amazonian face onto the table.

"This table is the property of the Malaysian government, purchased using taxpayers' money. You're going to lick every drop of your *mafakas* saliva clean. Do you understand me?" Johan whispers into his ear.

"Fuck you, too," Zamly responds.

Grabbing a handful of his long hair, Johan drags his face across the table, wiping the saliva off it. Zamly turns and twists his face to avoid contact with his saliva, but Johan's grip is too strong for him to break loose. When Johan lifts his face, the saliva is stuck to his nose.

Seeing the suspect's saliva-smeared face, the officers break into crazy laughter. Zamly desperately tries to wipe the saliva on his face against his shoulders, failing miserably. Giving up, he curses at the officers and threatens to make them pay for what they did. When he's done with his swearing and threatening, Mislan pushes the cutout photos of the individuals snapped by Tee. He notes recognition in the suspect's eyes.

"Here's the deal, we're going to round up all these clowns and let out that you, Zamly, were the one who led us to them," Mislan says matter-of-factly.

The suspect glares intently at the inspector.

"Then we'll release you earlier than your remand period, but of course with a little story to go with it. The story goes like this: you brokered a deal with the DPP to save your own neck, and that's why you were let off early. Oh, if you don't know what DPP stands for, it's Deputy Public Prosecutor. You know, the man who represents the AG, the Attorney General."

"You're bluffing," Zamly says, daring him but without conviction.

Johan grins. "A lot of people have made the mistake of calling his bluff, and most of them are now counting their days in prison. A few have even gone to meet their Creator. Call his bluff, and you may just add to the numbers."

Zamly's gaze wavers as he looks first at Johan, then Mislan, then back to Johan.

Mislan pulls out his cell phone and makes a call to Saifuddin.

"What've you got for me?" he asks.

"Oh hi, Inspector," Saifuddin answers sheepishly.

"Hi, what've you got for me?" Mislan asks again.

"You said two days. It's not even twenty-four hours yet," Saifuddin replies defensively.

"I lied. What've you got for me?"

"I haven't had any sleep yet. OK, OK, I know it's not your concern," Saifuddin says, chuckling. "I managed to pin down two of them and am still working on the rest."

"Good man, mail me their profiles," Mislan says, smiling for the benefit of the suspect who is watching him with interest. "That's enough for now to fry this bastard in front of me," he adds, striking the killer blow.

"Who's in front of you?" Saifuddin asks excitedly.

Mislan terminates the call without answering. Turning to Johan, he says, "We got the rest of them on the darkweb list."

"Bullshit," the suspect challenges him. "No one can break into the site, Ted told me so. He's the best, and no way anyone can break into it."

"So you do know Ted and the site," Mislan says.

Zamly realizes he has slipped and clams up.

"No one can, but it was not just anyone who broke into it. It was you. We used your username—FJ.Med—and your password to get in," Johan says. "By now this Ted guy would've put two and two together and figured out who the traitor is. You're a dead man, asshole, and you're still here only because they haven't buried you yet."

Mislan notes the suspect is terrified and is literally shaking. His cell phone beeps, indicating an incoming email. Opening it, he slowly reads the profiles sent by Saifuddin.

"Datuk Azamy Ramlee—D'Azram—and Datuk Kamal Yunus—DKYun. You know who they are?"

The suspect's shoulders hunch, his head bows, and he starts rocking to and fro, his thick, straight shoulder-length hair swaying in tandem. The officers know they've got him by the balls. They patiently wait for his sobbing ass-saving pleading, the I-was-forced into-it bullshit.

44

A TALL, SLIM GORGEOUS woman is leaning against his car on the driver's side toying with her cell phone when Techman steps out of the office building. Approaching his car, he ogles her. *Stunning,* he says to himself, *designer jeans, light blue blouse, nice shades, a touch of makeup, and slim arms with long pencil-like fingers. Must be an artist or somebody in that line.* He presses the auto-lock remote, but the woman doesn't seem bothered or make any attempt to step aside. *Is she waiting for me? Perhaps this is the chicks' new pickup trend,* he envisages elatedly, *must be my lucky day.*

Techman is actually half-correct in his assumption, the knockout woman is waiting for him, but it isn't a new pickup trend.

"Excuse me," Techman says, rather intrigued by the woman's behavior. "May I?" he continues, pointing to the car door.

The woman pretends to be surprised by his presence, hurriedly stepping aside and in her haste drops her handbag. Being the gentleman Techman is, although on this occasion he is hoping to score, he bends down to pick up the handbag for the stunning but clumsy woman.

As he bends down, the woman pulls out a .22 revolver from her waist, points it to the back of Techman's head and coldheartedly fires two quick shots. Techman's body slumps to the pavement. His head, bearing two tiny holes, slides under his brand-new red Aston Martin Rapide S, valued at close to two million ringgit. He never knew what hit him, and the last image his eyes saw before they lost their purpose was the tires of his car. The woman calmly blows a kiss to Techman and walks away, leaving behind the fake branded handbag stuffed with old newspapers.

———

Techman's passing makes the evening news. It's said that he operated a low-profile IT security company exclusively managing websites for high-flying individuals. To the IT community, he was a respected security specialist who was previously thought to have left the country for greener pastures. The police said they believe the motive for the killing was carjacking. They believe the victim had put up a fight, refusing to relinquish the car, and in the ensuing tussle was shot. What was not mentioned was that Techman was shot not once but twice with a .22, not a weapon of choice by carjackers, who prefer the .38 or 9mm.

An eyewitness said he was leaving the building and saw the victim talking to a woman beside his car. The woman was described as being in her late twenties or early thirties. about five feet five inches tall, well-dressed, slim, with short hair. She could probably be a foreigner. The police are pleading for the woman to come forward to assist them in the investigation.

Mislan is informed of the killing by Inspector Tee. He immediately asks if Tee can get a photo of Techman from the crime scene.

"What do you need it for?" Tee asks.

"My ace to play on my suspect and to pacify a traumatized friend."

"I'll speak to the IO."

"Thanks, let me know when you get them."

———

Detective Jeff escorts Zamly into the interview room, where Mislan and Johan are waiting. Bloody photos of Techman are laid out on the table. They watch as Zamly is ushered to his chair, his eyes fixed on the photos.

"Who's that?" he asks, pouting toward the photos.

"Take a guess," Mislan says, pushing the photos of the back of a man slumped on the road. "Two bullets in the back of the head execution-style, broad daylight, no witnesses, has to be pros."

"Who's that?" Zamly asks again, only this time his voice trembles.

Mislan flips open the last photos, which show Techman's bloodied face.

"Fuck!" Zamly yelps, pushing his chair back.

"Yes, he was fucked and soon you'll be, too," Johan says, chuckling.

"Your only chance of celebrating your next birthday is to work with us," Mislan offers.

———

Detective Jeff tells Mislan Interview Room 2 is ready and that Superintendent Samsiah has also been informed. Mislan instructs his assistant to escort the suspect to the interview room and he rushes off for a quick smoke. When he enters the interview room, Superintendent Samsiah and Johan are already seated and the technician gives them the thumbs-up that he is ready to roll. The video camera is focused on gloomy-looking Zamly, with the rest of them out of shot.

Superintendent Samsiah starts by stating the day, date, time, and venue, followed by introducing herself and the rest of them. She proceeds to ask Zamly to state his name and identity card number.

"Mr. Zamly," she says, "please listen carefully to the warning I'm about to give you."

Samsiah slowly and clearly reads the caution under section 113 of the Criminal Procedures Code.

"Mr. Zamly, do you understand the caution I just read to you? For the recording purpose, please answer yes or no and not by body language."

"Yes."

"Were you at any time forced or coerced or promised anything by me or my officers into giving this video statement?"

"No," Zamly says, shaking his head.

"Please look into the video camera," Samsiah says.

Zamly lifts his head to face the viewfinder.

"Thank you. Am I correct in stating that you're giving this video statement of your own free will?"

"Yes."

"Please state what you have to say."

As expected, Zamly sings like a *Malaysian Idol* wannabe. Being a journalist, he is detailed, sparing nothing. Sometimes too detailed and has to be guided back on track. The interview lasts almost three hours, and at the end they are all physically, mentally, and emotionally drained but—with the exception perhaps of Zamly—satisfied.

45

SITTING IN HER OFFICE over mugs of tea and coffee, Superintendent Samsiah Hassan and her two officers, Inspector Mislan Latif and Detective Sergeant Johan Kamaruddin, cogitate on the video statement by Zamly, the war-torn-countries journalist—and soulless flesh trader.

Zamly is one of many agents engaged by a syndicate to recruit or purchase young girls and women from all over the world to be contracted out to the country's rich and powerful. His hunting grounds cover Central Asia, Thailand, Indonesia, and the Philippines.

According to Zamly, once a month at varying dates, a lavish party is thrown by the syndicate at a mansion in Kenny Heights, where the newly acquired girls and women are showcased to mingle with the invitees. There is nothing about the party that can be deemed illegal or out of the ordinary, except of course for the illegally brought-in girls and women. The rules are simple: no sales or bidding or hanky-panky, just eat, drink, and feast your eyes on the beauties. Attendees are strictly by invitation; no friends or acquaintances of invitees are allowed in without prior approval.

A day after the party, bidding is opened through the dark web site, *DreamsAreForReal*. To be a member of the site, one has to apply through an introducer and be recommended by two referees who are already members. It takes roughly seven days for an application to be approved or rejected. All vettings are, or were, handled by Techman, who administered the site. Zamly doesn't know all the members, but he gave the names of some politicians and corporate figures he knows are members, and they're mainly Malay. As for the girls and women, he said Mongolians seem to be the flavor of the moment.

According to Zamly, their victim, Jariya Praphasirat, was murdered at the last party. After the party ended and the guests left, the girls and women were herded into the mansion's annex. There the anxious girls and women were made to stand in a semicircle around Raja Eze and forced to witness the killing. They were told the same fate awaited them should they even think of escaping or not complying with the demands of their contractual owners. She warned them that her reach is long and wide, extending into the girls' and women's countries of origin.

Jariya was said to have run away from the apartment where she was being held by the contract owner. Without legal travel documents she didn't manage to get far, however. Soon after escaping, she was detained by the police at Jalan Stadium Raya bus station. A bus station that services northbound buses, including to Hat Yai, Thailand. She was handed over to Immigration. The news of her arrest reached the syndicate and eventually Raja Eszura. Through her numerous contacts within immigration and police from her father's previous position as the home minister, she was able to secure Jariya's freedom into her care.

When all the girls and women were gathered, Jariya was brought out. She was stripped to her undies and tied to a chair. Raja Eszura told the girls and women that Jariya was an ungrateful bitch. She was rescued from a life of poverty and given all the luxury a girl of her upbringing could never dream of, but instead of being thankful, she tried to escape. As Raja Eszura spoke, she was pinching Jariay's body with an instrument. Jariya flinched in pain. Tears rolled down her cheeks, but she never once cried out. At times, the girls and women thought they saw her smile as if she welcomed what was happening to her; as if she had accepted her fate. Several times, Raja Eszura screamed at her, asking her to beg for mercy, but Jariya looked at her with defiance. That angered Raja Eszura and she kept pinching Jariya harder and harder.

After what seemed like forever, she finally gave up on Jariya. She said something to the contract owner, and they both laughed; she then nodded to her brutes. Two of them, wearing rubber gloves and one carrying a plastic container, stepped forward. One grabbed Jariay's hair, holding her face upward, and the other poured acid from the can onto her face. Even then, Jariya didn't scream or cry out in pain, but her tiny body wriggled and writhed in sheer agony.

The girls and women watching started crying and screaming when they saw what was being done to Jariya. One of them fainted, a few puked. Some were screaming and running hysterically, seeking to escape the room.

Pandemonium broke loose. The room stank with the smell of burning flesh and acid. That was when Raja Eszura together with the contract owner left. Before leaving, she nodded to the man holding Jariya's head, telling him to finish her off.

Zamly maintained he was not present, and what he related was what was told to him by one of the girls whose contract expired and who was recycled by him. None of the officers believed his claim of not being present; his description of the incident was too detailed and graphic. They knew if he admitted to being there he could be charged as an accessory to the murder, which he probably understood as well. They needed to get at least one witness to put him at the mansion when their victim was murdered. Perhaps one of the girls or women there whose contract had expired. It was decided to leave it at that for the moment, and to use him to get to the bigger fish.

"It's such a vicious world out there," Mislan says.

"Human trafficking is a big business; 200 billion US dollars per year with fifty percent of it coming from prostitution," Samsiah says. "Our country sadly is among the top on human trafficking lists although the government denies it."

"These are soulless people, living on income from sex slaves," Johan says indignantly.

"I suppose you're right, Jo. We tend not to take sex slavery seriously."

The office falls silent momentarily as Mislan walks to the cabinet to get an ashtray. He holds it up to Samsiah, asking if he can smoke. Samsiah, understanding his need to calm himself, nods her approval.

"What still baffles me is the earring in the victim's stomach," Samsiah says.

Lighting a cigarette, Mislan says, "My theory is the vic knew she was going to die and reached a point of accepting it as her karma. She is a Buddhist, so she believes in reincarnation—and what she didn't want to lose is her soul sister, Nadear." Turning to Johan, he says, "Remember, Nadear said they went to a wat and asked the monk to bless them as soul sisters?"

Johan nods.

"Nadear also said they weren't to take the earrings off, meaning never to part their bodies from them or it would break their vow as soul sisters. I guess the vic thought she would be buried with the earring in her, and thereby she and Nadear would remain soul sisters in their next life."

"Hmmm, interesting," Samsiah says. "Little did she realize her action or desire to remain soul sisters with this Nadear was what helped us identify her and pin down her killer." Samsiah takes a sip of her tea. "I'd like for you to put the earring together with her ashes," she instructs. "I know it's evidence, but she needs it more than we do. We can always find other evidence to nail them, but she has only that one earring to find her soul sister."

Again the room falls silent.

"Ma'am, we're going after them, are we not?" Mislan asks.

"I wish I could say yes, but once this goes upstairs," Samsiah tilts her head up toward the upper floor, "I'll have no say."

"What about our vic, Jariya? They can go after the human trafficking and whatnot, but the murder case is ours," Mislan pleads.

"In this case they're one and the same."

46

It's Sunday, and Daniel is coming home. Mislan sits by the bedroom window overlooking the guardhouse, waiting for the black Toyota Vios, which he'd bought his ex-wife, to come through the main entrance to the apartment complex. His mind is still bugged by the fact he may be denied the prospect of getting his closure. A closure asked of him by Chew, the forensics supervisor, and after meeting the victim's mother it became a closure he wanted. A closure she deserved.

Superintendent Samsiah had promised she would try and make a case with the chief of police for her unit to wrap things up. She did say the case has outgrown the unit, and for him not to put much hope in being given the go-ahead. She did, however, say she believed in the police force to do the right thing.

He spots the Toyota Vios approaching the guardhouse and walks to the front door to wait. After a few minutes, he hears the elevator bell, then Daniel's voice calling out, "Daddy, I know you're behind the door."

Mislan smiles to himself. The grille door lock clicks and he opens the door, beaming as he says in greeting, "Kiddo." He hugs his son, and they walk in together. Once inside the bedroom, Daniel plonks into the wingchair and turns on the television to the Discovery Channel.

"How was your holiday?" Mislan asks.

"OK."

"Make any new friends?"

"Mm hmm."

Mislan knows Daniel doesn't like talking about his stay with his mummy. He feels talking about it may make his father jealous or unhappy. Mislan understands his son's kiddy rationale and he never pushes it.

"Daddy, Sister is getting married," Daniel says, referring to the maid.

"Oh, when?" Mislan asks, surprised to hear it for the first time from his son.

"Wednesday."

"Which Wednesday?"

"This Wednesday."

"You mean three days from today!"

"Mm hmm."

"How do you know, kiddo?"

"Sister and Mummy talked."

"Shit," Mislan cusses.

Mislan knows how close his son is to the maid. Since his mother left, Ani has been with him through and through; they are more than just maid and charge. She is his friend, perhaps even like his surrogate mother.

"How do you feel about it, kiddo?"

Daniel doesn't respond. Mislan moves over to the wingchair and finds Daniel crying silently. He hugs his son, saying repeatedly, "It'll be OK, kiddo. Daddy will take care of you."

———

That evening when Daniel goes to the swimming pool to play with his friends, Mislan calls his ex-wife. After three rings, she answers, "Hi."

"Hi, are you driving, can you talk?"

"No, I'm staying at my sister's house. Yes."

"Kiddo just told me about Ani."

"I see."

"How did he take it? Did he say anything?"

"Devastated, of course, but you know him, he'll keep it all bottled up."

"Did you speak with him, find out what he wants?"

"I don't understand."

"I mean what his preference is?"

"You mean where he wants to stay . . . with you or me?"

"Hmmm."

"We talked casually."

"And?" Mislan asks, sounding anxious.

"He didn't directly say it, but says you're always not home, and without Ani, who is going to take care of him? His meals, school uniforms, and so on."

"And?"

"I asked if he wants to stay with me."

"And?"

"He doesn't think you'll allow it."

Mislan doesn't like the way it was said by his ex; it sounded to him more like a sneer.

"It's not what I want, but if kiddo feels he wants to be with you, I won't stand in his way. I want the best for him, with or without me. I'll have a chat with him and talk to you again."

———

Lying in bed, Mislan mulls over what he's going to do about his son. When his mother left, Daniel was devastated, but his child's mind healed when Ani came into their lives. Mislan is unsure if his son will recover from a repeat of a similar trauma.

Out of the blue, a question pops into his mind. *Where the hell is Fie? Why hasn't she returned my calls? Why aren't there any more WhatsApp songs?* Daniel nicknamed her Pretty, which indicates he likes her. Daniel gives his female friends nicknames if he likes them. Otherwise, he won't even say a word or make any mention of them.

Mislan picks up the cell phone and calls Dr. Safia's number. Instantly, it goes to the mechanical female voice saying, *The number you just dialed is no longer in service or is out of network coverage.* Terminating the call, he sends a *WhatsApp* message. *Hi* is all he texts. He notes the message doesn't go through, as there is no check mark indicating it has. He puts down the cell phone and sighs. *What the hell is going on? First, out of the blue, the maid is getting married, not next month or at the end of the year but in three days. Then Fie goes MIA. It's like someone up there woke up one morning and said I feel like fucking up Mislan's life. Poof, and everything came crashing down. It didn't even fall apart piece by piece, it just bloody crashed.*

————

That evening, while having dinner with Daniel at one of his son's favorite outlets—Taiwanese Noodle House, Ampang Point—Mislan receives a call from Superintendent Samsiah.

"Ma'am."

"Lan, I'm afraid I've some disappointing news," Samsiah says.

Mislan already knows what she has to tell him and remains silent.

"The case has been taken over by ATIP. We're to forward all our investigations to them tomorrow morning."

Mislan remains silent.

"Lan, are you still there?" Samsiah asks, full of empathy for her officer.

"Yes."

"I'm sorry. The Chief of Police extends his commendation to you and Johan for the effort and dedication both of you put into the case. He'll make a mention of it for citation."

"Thanks," Mislan says, thinking to himself, *Like I needed it.*

"Lan, are you all right?"

"Yes, ma'am, I'm fine."

"I'm really sorry."

"Don't be. It's not your fault. I know you did your best. For Jariya's sake, I hope those bastards get what they deserve."

"I'm sure they will, and I'm sure Jariya's soul can now rest in peace. Have a good rest, and I'll see you tomorrow."

Terminating the call, he focuses on his son enjoying the noodles with chopsticks. It was here several years back, eating the same dish, that he learned how to handle chopsticks.

"Kiddo, I spoke to Mummy," he says, observing his son's reaction.

The kid looks at him but says nothing. He sees sadness and hope in his son's eyes.

"With sister getting married and leaving, do you want to stay with Mummy?"

"Hm mmm," Daniel answers, his eyes on the noodle bowl.

"Have you discussed it with Mummy?

Daniel nods.

"What did she say?"

"OK," he says without elaborating.

Mislan understands: his son will not say what he told his mother, will not say that his father is seldom home, and, with sister gone, he's afraid that no one will be there to care for him.

"I'm fine with it, kiddo," Mislan says, forcing himself to brave a smile. "I want whatever is good for you, and I want you to be happy."

———

That night, with a shattered heart, he thinks hard about giving it all up. About throwing in the towel, then calling Police Sergeant A'Sark and asking him as a favor to buy him a gun. At his own leisure, he will go after the country's bastards—vigilante justice. The thought soothes his anger, bringing a smile. He turns to his side, listening to Daniel's peaceful breathing, thinking, not being a good father, perhaps it's better for his son. As he holds his son's tiny hand, Mislan fades into a dreamless sleep of exhaustion.

Epilogue

Jariya Praphasirat was given a decent wake by a Buddhist association in Brickfields. Her ashes and the earring were handed to the Thai Embassy to be forwarded to her family.

Forensic Pathologist Dr. Nursafia Roslan spends sixteen hours a day at the hospital, submerging herself in work and trying very hard to forget her past and begin a new life. She still listens to music and lives by song lyrics.

Daniel left to live with his mother in Johor. The mother managed to enroll him in a public school close to where they live. Mislan makes it a point to talk to his son every day, even only just to say goodnight.

Abdul Mukmin Burhan Tajuddin returned to his hometown in Penang and was never heard of again.

Zamly left the country immediately after his release, fearing for his safety. The High Commission of Malaysia office in Islamabad received a report of the discovery of his mutilated dead body in a cheap hotel in a red-light district. The Pakistani police found two blood types at the scene and believed Zamly was with a young girl when he was attacked and killed, probably by the girl's family.

A joint operation by Anti-Trafficking in Persons & Anti-Trafficking in Migrants (ATIP) and Immigration raided a mansion in Kenny Heights. The raid rounded up seventeen foreign girls and women without travel documents and thirty-one elite Malaysian personalities. Of the thirty-one, only two were ethnic Chinese while the rest were Malay, with fifteen of them the recipients of state or federal awards. The thirty-one locals were released unconditionally, while the seventeen foreign girls and women were charged in court with illegal entry into the country and immediately deported.

Nothing was mentioned of Raja Eszura, the daughter of the former home minister or the soulless activities she operated.

On Mislan's drive home after a late Monday night at the office, a motorcycle pulled up alongside his car as he stopped at the deserted traffic light on Jalan Ukay Perdana. The pillion rider approached the car. When Mislan lowered the window, the pillion rider fired two shots into the car, and they sped off into the night.